C W SCHWARZ

The Cache

A Black Hawk Bend Mystery

For mom and dad, who started me on my own STEM adventure.

Contents

Chapter 1

Renn hiked alone in the golden woods, and it annoyed her. A fluttering breeze rippled oak, maple, ash, and birch branches around her in various states of undress. Shadows played on the trail that stretched before her. Occasionally the sun twinkled through the leafy canopy.

She paused at the crest of a small rise in the trail and looked over her shoulder. Jack stood about twenty feet behind, arm extended and leaning against a slender birch trunk. His face, still tan even into October, tilted up to meet the sun, his eyes closed. He appeared to be absorbing the sun's rays like a dog. Was he sniffing the wind, too? What a goof.

Renn brushed an orange leaf off her teal quilted vest and flipped her long ponytail behind her shoulder. Then she raised two fingers to her mouth, whistled, and turned to resume her trek. They were wasting time.

"Wait up, Renn," called Jack.

His voice—pleading, cajoling, a little whiny—pressed a well-worn button in her psyche. Give him an inch and he would take a mile. "Catch up, Jack."

And he did. She could hear his footfalls, crunching leaves and kicking stones on the trail, growing closer by the step.

"What about stopping to smell the roses? Ever hear of that?"

Now is when he would poke and prod, looking for a chink in her armor. He could be stubbornly persistent, but she was obliged to provide a token resistance. "Do you *see* any roses? There's some moss you can sniff if you really want to."

Jack's stride fell into step beside hers, and she looked up to take in his sandy blond hair. Why had she invited him to come along today? Oh yes, to celebrate the milestone. This might be her last excursion for a long time. She had a strange desire to mark the occasion.

"This is kind of boring," her friend remarked. "Have you really been doing these by yourself all year? Are we almost there?"

Renn laughed. "I knew you'd enjoy this, Jack."

"I'm giving it a chance, I promise." He ducked his head under a low-hanging branch, almost colliding with Renn's in the process. "So you got your app, then you pick a ..."

"Geocache."

"Right, you pick geocache from the list. Then you just start hiking towards the GPS coordinates until you find the... geocache. I get it, you're Captain Jack Sparrow."

Renn pulled her phone out to check their heading. The compass on the geocaching app indicated they were right on target, about a mile away. She waved the phone at Jack before returning it to her jeans' back pocket. "He would have gotten around a lot easier with one of these. Anyway, it's about the journey, not the destination."

The irony struck her even as the words left her mouth. Here she was, the most goal-oriented person either of them knew, talking about the journey. She found the first geocache in the spring of that year under a park bench a few blocks from her house. She knew, even then, that this day was inevitable.

There were a dozen caches hidden around Black Hawk Bend, and this was the last one she had to find. There was a reason she hadn't joined Jack and their friends during their Pokémon GO phase; she knew herself well enough to understand she'd have to catch 'em all.

But had she enjoyed the journey?

She slid quickly past another intruding branch and pulled it after her, releasing it like a whip into Jack's torso. "Keep up Jack-o," she called, daring him to keep pace with her sprint that could traverse a soccer field in mere seconds.

"No fair, Rennie," Jack huffed as he sped up. "Wait. Up."

She dashed through the woods, preferring the straightest path to the marked one. Autumn colors blurred around her, and branches slapped harmlessly off her body as she took shortcuts through the underbrush. She *was* enjoying herself, chasing this goal. In contrast to other parts of her life, responsibility didn't weigh on her here. No checklist needed to be filled out, and no extra credit would be given. This goal was simple and raw, and she would miss it.

No sooner had Renn gotten her endorphins flowing, then she came to a sudden halt on the trail, panting with hands on hips and elbows out.

Jack barreled to a stop beside her and bent over, hands on knees. "I. Caught you. You're slowing down."

"You wish. Look." Renn pointed at a tall, gleaming fence, slicing the woods in two as far as the eye could see in either direction.

And her goal lay on the other side.

She approached the fence and laced her fingers through its diamond-shaped mesh. She shook it, testing first its reality, and then its strength. This thing stood eight feet high, easy.

3

How was she going to get to the cache?

"Come, look at this," said Jack from a ways to her left. She stepped off the trail which wound on past the barrier and walked over to Jack. A sign, posted at eye level on the fence, read, 'No Trespassing'.

"Who do you think put it here?" asked Jack.

Renn had not considered who; she didn't really care.

Jack turned his back on the fence. "Good try. Let's go back."

Renn took out her phone as she walked back to the trail. The compass pointed right through the fence and the distance showed half a mile. She craned her neck and tried to see the bends in the trail through the colorful foliage. Stowing the phone, she tested the fence again with a shake. It was climbable. But what were the consequences? You shouldn't have to climb fences while geocaching. Had someone bought the land after the cache was planted? If so, why was it still alive on the app? "I know, we probably should, but we're so close."

"It looks pretty new," said Jack. "What if they have cameras or guards?"

He was prodding again, looking for a chink. And if he could get her to crack a smile, so much the better in his book. Annoying, but also a little endearing.

She glanced over towards Jack. He crawled, down on his hands and knees, looking over a bush.

"Someone's coming." He turned his head and hissed, "Let's get out of here."

Renn shook her head in wonder at his level of commitment to the farce. Then she started climbing the fence. It flexed back and forth as she shifted her weight, but the going wasn't too bad. Soon, she stood with her arms thrown over the top.

She just had to get her body over, but couldn't figure out an elegant way to do it.

Something crashed through the bushes. "Ahhh, a bear!" Jack wailed.

Renn sighed and turned her head to pay him the attention he so obviously craved. He lay on his back, obscured by an enormous black and white furry shape. It licked him furiously.

"Renn, get your Bear off me, please."

She fished a baggie from her vest pocket and tossed him a treat. "Try that. It might not compare to taste of Jack though."

Getting over the fence was awkward, but quickly accomplished. From the other side, she fished out another treat and held it through the fence for Bear. Jack knelt on the trail, dusting himself off and wiping a plaid flannel sleeve across his face. "This is a bad idea, Renn. What about Bear? He can't follow."

"He'll be fine here. Won't you, Bear? Newfi's are very loyal. It's only half a mile more, Jack. Let's go, in and out. Then I can put the caches behind me for a while."

Jack grunted and lumbered to the fence. He climbed ponderously and complained loudly. Renn suppressed an urge to giggle. She had won this round. He landed with a thump beside her. She admonished Bear to stay and fed him a final treat.

"Let's go, then. You're getting a proper initiation into geocaching."

The woods seemed different on this side of the fence. The shadows were longer, the colors more muted. An eerie silence blanketed them, and every crack of a branch under their feet pierced it like a needle. The day was getting away from her. They'd spent longer than planned on the hike, putting her schedule in danger. She'd planned for time to help mom with dinner, time for homework, and time to study for her biology test. Then half an hour to work on an ACT practice exam, if time allowed. They had about thirty minutes to find this cache and get back to their bikes.

They walked in silence now, as if a spoken word would further contaminate the space they invaded. Renn walked a few steps behind Jack, letting him blaze the trail. He might be in a bigger hurry than her to get out of here.

Jack was a true friend. They'd known each other since the second grade, rode the bus together for years. She even kissed him once after declaring that they would marry. Back then, he was one of the few kids who didn't make fun of her Asian features, so exotic to the Midwestern kids. Boys eventually became gross, and she had her girlfriends. They lost touch for the rest of grade school. But when times got tough for her in junior high, and her friends revealed their true characters, Jack was there. And their friendship had continued on into high school.

They arrived at a small glade dominated by a tall majestic maple with burning orange leaves. Renn held her phone in front of her and turned all the way around. "We're here. Start looking around."

Jack kicked at piles of fallen leaves. "What are we looking for exactly?"

"Hard to say. It's probably a small container, like a metal or plastic box, or maybe it's a canister of some kind. Let's check the base of this tree."

She got down on her hands and knees and brushed away leaves all around the trunk of the maple. She found no recessed spaces to tuck away a cache, and it didn't look like anything had been buried. Jack walked around the edge of the glade, checking the surrounding trees. Renn blew a strand of hair off her face, stood up and brushed herself off. She walked around the area again with her phone.

The GPS tracking on the app was only approximate. She'd found caches several feet away from where she thought they'd be. They might be easy to spot or well hidden. One was tucked into the blind side of an I-beam on a bridge. She found another one stuffed into the crack between boulders. One even hung in plain sight in an apple tree. Unfortunately, the container was a fake apple and they were in season, so she'd searched for an hour before noticing its glint, a little shinier than its neighbors. She hoped this wasn't another one like that.

"I don't think it's here anymore," Jack said. "Are they all this hard to find?"

"No, not all." Renn stood in the clearing of the glade and let her gaze wander. "I guess it's possible someone muggled it."

"I'm sorry, are we role playing now? Is this the forest by Hogwarts with the spiders?"

Renn bent down, selected a small stick, and flung it at Jack. "Shut up, you. It's a geocaching term. It just means that a non-geocacher stole it. I guess it came from Harry Potter, though."

Her train of thought picked up some steam and she continued to muse, to no one in particular. "Or maybe it's archived. No, then it wouldn't be on the app anymore. It's still an active cache, but there are a few DNFs."

Jack was trying to carve something into a tree trunk with the stick she had provided. "You're geeking out on me here, Renn. Earth to Renn."

"Did not find, get it? And you're calling me a geek? I've got three words for you Mr. Football Star." She selected another branch, larger this time, and pointed it at him. "Kerbal. Space. Program."

Jack clutched his heart with both hands and fell to his knees. "How could you? You wound me."

Renn looked at Jack kneeling by a tree, then looked back to the burning maple. "Come here. I need to stand on your shoulders."

"Oh, come on. How about I stand on your shoulders?"

"Because you'd crush my delicate bones. Now, please. I need to check the place up there where the trunk splits into three. See it?"

Jack sighed and nodded. "It's worth a shot, I guess. But if it's not there, we're going, okay?"

Renn took a long look around the clearing. "Deal."

Jack walked over to the big tree and knelt in front of it. Renn got a knee up on his shoulder, then a foot, then both feet, and finally shimmied her torso up the tree.

Jack writhed beneath her feet.

"Will you hold still?" she griped.

He muttered something about soccer cleats and stabilized enough for Renn to stand up straight. She barely stood tall enough to reach into the nook, much less see into it. She probed around blindly for something more substantial than loose leaves, stretching and pushing up onto tip-toes.

Jack howled and squirmed in pain, whether real or mock she couldn't tell. Renn hugged the tree with her free arm, but soon lost her balance. She groped for some kind of handhold to climb up with, but the tree was too smooth and slipped under her hand. Wait. "Hang on, Jack, I got something."

She lost her footing and started to fall back. Instinctively, she twisted to go down forwards, maybe even tuck and roll. It wasn't pretty, but once she regained her wits, she found that she clutched a metal tin in her right hand.

Goal achieved.

Still lying on her back, she held the tin in the air and turned it around. It was gray, unadorned, and rusting in spots. Her year of geocaching was about to come to an end.

Jack yelled and leapt to his feet, frantically brushing off his jeans.

"You okay there?"

"Spider," said Jack, checking his shirt and hair. "I hate spiders."

"Just hang on, we'll be out of here soon." She sat up and worked the rusted lid off the tin. Even though Renn had found several caches so far, the excitement of opening a new one had not gone away. "Come, have a look."

She dumped the contents onto the ground between them. Out tumbled an old Batman Pez dispenser, an Indian arrow-head, and a troll doll with wild orange hair. Renn's experience with such things was admittedly limited, but these seemed a little more eclectic than usual.

Jack studied the troll doll and said, "We came out here for this junk?"

"It's called swag," said Renn. "People can bring a new item and exchange it for one in the cache. It's a tradition. See, I brought one along." She pulled from her pocket a set of dog tags. "These are from my old dog, Sparky. Remember her?" She ran the tags through her hands with tender care and placed them in the tin. "Now what should I take?"

Jack brushed his hand through the swag and picked up an item she hadn't noticed. He held it up for them both to see. It was a small, blue, plastic cylinder a little over two inches long and not quite an inch in diameter. Close to one end were five rings, with numbers imprinted on them. It looked like a combination lock.

"What do you think about this?" he asked. "It looks like there might be something else inside it."

Renn took the piece and tried to pull it open. "Yeah, but it's locked. Well, I don't want the ugly troll, and who knows how old that Pez is. What about the arrowhead? It's cool, right?"

Jack's attention fixed itself on the blue cylinder. "I vote for this. Don't you want to know what it is?"

Renn shrugged. "Okay, we'll take the mystery lock for the dog tags." She brushed past the arrowhead and pulled a small notebook and pencil from among the swag. On the first available page, she signed it 'Wren' and added the date. "The last log entry is from about a year ago, signed by a 'Unicorn'." Renn showed the book to Jack, but he was still preoccupied with his new toy. She put Sparky's dog tags in the tin with the notepad and pencil. "If you really want it, you can have it. I left my swag and signed my name. That's all I need." Renn resealed the container and tossed it up into the nook of the maple. On her first try, she heard it land neatly with a metallic thud.

Her thoughts turned to her dog, and then to her chores and homework. This had been a pretty good day, but it wasn't over yet. She took a moment to redo her ponytail and check her clothes for stray leaves. "Ready to go?"

Jack had crossed to the far side of the glade and looked to be marching off in the wrong direction. She checked the compass on her app to make sure she wasn't turned around. "Hey Jack, the fence is back this way."

"I know, I want to see what's over the ridge here," he said

10

as he hiked in the opposite direction of home.

What was this about? Wasn't he bored with the whole geocache thing? She shrugged and followed. In about five minutes, they crested the ridge and came upon a deep ravine choked with brush and brambles. Beyond that lay a large, manicured lawn, and beyond the lawn sat a large building. She made out a loading dock and a couple of dumpsters. "What is it?"

Jack showed her the blue cylinder again, and now she could see it had an icon carved into one end.

"Do you know where we are?" he asked.

"Not a clue. Enlighten me."

"That," he said, pointing at the building, "is Silver Labs. And this," he continued, pointing at the icon on the blue cylinder, "is Silver Labs, too."

Chapter 2

"Silver Labs. They do techie stuff, right?" Renn studied the building but saw nothing special or interesting.

Jack tapped his finger against the blue icon. "They do *everything*, Renn. Jason Silver is some kind of computer engineer, but they're into manufacturing, transportation, health, manufacturing—you name it." He waved his hands around now, using the thing to point at the building.

Renn couldn't help but be amused at Jack's boyish enthusiasm. Not ten minutes ago he was dying to head back home. She checked the time and updated her schedule in her mind again. "Let's get out of here."

They retraced their steps along the trail, Jack chattering away about products and inventions from Silver Labs. They got back to the fence and found Bear, his thick, black fur sprouting through the mesh like a Chia Pet. He stood when he heard them approach. His great tail swooshed and his big, pink tongue lolled out of an open, smiling mouth.

The woods brightened again as they retreated from Silver Labs. They found their bikes parked at the trailhead, and Bear rushed to inspect them diligently. Renn took a drink from a water bottle stashed on her bike when her phone buzzed. A message from Mom popped up, asking if she had heard the news.

"What news?" she thumbed back. She gaped at the reply, too shocked to respond.

"What is it?" Jack asked after taking a swig from his bottle.

"Stella disappeared from the Raptor Center this morning.

"What does that mean? Who's Stella?"

Renn was rooted to the trail, her phone dangling forgotten at her side. "Stella is a bald eagle who's lived at the Raptor Center for a couple of years. She had a broken wing." She typed a hurried reply to her mom and stuffed the phone into her vest pocket. How long had it been since she'd seen Stella and Ranger Scott? And how could an eagle just up and disappear like that?

"Listen, Jack, I'm going to swing by on my way home, just to check it out."

Jack looked up at her from a squat, one hand petting the big dog. "Want me to come with? I don't mind."

Renn knew Jack had no interest in the Raptor Center, or an abducted animal. He was just a true friend. "No, it's okay. You go on. I have Bear."

They exchanged waves and she watched him ride off. She should go, too. Every item on her schedule tugged at her mind. But Stella's disappearance grabbed her by the neck and yanked back. She resigned herself to a late night of studying and mounted her bike.

The Raptor Center wasn't far, but it was the opposite direction of home, and a good ten-minute ride at a brisk pace. She took it slow enough for Bear to keep up. She had ridden this way before. Her wingman was Sparky the Bearded Collie, and ribbons streamed from the ends of her handlebars. First came Hawk camp, then Osprey and Falcon camps. Her earliest

13

memories of learning biology were out here, studying the animals and plants of the northern Illinois woods, near the Mississippi river. In fact, she'd wanted to be a vet for a long time after those camps. Above all, Ranger Scott had instilled in his campers a respect for the natural world.

She pulled onto a gravel road and pedaled under the roughly hewn log arch that marked the entrance to Black Hawk Park. Beyond the gravel parking lot, Renn could see the familiar Ranger Station. She pedaled onto the grass and continued past it. Behind the station sat several elevated wooden cages with chicken wire fencing and slanted roofs. The bike fell to the ground, unheeded, as Renn stepped up to an empty cage. A metal plate on the front read "Stella. Southern Bald Eagle."

Once, she had stood in front of one of these cages on top of an old apple crate. Then, she had sported pigtails instead of a ponytail, and she had examined an old red-tailed hawk to diagnose her injuries. What was she doing here now? What did she think she could accomplish, staring at an empty cage? Her mom's report of the missing bird was real, as real as the fence that split the woods in two.

Just as she made up her mind to go, she heard a door slam. A tall, thin man wearing forest green rounded the corner of the station. His head tilted down, exposing the wide brim and dented top of his ranger's hat. "Mother Mary and Aunt Jemima, we don't need any more rubberneckers today. You just be on your way."

She crossed her arms and stood her ground.

"I don't know what you think you're going to see." He lifted his weathered, rugged face and a look of recognition filled his eyes. "Why, Adrienne Chao, is that you?"

Renn ran to him and hugged him tight around his chest. He

patted her back awkwardly before she broke away and met his gaze. "My mom told me the news. I was close by and wanted to come see. I can't believe it, Ranger."

Ranger Scott scratched his scraggly salt-and-pepper beard. "You and me both darlin', you and me both. I'm sorry for the rude reception. You wouldn't believe how many folks have dropped by today to gawk at an empty cage. And then there were the reporters and the police."

"If you don't mind me asking, what happened?"

The ranger recounted his story in a soft, monotone voice. He had checked on Stella and the other birds in the morning, but decided to make his rounds before feeding them. He'd been a few hundred feet down the road when he'd heard her distinctive call. She called like that sometimes when he had food, always when he was around the cages. He remembered standing there, thinking about going back. But then she quieted down, and he went on. Only after he finished his rounds and carried a bucket of food around back had he discovered her door open and the cage empty.

He looked ten years older than Renn remembered. This must have really shaken him up. "Is it possible someone let her out?" she asked.

Ranger Scott removed his hat and ran his nut-brown hand over his graying crew cut. He spoke with the well-practiced tone of a teacher. "Good question, Renn. Look over here." He led them behind the cage where the door stood half open. "Do you remember the extent of Stella's injuries when she arrived?"

"Um, she had a broken wing and several broken tail feathers, right?"

"Right, and she also has a bad eye. We determined early on

15

that Stella would never be fit enough for release back into the wild. If I opened her door, like this, chances are we'd still see her sitting inside after a whole day. Then there's this." He pointed down to the bush below the cage door.

Renn followed the ranger's gesture and bent to look closer at the bush. Some leaves had dark reddish marks on them. "There's blood here."

"There was a lot more than what you see. I collected most of it for evidence." Ranger Scott looked grim as he continued. "Stella still couldn't fly, so if she were loose, she'd only be able to travel by foot. I've been all around the area and haven't seen any sign of her. She could only have been missing for half an hour at the most by the time I got back."

Renn touched a bloody leaf and rubbed the inky reddish stuff between her fingers. "Is this Stella's blood?"

"I've been so busy dealing with people today, I haven't had time to answer that question yet. I was just about to try when you showed up."

Renn gave Ranger Scott a look that said, "Don't let me stop you," and "Can I help?" all at once.

This reaction from his former student clearly didn't surprise the ranger. He chuckled and said, "Adrienne, do you know the difference between bird blood and human blood?"

Renn smiled, transported back to her childhood. He might have been asking her to differentiate ash and oak leaves or teaching her the call of a barn owl. "No, not really."

"Well, come on then." He led her around and into the ranger station. The small space was combination tourist information center, office, and small laboratory. In the back sat a counter with a sink, coffeemaker, and microwave. On the same counter sat a microscope and a small rack of glass slides, vials, and test tubes. Ranger Scott reached below the counter to swing open the door of a mini fridge. He pulled out a Ziploc bag that held several snipped branches and leaves from the bush. At the bottom of the bag, Renn saw a pool of partially congealed blood.

As he worked, he lectured. "There are two key differences between the blood of birds and that of mammals. First, red blood cells in birds have nuclei, and mammal blood cells don't." He retrieved a glass slide from the rack and picked a leaf from the baggie. With the leaf, he smeared some blood on the slide and prepared it for viewing under the microscope. "Now, with this microscope, I don't think we'll be able to see nuclei. But the other difference is that bird cells are more oval shaped, while mammal cells are more round."

"Because of the nucleus?" asked Renn.

"Hmmm, perhaps," he answered. He placed the slide under the microscope and pulled it closer to the edge of the counter for easier viewing. He turned the magnification knob to the 40x setting and looked through the lens. The tall man hunched and fiddled with the focus, studying the sample for several seconds. Finally, he stood and stretched his back. "Well, have a look. Let's see what you think."

Renn tilted her head and looked through the eyepiece. The view was fuzzy at first as her eyes and brain adjusted, but soon she made them out. A field of round, purple capsules. Some of them clumped together while others roamed free. The clumped ones reminded her a little of fish eggs.

She ran through the parts of a cell by rote. It would be on her biology test anyway, the one she should be studying for right now. Maybe her teacher would give her extra credit for field work. A knot formed in the pit of her stomach. One strand of it represented the homework she was neglecting. Another, the horrifying, incomprehensible crime of stealing an injured bald eagle. If it turned out to be some sick prank, there wasn't a pit deep enough for the perpetrators.

She should get on her bike, ride home with her dog, and resume her normal life. What could she possibly do to help Stella now? The deed was done and couldn't be undone. A line of tears wet Renn's cheeks, and she huddled over the microscope even more to hide her face. Why did some of the most significant moments in life jump out of nowhere and slap you in the face?

No. This wouldn't be the end of Stella's story. There had to be something she could do. She turned away from the ranger and wiped her eyes.

"Well, what's the verdict?" Ranger Scott's question echoed in her head.

The verdict was that this pond scum would not get away with taking Stella.

The verdict was that if Stella still lived, Renn would find her.

The verdict was, "They're round. That's not Stella's blood."

The ranger looked pleased with his student, and the approval made the knot in her stomach loosen.

"I have to agree. That is definitely human blood."

"Stella must have injured the stupid bird-napper. I wonder if she used her beak or her talons."

"Either way, I wouldn't be surprised if they have some pretty nasty gashes."

Renn crossed her arms and leaned back against the counter. "Well, the police will catch them, right?"

Ranger Scott grunted and shook his head. "I don't reckon the police will do much. They took a bit of the blood and said they'd look into it, but I don't know. I heard the deputy say something about his backlog of parking tickets. Parking tickets! All they have to do is search for a red truck."

Renn's head perked up. "What truck?" she asked.

Ranger Scott explained the presence of another pickup truck when he arrived in the morning, and its absence after he returned to find the cage empty. He didn't pay much attention, as it wasn't unusual for someone to be out for an early morning hike.

Renn racked her brain, exercising it on a new kind of problem, one that would be graded on a scale of life and death. "Anything else you can remember?" she asked.

The ranger shook his head, his features downcast. "I'm afraid not. It doesn't seem to be very much to go on."

Renn gave him a quick hug. "If there's anything I can do, please let me know. And if I think of anything, I'll get back in touch."

Renn didn't know how, but she *would* think of something.

Chapter 3

Jack reached into his locker and rifled through a mess of papers, books, and clothing. He grabbed a rolled-up towel and sniffed it, reared his head away from its rankness. A second roll smelled less offensive, so Jack tucked it under his arm and shoved his backpack and the older towel into the cramped space.

This would be a great week. The Black Hawk Bend Scouts were on their way to state. They had a shot for the first time in ten years. They played Central High, one of the toughest teams on their schedule, this Friday. If the Scouts won, their chances looked very good. So that's what they were going to do with Jack's help.

Some people preferred the glory of the offense, moving the ball down the field, running in for a touchdown. He liked the grittiness of the defense. What a rush, to slip past the offensive line and lay out the quarterback, ball in hand. Yes, he was in touch with his inner caveman.

The after-school traffic quickly thinned out after last period. Jack headed for the wide central staircase of the school, composed of two staircases back to back, spiraling in opposite directions. His teammate Ryan flew out from the stairs and into the opposite wing of the school. He identified Ryan by his long black hair, not as long as Renn's, and more stringy.

Jack heard laughter and it gave him a bad feeling. He stepped past the staircase and stood in the archway leading to the other wing. Ryan and another teammate, Bernie, stood around a boy, blocking him in at his open locker. The student's backpack sat at his feet; he tried to pull another book from his locker.

"What's up, Dominique? You gonna take all those books home?" Bernie's gravelly voice echoed off the linoleum floor of the empty hallway. He pronounced the name oddly, putting extra emphasis on the last syllable: 'DominEEK'. A girl's name.

Jack knew both of them well enough to understand the dynamics at play; Bernie the ringleader and Ryan the willing follower. Bernie wasn't happy unless he was tormenting someone. It made him a vicious opponent on the football field.

"Can I have my book back, please?"

Bernie held a fat textbook, riffling through it. "Jeez, you ever do anything but study, DominEEK?"

"Get a life loser," Ryan added with enthusiasm.

Jack got a closer view of the victim and recognized him from his advanced math class. There were only two African American kids in it. Medium height and a little chunky. Dominic Marshall. Dominic was better at math than him, a fact Jack only grudgingly admitted.

He checked his Fitbit and glanced down the stairwell. If he arrived late to practice, there was a good chance he'd get to experience Coach Kelley's killers. He stepped back out of the arch and into the stairwell, and glanced over his shoulder at the unfolding drama. "Bernard, Ryan," he shouted. "Yo, do you want to be late? Let's go."

Bernie spared him a venomous glance. Dominic also looked at him with a pleading in his eyes, a buried cry for help mixed with fear.

Jack paused a moment longer, then hurried down the stairs. The idiots could run killers for all he cared.

* * *

He rushed down the first-floor hallway towards the locker room. As he passed the Chemistry room, a familiar voice rang out, "Ah, Jack, I'm so glad I caught you. Do you have a minute to help me out?"

He suppressed a groan and turned to face the voice. Mrs. Anderson stood by the door, wringing her hands. Her brown hair balanced precariously atop her head, like a fluffy game of Jenga. She wore even more costume jewelry than usual.

There could be only one reason for stopping him like this. Another time he'd have been happy to help. But this wasn't another time.

"Hi, Mrs. Anderson. I'm sorry, but I'm going to be late ..."

"Thank you, Jack. I'm sure it won't take but a moment. I am at my wits' end with this machine. Such a frustrating contraption."

Mrs. Anderson could go on like that for a long time. She had the ability to wear a person down with nothing but words. On the other hand, Coach Kelley's killers could wear a person down in a much more painful way.

"Coach will be mad if I'm late again."

Mrs. Anderson waved thick rings with gaudy gems in a dismissive gesture. "Oh, you let me worry about Mr. Kelley, dear. I'll write a note if it comes to that. Now be a dear and look at this piece I'm trying to finish for Mr. Harvey. It's not nearly as complicated as that last one. I promise."

Jack shifted back and forth on his feet as he cast a yearning glance down the hallway. Then he followed Mrs. Anderson's trail of perfume into the Chem Lab. He didn't see the 'contraption' in its usual spot. Dozens of plastic cups now occupied the space.

The harried teacher rounded the corner of a black resin countertop. She had a way of reaching out to touch the nearest piece of furniture at hand as she walked, too lightly for physical support, possibly for reassurance. "We had to move it yesterday to make room for my third period crystal growing experiments. It's over here now." She gestured over to a counter along the side of the room where several microscopes sat beneath reddish-brown cabinets with wood-framed glass doors. "There's no good spot for it."

Jack dragged his hands through his mussed hair and looked for the printer. He thought he might know the problem already. He rushed over and started his examination. About the size of a microwave oven, and hollow like one, the machine didn't have walls across the sides or front. In its interior, a print head extended from the device's ceiling. A control panel along the top front edge near the right side read '3DPlot'.

Jack examined the printer with a keen eye. "Is this the first thing you've printed since you moved it?" A piece sat in the print bay on the build plate. He couldn't tell if it was finished or not because he had no idea what it was supposed to be. It looked a little like half of a star shape. It had large spikes and between the spikes, thin strands of filament hung like Christmas tree lights.

Mrs. Anderson leaned over to examine the shape, and her perfume threatened to overpower him. "Impressive, isn't it? It's for Mr. Harvey's geometry collection. A stellated dodecahedron. Well, half of one. I have to print the other half next."

It didn't show any warping around the bottom, nor did it sag to one side. That busted his hypothesis that the build plate had become unleveled when moved. She'd probably asked a couple of boys in class to move it, not realizing how delicate it could be.

The teacher pointed a finger at the stellated dodecahedron. "See, these strings on the ends ruin the whole piece. Very disappointing."

Now that Jack better understood the intended shape, it gave him an idea. "Can I check a setting on the laptop?"

Mrs. Anderson assented and pointed to the cupboard under the counter. He retrieved a beat-up laptop, powered it up, and brought up the software that configured the printer. He opened the settings and scanned through them until finding the right one.

"Here, do you see this setting called 'Retraction'? You should check it before trying this piece again. It retracts the filament into the nozzle before traveling across empty space to lay down a new section of material. That prevents any strands from being dragged across by the nozzle. That should take care of the problem."

His teacher wrinkled her brow and flipped her gaze between printer and laptop, printer and laptop. She didn't look convinced that such a simple thing could cause so much frustration. But she smiled and patted Jack on the shoulder. "Oh, dear me, thank you so much, Jack. I'll give it a try. I don't know what I would do without you. You have such a way with machines."

He smiled at the compliment and returned the laptop to its

home and took another look at the printer's nameplate. It had a model number and a logo. He fished in his pocket for the blue combination lock he'd found earlier with Renn and turned its end up exposing the logo. They were the same, of course, because this was a Silver Labs printer. The logo had a stylized set of initials, 'SL' in the style of a circuit board. Straight-line segments, like little wires laid between pools of solder, made up the intertwined letters.

"What do you have there, Jack?"

He held out the lock for her to examine. "My friend and I found this, but we don't know what it is."

"Why, it's a cryptex," she said without hesitation. "You know, from *The DaVinci Code*? That Dan Brown is one of my favorites. Wherever did you find it?"

Jack gave an abbreviated version of their cache adventure and wondered anew at the potential connections with Silver Labs. What did this cryptex have to do with a billion-dollar company out of Silicon Valley? Could it be tied directly to Jason Silver, its founder and CEO? He spun one of the rings on the lock. There were five of them with ten digits each. That meant one-hundred thousand possible combinations. His chances of guessing were not so good.

"Could it be stolen?"

What?! "No. We didn't steal this, Mrs. A. We just found it." He bristled at the accusation.

"Oh, I wasn't implying that, Mr. Henderson. I'm referring to the reports of attempted theft from Silver Labs a couple of weeks ago. Do you remember hearing about it? I just wondered if it might be something someone took. Oh, but they caught that poor young man, didn't they?"

He turned the cryptex in his fingers and tried to probe its

secrets. Could someone have stolen this from Silver Labs? He didn't think so. The cache they found had been there for quite a while. Renn said the last entry was, like, a year ago or something. They couldn't be connected.

"Thank you for your help, Jack. Should I write you a note for Stan?"

Oh crap. He checked his Fitbit. He was already five minutes late for practice.

Chapter 4

Dominic Marshall sat at the weathered practice piano and ran through a series of two-octave arpeggios, first starting on C, then D, and continuing up the keyboard. The notes filled the small apartment with sound. The weathered practice piano was half a key out of tune, but the B flat just below middle C, and the F an octave above, stood out as especially offensive. He pushed on through the sour notes to finish the exercise. A person learned to tolerate a lot of things.

"Get your damn hands off me."

He wrung his hands together and shook them out at his sides while he tested the words out loud. No, cursing seemed like too much.

"Get your lousy hands off me, Bernard. Bernie. Take your hands off me, Bernie, or you'll be sorry."

Dominic shook his head and sat up straighter on the hard, wooden bench. He spread out sheet music for Bach's "Minuet in G Major", a favorite of his, and began playing. The fingering patterns came easily, imprinted in muscle memory. By the time he finished, he realized that he attacked it with more tempo and intensity than Bach had probably intended. He started over, but the notes came stiff and tense.

"Bernie, let's be reasonable." He paused and laughed to

himself. "That's stupid. You've got to think of something good to say."

It bothered him that he couldn't think of female versions of either Bernie or Ryan. Was his the only name that gender-flipped so easily? He preferred Dom. Nice and short, hard to abuse.

He experimented with some improvisation. Music appealed to him for many reasons he did not fully understand. But it also attracted him in a way that made intrinsic sense. It was so mathematical. Each note corresponded to the frequency of a string vibrating when struck by a hammer in the piano. Notes, octaves, scales, chords. All worked together, and as long as you learned the rules, you could create beautiful music.

Sitting at this worn-out instrument allowed him to get out of his own head, though he doubted even Bach would be enough to get him through the school year. The latest attack rewound and played again in his mind's eye. He had been afraid that Bernie and Ryan would shove him completely inside his locker. Maybe, as a sophomore, he was finally too big for that particular trick.

It seemed like they never ran out of tricks. He'd been bullied in hallways, on playgrounds, in classrooms, on the way to and from school, online, and in locker rooms. Man, locker room bullying was the worst. Last week, he'd rushed so much to get dressed and get out of there that he accidentally put his underwear on backwards.

"Ha! Look at DominEEK!" the kids had teased. "Hey, did you know that the hole is supposed to go in front? He didn't know, haha."

"You can go straight to hell, Bernard," he whispered.

He shook his head again and started improvising a melody

with his right hand. He let it rise and fall, creating a tune that he imagined Bach could have written. Almost a random walk along the keyboard. Then he tried the same thing with his left hand. He imagined a melody that would provide an interesting counterpoint for his right-hand tune. Next, trying to keep both in his mind, he tried to play them together. He got about two measures in when it fell apart. His mind couldn't track both lines at the same time without seeing it written down. He had read that Marvin Minsky, the pioneer of artificial intelligence, had this ability—to improvise a point-counterpoint out of thin air. Create something new and beautiful, but also complex and stable.

He couldn't even formulate a cogent sentence and send it out of his mouth. And did anyone ever stop to help? Not a chance. Another football player had seen them today, catching his eye but doing nothing. Those guys all looked after one another. He felt like a minnow swimming with sharks. His only chance was to get out of the deep water.

"Dominic!"

He startled, lifted his head from his reveries, and looked towards the kitchenette where he saw his mother pulling dishes down from the cupboards.

"Sorry, Mama. Did you just get home? I'll help you with dinner."

"Aw, sugar, I been home for a while. Food's ready to be eaten! Come, set the table now before it gets cold. Lord Almighty, what am I going to do with you, baby? Always got your head in the clouds."

Dom understood the question was not directed at him, even though there was no one else in the apartment other than their cat Boots. Rhetorical questions made him a little

29

uncomfortable. He still felt like he should have a ready answer, but he had none. He wondered if she heard any of his comments for Bernie but didn't ask.

The piano bench creaked as he rose and wound his way around the sofa and dining table to the kitchenette counter. His mother passed him plates, cups, and silverware across the counter, and his mouth watered upon sniffing her mashed potatoes. After setting the table, they sat down to their meal, held hands, and said grace.

"You playin' that thing just beautiful these days, baby. I swear, you gonna be the Duke one day."

"Thank you, Mama." He fashioned himself more as Thelonious Monk than Duke Ellington, but the compliment still resonated.

"But you got to get that head out of the clouds. Pay attention to what's going on around you! Life be passin' you by, baby, and you none the wiser."

"Yes, Mama." Dom took a drink of ice water and stared at his mashed potatoes.

"You finish your homework yet?"

That question had layers. Of course he'd finished his homework. He could do it in his sleep.

"Yes, Mama, but I ain't going back there."

His mother arched an eyebrow and took a bite of her buttered Hawaiian bun. "Mmm hmm. How do you s'pose that?"

Dom looked up and spoke fast to fit his prepared argument into a brief window of opportunity. "Mama, I could do all my reading at home, get the homework, and drop it off on Monday morning. I don't get anything out of class anyway."

"Because you don't pay attention, Dominic." She had stopped eating. "Those teachers are there to help you. You got to get a good education." She struck the word 'got' like a hammer on a piano string. Even Boots swiveled his head towards the sound.

Dom withered in his seat. He didn't have a response prepared. He managed a forced whisper. "But I don't like it there."

"Baby, whenever those kids give you trouble, you go talk to a teacher. That's what they for." Her voice softened, and she muttered something under her breath that sounded like, "Too good for them."

Dom took up his prepared argument again. "I could get my GED and start college early. Or I could take some college classes now." At least it would get him away from high school for a while.

"No." The hammer struck again. "GED is what you get for quittin' school. You is too good for that, Dominic. You can do it right. You can be the first one."

Both their plates sat untouched now. They were in a battle of wills, one that Dom had never won.

"I don't feel good. May I be excused?"

The force of her will pressed on him as they sat there in stony silence. Finally, she waved her wrist and picked her fork up. Dom pushed back the chair and hurried to his room, shutting the door behind him. He flung himself onto his bed and lay there with his eyes clamped shut for a long time.

When the pressure in his head receded enough for him to think clearly, he opened his eyes. Above his head, a poster of Einstein greeted him with words of wisdom, 'The significant problems we have cannot be solved at the same level of thinking with which we created them'.

Dom reached for his phone and earbuds sitting on the nightstand. He put them in and started his jazz play list. After two songs of lying there and breathing, he swung his legs off the bed and sat up. In front of him sat his desk and bookshelf, strewn with papers, books, games, and puzzles. He plucked the Rubik's Cube off his chessboard and lay back on the bed while shuffling it from its solved state to a random one.

His mind turned the corner from randomizing to solving, and the turns slowed down, each one careful and studied. Dom tried to absorb all the effects and side effects of each action he took on the cube. Lining up an edge was trivial. Solving for one face was easy. After that, putting other faces in order messed up the one already solved. You had to plan several moves ahead and live with temporary chaos until a new order clicked into place.

What was his next move? What words could he say? His life twisted into chaos and he couldn't solve it. He didn't know if he had the courage to go back to that place again.

That night he tossed and turned for a long time before falling into dark dreams.

Chapter 5

Renn pulled into Jack's driveway and pushed the button to shut down her mom's Prius. She picked her school planner off the passenger seat and it fell open to the day's date. Lists, notes, and doodles filled the page. Sticky notes protruded from between pages, reminding her of appointments and due dates. She reviewed today's items, her eyes following her finger down the planner's inked-up page. She had not forgotten anything.

The current item on her list read, 'Jack's house. Cache swag nonsense'. She knew why he wanted her to stop by, but it was okay. She had news for him, too, about Stella. Renn drew a line through the item, tossed the planner back onto the seat, and stepped out into the chill October air.

The front patio light was on and she heard the doorbell chime throughout the house when she pressed the button. Footsteps pattered down the wooden staircase beyond the door. It opened and Jack's little brother, Timmy, pushed open the storm door a couple inches for her. "Hi, Rennie," he sang in his high, seven-year-old voice.

"Hi. Timmy, how's my little man? Got a girlfriend yet?"

"No, silly," Timmy giggled.

"Good, I don't think I could bear it." She reached to tousle his hair, but he ran off into the living room.

"Over here, Renn." Jack's voice came from the kitchen, and she found him sitting at the breakfast bar eating a bowl of Frosted Flakes. Jack's mom bustled around the kitchen, cleaning up after dinner. She waved at Renn and shined a warm smile.

"Dessert of champions?" asked Renn, gesturing at the bowl.

"You know it. Want some?"

"No, thanks, I prefer to get my calories from, ya know, food." She sat on one of the empty barstools.

"So picky you are." Jack slurped the last bit of milk from the bowl. "Hey, what was the date of Unicorn's log entry?"

"Jack, don't be rude," his mother called from across the kitchen. "I'm so sorry, Adrienne. Can I get you anything?"

"No, thank you, Mrs. Henderson. I'm good." Renn pictured the logbook and tried to remember the date on the page. "I want to say June or July of last year. I don't remember the day."

"No problem. That's sixty-one days. With different date formats, I have lots more combinations to try."

"You think you're going to crack it?"

"I do. I mean, it was meant to be opened, right?"

Renn rested an elbow on the counter and her chin on the heel of her palm. "Oh, really? How do you figure that?"

"Simple," said Jack as he pushed his empty bowl to the other side of the bar. "Suppose whoever hid this wanted it to be a secret. Why did they put there? Why does it have the Silver Labs logo right on it? It just makes no sense."

"I guess it's not what I would have done. I'd lock it up and hide it, but not in a tree."

"Exactly." Jack pointed at her. "Exactamundo. Hey, did you know that someone tried to rob Silver Labs a couple weeks ago?"

Renn picked her head up and sat straighter. "No, I didn't hear that."

"Mrs. Anderson told me about it yesterday. I guess they caught the guy, some intern or something, tried to smuggle out some data in his thermos. She thought this cryptex, it's called a cryptex by the way, might have been the thing he tried to smuggle. Isn't that crazy?"

"Well, that's another explanation for why it looks like a secret. Maybe someone took it and hid it."

Jack shook his head. "I'm not buying that. Come on, let's move to the living room."

Renn hopped off her stool and watched Jack slide gingerly off his. He walked with a slight limp.

"Coach Kelley's killers," he said. "It's Mrs. A's fault."

"Right, somehow I don't buy that." Renn walked back across the entryway into the living room. Timmy sat cross-legged on the floor, playing Mario Kart on the big screen. She took a seat on the L-shaped sectional behind him, and Jack fell into it at the other end.

"Listen," Renn leaned in conspiratorially, "someone abducted a bald eagle from the Raptor Center. There was blood evidence and everything."

"Ooh, blood. Do tell."

The music changed on the TV and a menu screen came up. Timmy lay back on the floor and interjected, "Rennie, want to play Mario Kart?"

Renn could think of nothing she wanted to do less than be humiliated by a seven-year-old. "Not now, kiddo. Let's see you play again."

Timmy sat up and started another race. "Okay, watch!"

She told Jack about Stella, the blood by her cage, and the red truck, speaking in hushed tones to stay under Timmy's awareness. "How do I find the scumbag who took Stella, Jack?"

"You said the blood was human?" said Jack. "He must have gotten quite a cut. Maybe he went to the hospital where your Aunt Jamie works. Just ask her."

Renn bounced on her cushion. "You're a genius."

But then she sagged a little. "I can't ask Jamie to get involved like that. There are privacy laws and stuff. She could lose her job."

Timmy finished another race and lay back again. "Rennie, will you play now?"

"No way, man, you'll beat the stuffing out of me."

"I'll give you a head start. And I won't take any power-ups whenever I'm in front."

Jack shook his head in silent warning, and Renn smiled.

"No deal. You're too good for me. We'll watch you again though."

They talked more about the problem, and Jack came back around to the hospital. "You should ask her. See if she's willing to help. It's not like you even need to know the dude's name. You could just look for the red truck. They probably have video or something, right?"

"You mean security cameras? That might work." Renn thought about this option for a while before sagging back onto the sofa. "But even if we get a good picture of the truck, even its license number, how do we track it down?"

"I don't know. Find someone who knows how to do that. It can't be that hard."

Renn chewed her lip. "Can't be that hard. Right."

They sat for a while, watching Timmy zoom and spin and

jump through brightly colored shapes hanging in the air.

Jack's dad walked in and said, "Okay kiddo, time to brush your teeth. Hi, Adrienne."

"Nooooo. One more game. Please?"

"Okay. Just one more," came the stern reply as he retreated.

"Rennie, will you play now? Just one?"

Renn sighed. Oh well, how bad could it be? "Just one game."

Timmy held nothing back and destroyed her even worse than she feared.

* * *

The problem of Stella niggled in her brain all night and through school the next day. If she started bringing other people in, she couldn't know if they would do their part. She'd have to *manage* them. And even then, they'd probably mess it up. It would be easier for her to do it herself, if only she knew how.

Renn wandered the hallways of Black Hawk Bend High after the last bell of the day. She thought about Stella. What must the poor girl be going through? Wouldn't it be worth the trouble if Renn, against all odds, somehow found her? The biggest problem was tracing the truck, assuming she could even get a picture of it. It wouldn't hurt to explore some options. She came to the school announcement board and stopped short. A vague memory inspired her to scan its myriad pieces of colored paper.

The board must have been ten feet wide and five feet tall. Small bits of the underlying cork board peeked through over-lapping papers here and there. Her school's government committee had organized a color run for charity. That was over a month ago. A Bollywood dance competition advertised for teams to compete. Study groups were underway for the ACT and SAT. Her own self-study program wasn't going so well. Oh, interesting. The field trip to Silver Labs was this week. Surely Jack remembered, but she would mention it.

She lifted a corner of the week's cafeteria menu, and her memory solidified. A plain white sheet of paper advertised help with computer services, recovering deleted files, investigations into cheating girlfriends or boyfriends, and the like. It had the word 'discreet' which, to Renn's mind, brought up images of hackers and the darknet. The bottom of the page was cut into tabs with the words "text TECH HELP to" and a number. One strip was torn off. She punched the number into her phone and typed the message, but didn't hit send. Talk about a long shot.

She tried to think of any other options as she left the school. None came to mind. On her way down the front steps she clicked send and sent her plea out into the universe. Now, she just had to call Aunt Jamie about that video. She couldn't say why, but the whole thing reminded her of playing Mario Kart with Timmy. She was up against forces she couldn't understand, much less compete with. The western sky was streaked with lavender, and hints of red and purple. It would be dark soon.

Chapter 6

Clara leaned into her stretch. The heel of her elevated right leg rested on the ballet barre. Her torso leaned to the right, and her left arm arced over her head, almost touching the foot of the raised leg. She pointed her right foot even as she turned the left one out almost ninety degrees. Breath hissed between gritted teeth as she stretched, and she pursed her lips to silence it. Hissing was not ladylike, and her teacher would not approve. Nor would her mother.

Between stretches, the other girls murmured gossip among themselves about this boyfriend and that new outfit. Clara paid no attention as she straightened her torso and slid her foot along the barre, settling into a straddle stretch. Next to her, Lacy adopted similar poses. Clara saw both of their reflections in the mirrored wall. Lacy had a perfect dancer's body. You could mount her on a musical jewelry box.

Their two bodies reflected from the wall mirror in matched poses, but there the resemblance ended. Lacy had pearly white skin with silky black hair in contrast to Clara's olive complexion and brown hair with loose curls. Lacy was perfectly sized and proportioned while Clara's short legs didn't quite raise her to an adequate height. And Lacy was the epitome of supple grace. Clara wondered if her mother might like to adopt her.

"Did you hear what happened?" Lacy said. Clara hummed a questioning sound.

"Someone sneaked into the woods, like where they keep the injured birds and stuff, and stole a bald eagle. Just stole it!"

Clara had heard something about it around school that day. She whispered, "Ay, what a dummy. What would you even do with an eagle?"

"I don't know, make eagle soup?"

The girls giggled and quickly glanced towards their teacher across the room. They shifted poses to a stretch in attitude.

"Maybe you can train it," said Clara. "You know, to catch fish and rodents and stuff."

"Oh, gross," Lacy said.

"Not to eat, silly. To get rid of them."

"Last summer my cat brought a dead mouse and dropped it right at my feet. I almost screamed."

They finished their barre work and transitioned into some simple cool-down stretches.

"I would love to fly," Clara sighed.

"What?"

"You know, fly. To soar on air currents like they do. It must feel a little like when you stick your head out the car window."

Lacy looked like she did not know anything of the sort. "Whatever. Listen, you want to go to the mall after? I need a new top for the party this weekend."

"Oh, sorry, I can't."

"But you are coming. To the party?"

Clara answered with her best noncommittal nod and shrug. "We'll see."

Lacy engaged Trish on her other side about the party, with greater success. Parties were fine. Except they were loud, and there were too many people, and they all acted stupid. At least this was one thing Clara and her mother agreed on. Their teacher called time and released them from their cool downs. Immediately the room bustled with random movement and chatter.

Lacy turned back around and teamed up on her with Trish. "Clara, you've got to come to the party,"

"Yes, you've got to. Everyone's going to be there, including Damien," added Trish.

"OMG, he's so fine."

"Who do you hope is there, Clara?"

"Oh, yes, who do you like?" asked Lacy.

Clara considered Lacy almost a friend. She got along fine with her, and the other girls, but she was already sick of the cliques and popularity contests, the intricate social dance that was high school. And she didn't like parties.

She pushed off the floor and stood over the two girls. "Sorry, I'm not going to the stupid party. I hope everyone gets lit, or whatever."

Lacy and Trish clambered to their feet, and both now stood over Clara. "You don't have to be all superior about it," said Lacy.

"Yeah, it's not our fault if you don't have a life," added Trish.

They turned away from her and retreated to a corner of the room where three other girls chatted.

Clara retrieved her giant pink and black duffel from the side of the room. From its vast interior, she pulled on sweatpants and sneakers, and found her glittered phone with the Hello Kitty design. Slinging the bag around until it hung behind her like a mountaineer's backpack, she waved bye to some girls and bent over for a drink at the fountain.

41

As she exited the studio, she checked her email and various social media accounts for updates. She saw a text notification, and it made her stop in her tracks and do a little dance of excitement, all the way around in a circle. She opened it and received her confirmation. A two-word message had come in near the start of practice. It said 'TECH HELP'.

TacoCat was back in business.

Chapter 7

Renn drove their blue Prius into the hospital lot and parked near the front lobby. It felt good to be taking action. Fortune favors the bold. That's what they say, right? Her hand floated up to the red and gold feng shui lucky charm hanging from the rear-view mirror. She had talked through her plan with Mom at dinner that evening and received nothing but encouragement. For one thing, Aunt Jamie had agreed to help, and having her approval went a long way. Mom asked if it was okay to look at the hospital's security video, and Renn had reassured her, although she honestly wasn't too clear on the legality of the whole situation. She would try not to worry about it. The charm's tassel ran through her fingers like water. Her mother had given her a tight hug and declared Renn the most responsible teenager she'd ever known. Her father would be so proud of her. That had brought a tear to Renn's eye. She slipped the charm off the mirror and around her wrist.

Her aunt waited just inside the double sliding doors, auburn hair popping against green scrubs. Apart from the freckles they shared, there was no sign that the two were related by blood. They hugged and Jamie held Renn at arm's length and studied her. "Young lady, you're getting more beautiful every time I see you."

43

Renn looked at her feet and smiled. "Thank you, Aunt Jamie."

"Are you still friends with that Jake fellow? Are you two an item yet?"

"You mean Jack? Stop, he's like a brother. Ew, that's just wrong."

Jamie laughed and dropped her hands from Renn's shoulders. "Okay, okay. Come on, let me introduce you to Ferdinand. He'll help you out with the video." She led Renn down a side hallway to a stairwell.

"Rennie, I'm very concerned about this situation. We haven't had any police or FBI here that I'm aware of. Isn't it a federal crime to harm a bald eagle?" She opened the door to the stairwell and motioned for Renn to take the lead. "Right down these steps."

Renn said, "Yeah, sure it is. But Ranger Scott said the police didn't seem that interested. They might not have even reported it to the FBI yet." She gripped the lucky charm while descending to the hospital basement. Renn wanted to work in a hospital someday, not as a nurse like her aunt, but as a doctor. She never expected to be sneaking into the basement as a … what? A private eye?

They emerged into a concrete hallway, absent any drywall or ceiling tiles. Bare florescent lights hung from the ceiling below stacks of pipes that led to and from places unknown. Jamie guided them to a door with a frosted glass window stenciled with the word 'Security'. She knocked and opened the door, revealing an office cramped with monitors and file cabinets. A round Latino man with a glossy bald head and a handlebar mustache stood and smiled at them.

"Miss Jamie, it has been too long since I've seen you live and in color."

Jamie kissed him on each cheek and replied in fast Spanish, impenetrable to Renn's conversational skills. Then she turned and said, "Ferdinand, let me introduce my niece Adrienne Chao."

Ferdinand took Renn's hand, bent from the waist, and lightly kissed it. "Adrienne, your aunt has told me of your quest and I am sympathetic. If it is in my power to help you, I will do it."

Renn curtsied a little, not knowing what else to do. She didn't know what to make of this strangely magnetic man. She looked at Jamie for reassurance and said, "Why, uh, thank you Mr., er, Ferdinand."

Jamie leaned in and gave Renn a quick hug and stepped towards the door. "Okay, Renn, I've got rounds. I'll leave you to it."

Ferdinand led Renn to a chair that sat in front of a large monitor, the fat kind, as deep as it was wide. Next to it sat a smaller, thin monitor behind a keyboard and mouse on the desk. "This happened sometime on Sunday morning, yes?"

"Yes, that's right."

He clicked on a file, and the fat monitor filled with a black and white video that started playing. The video had no sound.

"Um, Ferdinand, do you have it in color? I'm looking for a red truck."

His face adopted a troubled expression, either because he had bad news, or because it pained him to deliver it. "I am sorry, Adrienne. The camera is only black and white."

Renn took a seat in the chair. She would have to watch carefully. With a bit of luck, she would see evidence of an injury that matched their hypothesis of what had happened the morning of Stella's abduction. "It's okay. Thank you so much for your help, really. It's so... helpful."

This seemed to reassure the security guard, and he took a seat in a cracked leather office chair that creaked as he settled into it.

She put the video on fast forward and watched cars zoom up to the lobby doors, and zip away just as fast. She looked for pickup trucks and for anyone favoring an arm. More than once, she rewound the video a bit and played it at normal speed. Ferdinand gave her a pad of paper and a pen, and she noted down some timestamps. As she watched, she ran the charm's tassel through her hands.

This was probably going to be one big dead end. The man's wounds might be minor enough to treat at home, or he could have gone to a different hospital. There were so many possibilities, and so few of them would help her. This was not like chemistry where the right formula spit out a solution and tied a bow around it. Nor was it like biology where you only needed to memorize the parts of a cell. This was so open-ended, with no grade given at the end. But it was for a life, Stella's life.

Renn's phone buzzed and jerked her to attention, causing her to worry about how much video she had missed while her mind wandered. She checked her phone and found a text. Reading it, she sat up straight in her chair and paused the video. It was from the number she had texted for help. The TECH HELP person had replied and agreed to help. A smile came to Renn's face, but faded as she read on. He would help her for a fee of fifty dollars. The text was signed 'TacoCat'. Was that some kind of hacker handle? She pictured a furry little kitten wrapped in a tortilla. Renn gave this TacoCat a basic outline of what she wanted. He better not be wasting her time. She punched the play button on the parking lot video and sagged back in her chair.

"For luck?"

She paused the video again and looked over at Ferdinand. "Excuse me?"

He pointed at the feng shui charm that lay on the counter in front of her. "A good luck charm?"

She nodded. "I can use all the luck I can get right now."

He pulled open a drawer of his desk and fished around in it. With a look of delight, he pulled out a small doll and tossed it onto the counter next to her charm. Knitted from yarn, it appeared to be a woman with a colorful dress, wearing a headscarf. The eyes were nothing more than single stitches of black string. "My daughter gave me this many years ago. You tell her your problems, and she will fix them while you sleep. You tell her."

Whatever, it couldn't hurt. She picked it up and silently voiced her problem and her wish to the doll. Find the red truck. Find Stella. Then she set it back on the counter next to her own charm and returned her attention to the screen.

Thirty minutes later, she jolted to attention and paused the video. Sitting right in front of the lobby doors was a pickup truck. Renn let it play at normal speed. She watched a man get out of the passenger side. He had a bandage wrapped around his right arm, which he held gingerly with his left hand.

"That's it!" shouted Renn, as she leaped to her feet and pointed at the monitor.

Ferdinand walked over and studied the image frozen on the screen. "What do you know, my child? Luck is with you!"

Together they played the video forwards and backwards until Ferdinand extracted two screenshots. One showed a direct, if fuzzy, view of the license plate while the other showed a blurry picture of the man's face. Ferdinand clicked a few times, and the printer whirred into action and spit out the two pictures. Her only lead had panned out.

If TacoCat came through with information about the person or the truck, Renn would figure out how to get the money to pay him. Then she would get justice for Stella. She picked up the knit doll and offered it back to Ferdinand. "Thank you for your luck. It has given me some hope."

The big man enclosed her hand between both of his and looked her in the eyes. "Faith, hope, and love, Adrienne. You need all three."

Uncharacteristically, Renn leaned in and kissed him on the cheek. Then she hurried off to find Jamie and share the good news.

Chapter 8

Clara slammed the door of her bedroom and collapsed against it, her shoulders heaving. Her mother could be the most infuriating, frustrating, unreasonable person in the world. What were they even fighting about? She wasn't sure, except it had something to do with Clara not applying herself. If only she worked harder on her dancing, or her homework, or something, she could be remarkable. She would be Mamá's best little girl.

Clara threw her weight against the door, hitting it with her forearms. She allowed herself a soft shriek of exasperation, timing it to coincide with the impact on the door. Her younger siblings would know better than to intrude, but she didn't want to draw the attention of her mother, or Papá.

She used up a little more frustration leaping onto the quilted comforter of her bed. For a while, Clara studied the soft rose color of her ceiling. She killed time scrolling aimlessly on her phone until she noticed that her new client had sent pictures of a license plate and a grainy image of a man's face. Clara dabbed away her tears and sat up. Where had she gotten these pictures? It didn't matter. Now it was her job to trace them and come up with a name to match the face. But first she had to blow off some steam.

Clara moved to her desk, its surface dominated by a large curved-screen monitor. Next to the keyboard sat a bulky pair of gaming headphones and a T-shirt. She folded the shirt into thirds lengthwise and draped it over her head so it covered her ears. Over this she lowered the headphones, tilting her head both ways to test its fit and stretch out her neck.

Clara took a moment to calm herself and be mindful. She relaxed her feet and legs, clad with furry leg warmers over pink leggings, then shifted her attention up her body, currently covered by her favorite black Metallica tee. She checked her posture and rested her right hand on the mouse. The focus was on economy of motion, achieving the greatest effect with the least amount of effort.

She had seen plenty of gamers who twitched and squirmed like they were being electrocuted as they played, but she sat very still. Only the occasional movement of her head or a craning of her neck showed she was not in some Zen monk-like meditation.

She fired up the game.

Her fingers flew confidently over the keyboard, causing its embedded lights to flash and dance. She had customized her keyboard to make it easier on her shorter fingers. Clara typed quickly, her hotkeys and shortcuts translating her thoughts into commands.

She did not shout at the screen, or her game character, or her teammates. That was for amateurs. Well, amateurs and boys. Her teammates were also quiet. They all knew their roles and had played together enough to keep communication to a minimum. She heard an occasional "good shot" or "on your six" as she hunted the enemy players.

Clara's character jumped from building to building, down

stairwells, and behind burned-out cars. She observed enemies doing the same, lined them up in her weapon's sights, and took them down. It wasn't hard to wound by hitting a torso or a limb. The trick was to be accurate enough, and patient enough, to line up a good head shot. She achieved this about a third of the time. After her current kill, a head shot, the familiar victory message came up indicating the game's end. A long page of statistics appeared, and she spent a good half minute studying her teammates' and her percentages. When she clicked out, the game took her back to a main menu, and from there she clicked into league standings. She was still number one and had expanded her lead. This caused a smile to crack her stony expression. She felt a little better.

One of her teammates shot her a curt question on the voice channel about whether she was in for the next match. He sounded a little younger than her. Clara always listened in on voice, but never spoke. She didn't need the fragile male ego getting in the way of their good thing. She typed a quick excuse for ducking out. Better to end on a high note. She could bask in the victory for a couple of hours.

Clara pulled off the enormous headset and the shirt beneath, and set them next to her on the desk. She clicked over to email and brought up the two pictures. Someone had added their best guess at a license number in black marker at the bottom of one.

She had quoted a price that should cover time and expenses. TacoCat would set up the normal drop site procedure. She may not get much work, but she tried to think of herself as a professional. She had not gotten a job like this before. How to trace a license plate number? She didn't know anyone at the Department of Motor Vehicles or the Police Department.

A little googling revealed that information could be bought from private investigators or license check services, perhaps for less than fifty dollars. Okay, so one option would be to buy it and take it out of expenses. Maybe there was another way.

A knock sounded on her door. "Come in."

The door opened halfway and her father poked his head in and smiled at her. "Hey, nena, how's it going?"

"Hi, Papá. I'm all done with my homework."

They spoke Spanish, as was their habit at home. Both her parents thought it important for their children to be bilingual. It was also one more thing her mother got to criticize her about.

"You work too hard, Clara. You should go out more, have some fun. When I was your age—"

"Ay, I don't even want to know what you were doing at my age, Papá," Clara said. "Did they even have computers back then?"

"You are a comedienne. See, you should have more friends. Your mother worries, too."

"I seriously doubt that. Anyway, I have plenty of friends. And I have you." She went to her father, stood on her tiptoes, and kissed him on the cheek.

Her father, head dipped for her to reach it, backed out of her room and closed the door as he left. "Good night, nena."

Clara could not help but smile at her father's concern. He encouraged her interest in computers and lobbied for free time on behalf of her and her siblings. She needed time to slow down and relax. He needn't worry about her social life, though. She had gone out, what was it, two weeks ago, or three? Yeah, she was a social butterfly.

She might even have friends she'd never met.

Clara sat back down at the desk and clicked over to the game lobby. She typed out a message to her friends list. "Can anyone run a license plate check for me?" She had to wait less than five minutes for a response.

"np. Hit and run?" came the response from Death&Taxes999.

"Lol, no. Helping a friend. In return?"

She waited for half a minute. She assumed he was checking out her profile, gamer score, and general status in the community

His reply caused her to laugh out loud. "Let me join you for a match."

Still, she considered the offer. She checked his profile—not highly ranked. She preferred not to have him join one of her matches. At her level, one weak team member could easily mean a loss. She countered with an offer of her own. "Get your best team together. I'll join you for three matches."

"Awesome, we'll kick some butt, lol."

Clara passed along the license plate number and they agreed on a time to collect the information. She didn't know how this guy was going to dig it up, but she figured it wasn't her problem. She saved fifty bucks.

Helping people with her computer skills gave Clara a rush, but she found that following all the rules was so constraining. And a lot of the rules were just stupid, like being forced to buy five-dollar M&Ms at the movie theater instead of bringing your own. She would never take advantage of or hurt anyone, but hacking, by definition, involved a bit of rule breaking.

She sat and pondered her next step for a few minutes, then brought up Black Hawk High School's administrative portal. From a yellow sticky she kept in a desk drawer, she typed a long and complex password that got her access to her high school's database. Her client used a school email, so it was easy to search it, and bring up the student profile.

As she'd assumed from the email address, it was Adrienne Chao. She knew her by reputation, had seen her in the halls. A straight-A student, involved in student government, National Honor Society, Spanish Club, honors biology, school and club soccer, volunteer activities, just reading about this girl exhausted Clara. The profile gave her home address and her mother's name. No father was listed, but it didn't say why. She had not given a reason for wanting to track down the truck. Clara wondered what in the world it could be. Maybe there would be some follow-on work.

Clara shut down the computer and got ready for bed. She would fulfill her contract. And in the meantime, she would do what she was good at—stay low and keep her eyes and ears open.

Chapter 9

Jack leaned forward and flicked his friend Noah's ear, catching some of his hair twists instead. The lean wide receiver reached back in a failed attempt to grab Jack's arm and said, "C'mon man." The air buzzed with jokes, gossip, and the occasional spitball. Mrs. Anderson raised her voice to no apparent effect. Field trips and assemblies were to high school students as the full moon was to werewolves. And today they were going to Silver Labs, offering the perfect opportunity to do some research.

Jack saw Renn sitting in her usual homeroom seat near the window. She was making notes in her planner and ignoring the chaos with her characteristic focus. A piercing whistle cut through the din and drew Jack's attention forward. Mrs. Anderson removed two fingers from her mouth. She did not look happy. This time, she made everyone stand and line up single file to leave for the bus.

Jack and Noah chatted about Friday's game against Central. It would be an important step on their march towards the state championship. Mrs. Anderson started the line moving, and several people shushed each other as they emerged into the hallway. Jack and Noah exchanged light shoves.

Three yellow buses in front of the school waited to be

boarded. Jack leaped into the middle one, let out a whoop, and called, "Let's go people!" He liberally gave out high fives as he made his way to the back of the bus. It wasn't until he took his seat and looked up to the front that he realized the boy in the front row who had not raised his hand to Jack's was Dominic.

This realization caused a strange mixture of guilt and annoyance. The kid was just sitting up there with his head down, all glum and gloomy, like he was reliving all the negative emotions from his entire life. The episode with Bernie and Ryan was already a fading memory. Anyway, hadn't he tried to get them to leave Dominic alone and go to football practice? Yes, he had. He couldn't do anything about the dour kid in the front row, but he could enliven the mood in the back of the bus. He turned to share a joke with Noah.

The buses pulled up to the front entrance of Silver Labs, gleaming with glass and metal. Apart from the very modern look of the front lobby, the rest of the building struck him as drab, just an ordinary office building. All three buses poured students onto the sidewalk as two people emerged from the front doors. A woman wearing an upscale business suit led the way. She carried a tablet which she could seemingly read as she walked. Her brunette hair was tied up in a tight bun. Jack thought she had a hot librarian thing going on. A man carried a large cardboard box behind her. He was taller than her, but pudgier, and older, too. He wore khakis and a checkered, button-down shirt. He had dark-rimmed glasses and hair long enough to hide his ears, parted right in the middle.

The woman greeted the group in a professional, yet warm voice. "Good morning, students of Black Hawk High. My name is Julia Bouchard. I am the director of operations here at the

Silver Labs Midwest Campus. This is Dr. Lewis Edmunds, one of our senior engineers who happens to be employee number seven in the company. Your first question might be, why call this a campus when there is only one building? Well, you'll be interested to know that we're planning our first expansion next summer and we expect to have five buildings on our 150-acre campus in five years' time. Now, Dr. Edmunds will pass out visitor badges to everyone, then we'll split up into two groups. I'll lead one group, Dr. Edmunds the other. Any questions before we go in?" She had recited her introduction like a memorized sales pitch.

Renn sidled up to stand beside Jack. "Whose group are you going to be in?"

"I don't know. I was thinking about going with her," he said nonchalantly.

Renn laughed, "Don't be so predictable. Let's go with Lewis. He looks like the brains of the operation, anyway."

Jack realized that to press the point any further was to admit his shallowness. "Fine, we'll go with Dr. Edmunds."

Lewis held the box with one hand and pulled out handfuls of badges which he passed out to the students, teachers, and chaperones. One of the teachers raised his voice with a question. "Ms. Bouchard, could you explain why Silver Labs has a Midwest campus at all? It seems unusual for tech companies to leave Silicon Valley."

Julia flashed gleaming white teeth through a perfect smile at the teacher and delivered another silky-smooth speech, "Excellent question. As you may know, we have not actually left Silicon Valley and still maintain our global headquarters there. However, we saw an opportunity to recruit talent that might never choose to live in the Bay area. The traffic and cost of living are significant barriers for some people. As it happens, Jason Silver was born not too far from here and attended the University of Illinois. We actively recruit from area schools and feel that the Midwest lifestyle is an advantage that we now have over our competitors."

Pretty good speech. Jack wondered if she believed it

A girl raised her hand, and Julia gestured towards her. "Is Mr. Silver here today? Will we get to meet him?"

"I'm afraid Mr. Silver is not in the state at the moment. He spends about a quarter of his time here, and sometimes even chooses to vacation in the Midwest." She puckered her lips a little, as if she had just sucked the juice out of a lemon wedge. She consulted her tablet before looking around the crowd again. "It looks like everyone has a badge. Let me just remind you that the use of smart phones is prohibited during the tour. I'll take half of you in now, and Dr. Edmunds will follow with the other group in a couple of minutes."

Jack reached into his pocket, retrieved the blue cryptex, and held it up for Renn to see.

She pushed it back down with her hand and stepped in close. "Why did you bring that thing? Didn't you say it might be stolen from here?"

Jack huffed and said, "No. *Mrs. A* suggested that, but it couldn't have been. It's been in that geocache for, like, a year before this, right?"

Renn did not look mollified. "We don't know that, Jack. And what if we have to go through security on our way out and they discover it? It's obviously their property and you really will be stealing then."

"Bull—"

"Young people. Over here, young people," Lewis Edmunds

called out to gather the remaining students around him. The last members of the other group were just entering the lobby behind Julia.

Jack and Renn went over to stand by Lewis. Jack hoped they hadn't made the wrong decision in choosing him.

Lewis waved the stragglers into the group and addressed them in a much more casual manner than Julia. "Let's get the most important thing out of the way first. Star Wars or Star Trek?" A smattering of each came from the group with some laughter.

Jack shouted, "Wars!" and saw Renn roll her eyes.

"So, any questions before we go in?"

Jack shot his hand up while giving Renn a knowing nod. "Dr. Edmunds, we heard something was stolen from Silver Labs a while ago. What was taken?" He imagined Renn turning a shade paler next to him.

Lewis' expression became serious. "There was an incident, but I can assure you that nothing was stolen from the labs. We have increased our security, though, so sorry about that. Why the interest?"

"Oh. Um, I'm writing a report for class. This field trip is like research for me."

"Well, great, I hope you ask a lot of questions then." Glancing to the now empty lobby, Lewis said, "Looks like we can go in. Follow me, ladies and gentlemen."

Jack nudged Renn as they walked into the lobby of Silver Labs. "See, I told you so."

Renn rolled her eyes again. "So what? Did you hear the part about extra security? What if they find a piece of Silver Labs tech on you? What do you think they'll assume?"

Jack scoffed at the question. Nevertheless, he felt for the

cryptex in his pocket and resolved to leave it there. Glossy information sheets about the lab sat on the counter in the lobby; he took one of each. Another boy asked, "Do we have to turn in our cell phones or go through a metal detector?"

Lewis scanned his own badge against a black plate on the wall and they heard a buzzing noise as the door into the building proper unlocked. He pulled it open and answered, "No, nothing like that. But we ask that you don't take any pictures or videos. You will be allowed in and out with a reduced security protocol. We're keeping an eye on you, though." He smiled and gestured up to the ceiling where a half-dome concealed a security camera. "Let's go in, shall we?"

Jack walked just behind Lewis so he could keep asking questions. He found out when the company was founded and a couple other stats, jotting them down on a brochure.

Jack and Renn followed Lewis through the side door into a short hallway that opened up into a large office space packed with cubicles. The hallway continued beyond the cubicle area and the group followed it about halfway down. They stopped in front of a room with long windows in place of a wall from about waist level up to the ceiling. Jack gazed in awe through the glass. Several large machines sat in this room. Spools of material, all with a metallic look to them, sat on counters. Then he noticed a familiar darting movement in one of the devices.

"Printers," he said to himself.

Lewis must have heard him because he replied, "Right you are, my young Jedi. The Force is strong with you." He addressed the group. "This is Lab 151, where we keep our state-of-the-art 3D printers. We sell this model to companies for manufacturing parts, but we also use this lab to print pieces for our own use."

"This isn't like any printer I've ever seen," said a wide-eyed girl.

"I would think not," said Lewis. "They use metal spools and can print with sub-millimeter tolerances. You could print almost all of a working car with these."

"How much are they?" asked Jack.

Lewis narrowed his eyes and gave Jack a stare. "Bring your checkbook, did you?" He quoted a couple of figures off the top of his head.

"I want," said Jack, smiling. He wrote down the numbers.

"Well, let's move on then. Follow me, everyone." He led them to the far end of the hallway and into a stairwell. They marched up to the second floor and into another hallway similar to the one below, but shorter. Jack saw a large open space on this floor. They spilled out into a giant area strewn with couches and comfortable chairs. Two ping pong tables and a pool table were arrayed on one side of the expansive room. A few larger offices with walls of glass dominated the far side of the space. Employees were scattered throughout the room in groups of two or three. A young man and woman played a casual game of table tennis, laughing at some joke. This place was great.

Lewis worked his way to the front of the group and resumed his tour duties. "This is our open-plan workspace. We find it encourages collaboration and creativity. Or folks can just come up here to take a break."

Several people in the group slouched into soft chairs and a murmur of giggling wafted through the area. Jack nudged Renn and pointed to two white egg chairs. They ran over to sit in them, allowing themselves to become enfolded in their cocoon-like depths. They had to swivel the chairs to see each other. "Wow, these are great for privacy." Jack felt like he had to shout just to get his voice to escape its confines.

Lewis gave them a few minutes to explore and play, then gathered them back together. Jack and Renn hatched from their eggs and rejoined the group in the center of the open space. He used the time to gather a few more facts for his 'report'. They soon followed Lewis back the way they came, down the stairs, into the first-floor hallway. They had to walk single file because the other group was passing them by, heading up to the second floor. Renn walked behind Lewis, with Jack behind her. He offered some high fives to their passing classmates, then withdrew.

Dominic approached in the other line. He studied the floor in front of him, but suddenly glanced up and caught Jack's eyes. He looked profoundly miserable, so much so that Jack had to break eye contact. Jack looked further back in the line and noticed a short girl with curly brown hair staring at a point just in front of Jack. No, she was looking intently at Renn. Before Jack had time to wonder at this, the girl noticed Jack and her eyes dropped to the back of the boy in front of her.

They got past the other group and hung a left at the cubicles, and then another left into an auditorium. Jack figured they were just below the ping pong and pool tables. He insisted they sit near the front so he could ask questions. He gave Renn a toothy grin, pulled out the information sheets, and continued scribbling down notes.

The general chatter muted when the lights dimmed. A projector above their heads lit up a large screen on the front wall of the room and a voice began narrating:

"Our world is changing at a breakneck pace. We here at Silver Labs are dedicated to providing solutions to the most pressing problems of the next generation. Our software helps provide easy access to information, and we're working every day to reach people around the world. Our advanced manufacturing technologies make it possible to print the machines of tomorrow."

The voice nagged at Jack. He had heard it somewhere. Various images of smiling people and fancy technology streamed from the video, as well as flyover footage of Silver Labs headquarters in Silicon Valley. The scene shifted to an interior location. The big silver logo gleamed in the background while in the foreground stood Julia Bouchard. She looked different in the video, though. Her hair was down and her expression seemed happy and engaging.

"Welcome to Silver Labs. Join us as we explore how the problems of today are turning into the technologies of tomorrow."

Jack thought she looked ten years younger, but wasn't sure whether to attribute that to the old video or to the changes in her hairstyle and expression. He settled back in his seat to watch and listen, making notes of any interesting facts and figures.

"Are you really going to write a report about Silver Labs?" asked Renn.

"Maybe. You never know."

The video ended and the house lights came back up to a smattering of applause and whistles. Lewis stood up to take questions.

Jack fished the cryptex from his pocket and started fiddling with the combination while glancing at his notes.

Renn leaned over to look at his research. She looked up at

him bug-eyed. "Oh, no, you didn't," she gasped.

"Oh, yes, I did," he said proudly. "Did you think I was going to waste this opportunity?" One by one, he tried combinations based on all the facts and statistics he had been collecting.

The audience peppered Lewis with shallow questions, so Jack tried to ignore them and focus on his work. At some point the quiet drew his attention, and he looked up. Lewis stood at the front of the room, looking directly at him. Jack thought about Renn's comments on stolen property and panicked. He looked right and left, thinking everyone else must also be looking at him, too. Renn had her hand raised beside him, and he sighed in relief.

"What's your question," asked Lewis.

Renn shouted her question. "Dr. Edmunds, I don't think you ever mentioned whether you like Star Wars or Star Trek. Which is it?"

Laughter echoed through the auditorium. Lewis smiled broadly and clapped his hands together. "Ah, yes. I am an equal opportunity sci-fi fan. Both are excellent and instructive in their own ways. Thank you."

The auditorium door opened and Julia Bouchard stuck her head in. Lewis turned to her and they shared a quiet communication. Jack glanced at his phone and saw they should have finished five minutes ago.

Renn leaned her head in and said, "Sorry, Jack, I guess you'll have to do more research."

Jack shot her a smirk and held the blue cryptex up for her to see. He grabbed each end and pulled gently. They came apart and Renn gasped. An inner piece was connected to the right end of the cryptex. It was black with a rectangular silver end. It looked like a flash drive.

"Silver's birthday," said Jack with a satisfied nod.

Chapter 10

The next day, Renn was staring out the window in Biology class when her phone vibrated a notification. For some reason, she expected good news. Maybe some of Jack's confidence about opening his thingamabob had rubbed off on her. After class let out, she checked her messages. TacoCat had the information she wanted. It would be ready after school, and a drop site had been set.

The rest of the day Renn made her rounds from classroom to classroom in a distracted haze. There were no tests, nothing important to focus her attention. She thought about Stella, dreamed about the long-shot possibility of finding the missing bird. This kind of thing had happened before, so said the internet. But she hadn't found a case of eagle-napping with a happy ending.

Renn reviewed her list for the day during study hall. A covert pickup of information identifying Stella's abductor wasn't on it, so she wrote it in between soccer practice and homework. Depending on how long this would take, she was in danger of ACT study time getting squeezed out yet again.

By the time soccer practice finished, the twilight at the end of the day's hectic rhythms had given way to the calming routines of evening. Renn switched out her cleats for cross-training sneakers, but still wore her soccer shorts and jersey. Long strands of black hair stuck to her forehead and cheeks in a sheen of drying sweat. It was fine; she didn't expect to run into any of her friends at this late hour.

Lights installed behind translucent ceiling panels switched on as she moved through the empty hallways of Black Hawk High. Once she looked for them, Renn noticed the occasional motion sensor and security camera. In the distance, she heard what might be a floor-polishing machine. Why didn't Ranger Scott have any security tech out at the Raptor Center? It would have made the investigation a lot easier, possibly prevented the abduction completely. She reached the double-wide stairwell and started the long climb.

Renn stepped into the west wing of the third floor. She could no longer hear the floor scrubber. She didn't hear anything. For that matter, she didn't see much either. The motion sensors in the hallway hadn't picked her up yet, and darkness shrouded the depths of the wing. She stepped through the arch into the dim hallway, the only light spilling from the stairwell behind her. The head of her shadow, long in front of her, disappeared beyond the edge of illumination. Then the shadow's form flickered as the overhead lights noticed her. The flicker didn't go away; rather an electric buzz joined in, accentuating the creepiness. The flicker caused her shadow to blink in and out of existence. They hadn't yet modernized this wing of the school; it still had the old florescent bulbs and the old gray color on the brick walls. The effect made Renn feel like she was stepping into a 1950s horror movie.

Renn took a few steps and stopped. This was stupid. She could pick it up in the morning. She didn't care if anyone saw her. It was just an unused locker. No one would even notice

67

that it wasn't hers. She needed to go home and study. In her left hand, she clasped her phone and an envelope with five crisp ten-dollar bills. Renn turned to leave but stopped, facing a closed classroom door. She wasn't used to being so indecisive. She wasn't accustomed to chickening out.

The lights buzzed and flickered and revealed Renn's reflection in the narrow window of the door just as her phone rang, echoing up and down the hallway. She screamed and dropped the phone and envelope. Embarrassed, Renn grabbed her belongings off the glossy floor, and sat in the entry nook of the classroom, her back against the door, her chest heaving.

"What the what?" she demanded, noticing Jack's name on the phone.

"Whoa, it's just me," said Jack. "You okay?"

"You scared me half to death. This place is like a mausoleum at night. I was just about to turn around and go home."

"Did you get it?"

"Not yet," Renn leaned forward so she could glance both directions down the hallway, then leaned back again. "I'm officially creeped out."

"Well, don't quit now. You're really close. Call me back when you get it."

"No, don't hang up, Jack. You've got to stay on the line now. I'm switching you over to speaker."

"Fine. I solved my mystery, it's time to solve yours. Let's go, girl."

Renn slid her back up the door of the classroom and shook off her jitters. "Right. Tell me about what you found."

Jack's excitement became more sincere as the conversation turned back to the cryptex. "Okay, so it has eight files on it, right? One is a text file, and the other seven are .stl files."

Renn stepped out into the hallway and turned towards the dark end of the west wing. "Keep going."

"Do you know what .stl files are for?" he asked.

"Let me guess. Something uber geeky, like programming robots?"

"Close, but no. So, you know how I've been helping Mrs. A with the 3D printer this year? Well, one of the file types it uses is a .stl file. These files are 3D designs, and I can probably print them at school."

A section of hallway illuminated in front of her as a new motion sensor detected her presence. The new lights didn't flicker or buzz. "Hmmm, interesting. What are the designs for?"

There was a pause before Jack answered. "Well, it's a little hard to tell, and the text file is... well, it's interesting. You ever hear of a puzzle called a tangram?"

"Nope, can't say that I have."

"So, here's what the text file says," he continued. "The tangram is an ancient Chinese dissection puzzle. Well over six thousand different configurations are known from just seven simple pieces. But in order to reveal its secret, you'll have to put it together in a very specific way. Print the pieces in their specified colors. Put the puzzle together in its standard configuration while simultaneously satisfying the four-color theorem as well as the number matching problem. Only then will the riddle be understood."

Jack paused again, and Renn waited for him to keep reading. It dawned on her that he had reached the end. That was the end of the message. She broke into laughter and felt tension release from her neck and shoulders. "Oh, thanks, Jack. I needed a little entertainment."

"What do you mean?" Jack sounded hurt.

"I think you've stumbled onto someone's idea of a practical joke, that's all," Renn said. Then, mocking the instructions, she said in a low voice, "Only then will the riddle be understood," and chuckled again.

Jack snapped, "We don't know what it is, but someone put there for a reason. Why would you make a puzzle like that and then have it lead nowhere?"

Renn had an answer. "Oh, I don't know. Because people can be complete idiots?" But she continued in a conciliatory tone. "Look, I'm not trying to rain on your parade, but this just feels like somebody's idea of a joke."

"I don't think so, and I'm going to find out. I mean, I have access to the printer at school, so it's not like it will be hard for me to make the pieces. Then we'll see what the puzzle says."

Just to pour on a little more fuel, Renn muttered, "Probably something dumb like, 'So long and thanks for all the fish.'"

Jack's tone brightened on the other end of the connection. "Nice nerd quote."

Renn laughed again, her stress drained away. Jack didn't let everyone see his nerdy side, and she liked to tease him about it when she could. She swiped over to email to check TacoCat's instructions, then examined locker numbers on either side of her before homing in on one. "Okay, I'm here. Putting in the combination. I won't be happy with anything less than a treasure map now."

"Haha, very cute. You mean for my thing or yours?"

"All I know is this TacoCat had better come through, or I'm gonna be pissed." Renn unlatched the door and pulled it open to reveal a bare metal interior. She wasn't sure what to expect. She knew it wouldn't be TacoCat's school locker. A lone manila envelope lay on the top shelf. She pulled it out, flipped it over, and bent the metal prongs to release the flap.

"Well, what is it?" Jack's voice rang out from the hallway floor where Renn had laid her phone.

"Shhhh," she chided. "Patience."

She opened the envelope and pulled out a sheet of paper. It showed a picture of a man with additional information printed below. She recognized the face from the security camera footage.

"Huh," she said as she finished scanning the sheet.

"What is it?"

"His name is Owen Sutherland, and he lives here in town. This gives his employer, too. Wanna guess?"

"Um, I give up. Tell me."

"Quitter," Renn said. "Owen Sutherland works for Silver Labs."

"Whoa, that's a coincidence."

Renn thought it was probably more than a coincidence, but what it meant, she had no idea. She grabbed her own envelope and placed it on the shelf in the locker.

"So what's next?" asked Jack.

"I'm not sure. I have his address... I guess I'll go do some more investigating."

"Not on your own, Nancy Drew. I can come with you on Saturday."

He sounded insistent, but Renn's thought Nancy Drew was a pretty self-sufficient detective. Suddenly, she wanted nothing more than to get out of that cold, dark hallway. She wanted to get home to her mom and Bear and settle into an evening of studying. "I think I'm fine now, Jack. Thanks for keeping me company. I needed it. See you tomorrow."

"Okay. See you tomorrow—and Saturday."

They hung up and Renn raced down the dark hallway.

Chapter 11

Jack pulled his shoulder pads on over his head, followed by his red jersey with black accents. Teammates jostled him on either side. The excitement in the locker room was palpable and caused more laughing and slapping than usual. The smell of stale sweat permeated everything.

Jack loved it.

He loved the camaraderie and the excitement. There was no greater moment than running out onto the field under the Friday night lights and hearing the roar of the crowd.

Tonight they would take one more step towards the state championship.

Tonight they would be cheered like heroes.

Jack grabbed his helmet and affixed his mouth guard to its cage. He saw Noah, and they walked out of the locker room together, helmets under arms. Noah diagrammed a play he had invented, something they often did, by drawing in the air with his hands. Jack commented on its elegance when he felt a strong shove on his shoulder as one of his burly teammates pushed by. He would normally let that go, but when he recognized the player, his annoyance crossed a threshold into action.

"Bernard, what's your problem?" Jack said loud enough to

catch his attention over the buzz.

Bernie stopped and turned. Ryan walked beside him, and he stopped and turned, too. "I don't have a problem, Henderson. You might have a couple problems, though."

Jack adopted a casual but alert pose. "Oh, what are my problems?"

"First, you stick your nose in other people's business. And second, you know I don't like being called Bernard." Bernie punctuated each point with a thrust of his finger at Jack's torso, not quite making contact.

Bernie's "business" had been gnawing at Jack more and more. If he had it to do over, he would have done more to break up their bullying. As for his preference of name... "You stick to the game plan, Bernard. We can go all the way this year. Keep your head in it and we'll be fine."

Bernie took a step towards Jack and Noah. His ruddy skin turned another shade of red. "What are you trying to say? As if I'm a weak link or something. We're gonna do our job on offense. The way you guys have been playing though, Central is going to roll right over you. *You* keep *your* head in the game and try not to let them catch you with your pants down." This time, when Bernie pointed, he poked Jack's chest between his shoulder pads.

"Save it for the field, *Bernard*."

"Call me Bernard one more time."

"Oh, come on, Bern..."

Bernie leaned in for a hard shove, and Jack swung his arms down in between Bernie's and dropped into a crouch. Bernie had an advantage, being shorter and stockier than Jack; he had a lower center of gravity and could win a shoving match. Jack shoved back. He noticed that Noah had shifted position to restrain Ryan from moving in.

"I wasn't even going to say it," whispered Jack. He was low and close to Bernie's face.

"I've wanted a shot at you for a while, Henderson."

A small crowd had gathered around them. Then a piercing whistle blew and Coach Kelley's voice called out, "O'Rourke, Henderson! What's going on here?"

Jack and Bernie stood up from their crouch and turned to face their coach. He stood above them, his face lowered to a position directly in front of and between them. He yelled, "Listen to me. We're going out there to do battle with the toughest team we've faced all year. And you're either with me or you can go get changed right now. What's it going to be?"

Jack and Bernie shouted like military cadets, "With you, Coach."

"And you've earned yourselves an extra round of killers next week."

Coach blew his whistle and motioned for all the players to get moving, and they did. Jack emerged from the narrow tunnel into the bright lights that illuminated the field. The lights glared and the roar of the crowd jarred his senses. This was not a great start to the game.

* * *

Renn showed her ID at the gate. Cars lined the streets by the field, and the Lutheran church across the street sold parking as a fundraiser. Friday night football at Black Hawk High was a city-wide affair. She zipped up her gray windbreaker with lavender accents and made her way around the field towards the bleachers and concessions.

Parents, teachers, younger kids, and townies sat in the bleachers eating popcorn and looking out over the field, bathed by spotlights mounted on high poles all around. Students roamed up and down the sidelines in groups large and small, lining up at the concession stands, or congregating at the far end of the fence where it was darkest and most isolated. Teacher monitors wandered by and joked with a student or broke up a brewing fight—or budding romance.

Renn left the concession stand with her corn dog and Coke and found a few of her friends to hang out with. They piled on to the empty end of a bleacher and watched the waves of red and black flow across the field against the green and white Central Warriors. They picked out friends in the crowd and joked about events of the week. Almost everyone they knew was there. With a chill, Renn wondered if Owen Sutherland—the man TacoCat identified—might be there, too, sitting somewhere in the crowd. He could be a row behind or in front of them. Would she recognize him?

The crowd roared and the girls stood. A player in green and white separated from the group and sprinted towards the end zone with the ball. A couple of their Scouts tried to catch up, but the effort proved too little, too late. Central scored the touchdown and the crowd sat back down. Renn and her friends booed and hissed. "Come on, Jack," Renn shouted in his general direction. She couldn't remember his jersey number and didn't see him on the field.

Renn followed her train of thought further. She knew the entire town didn't come to the game; it was a long shot that Owen would even be here. But it was Friday night and people were out of their houses. Owen might be at the bar playing darts or gone to see a movie. What would he be doing tomorrow? If he was anything like her neighbors, he would be doing yard work, or laundry, or watching golf on TV. Plus, it would be daylight and easy to see a couple of kids snooping around.

Special teams for the Scouts and Warriors lined up on the field. A small contingent of Central fans carried on cheering the recent touchdown. A line of green surged forward, and the ball arced over the field towards the red line. One of Black Hawk Bend's Scouts managed to catch the kickoff and kneel for a touchback.

Renn looked again for Jack on the sidelines and spotted him. He had his helmet off and squirted water into his mouth. He would be free tomorrow and they would go over to Owen's. Going together was much better than going alone. She would be braver with Jack there. Owen wouldn't be able to fight both of them, if it came down to that. She should really wait for him.

The girls watched the game, cheering when their team got a field goal and booing after the Warriors scored another touchdown. A couple guys sat down beside them and talked her friends into walking around for a while. Renn scanned the crowd for a man with a hat and a bandaged arm.

"You guys go on, I have to do something," she heard herself say.

She hugged her friends goodbye and walked the three blocks back to her car; she had opted not to pay the five dollars to park at the church.

Not even fifteen minutes later, she drove past a large two-story home, shrouded in darkness. Renn could not see lights in any of the windows. She was right about Friday nights. She didn't slow down. After two more passes by the house, she calmed her nerves and convinced herself that this was her best opportunity. Renn parked around the corner, behind a hedge, and slowly walked along the sidewalk back towards Owen Sutherland's house.

* * *

Jack was out of the flow. Flow was this amazing state of mind that Coach talked about, on the edge between too boring and too challenging, when you got into a total immersion zone and time slowed down. Time had slowed in one way; it felt like this drive by Central would never end. Flow for Jack came when he played football or built something. But not tonight, not since the fight with Bernie.

Everything came hard. He'd never matched up against this offensive tackle before; the guy was big. He hit hard and Jack fell hard. He was totally failing at defensive end and beginning to wonder when Coach would take him out. All he needed was a quick move past the tackle and a good look at the quarterback. He could end the drive right here.

Jack lowered one hand to the freshly clipped grass. Central's call echoed up and down the line, and the noise from the stands faded into the background. His opponent adjusted his weight and grimaced through his face mask. The center snapped the ball hard, almost overshooting the quarterback and forcing him to catch it high. Jack watched the ball rise into the air and felt like he had all the time in the world. Bodies launched across the line of scrimmage. Jack faked left and darted right, intending to arc around and catch the quarterback in his blind spot. The sound of grunts and colliding bodies rushed in from all sides and caught up with him in one quick moment. Jack went down hard, but not before seeing the quarterback pass for a short completion.

Mercifully, the drive ended two plays later. The score was ten to twenty-one.

He paced the sideline as his Scouts began their own drive. Down after down, Jack willed the ball farther down the field. Their strong passing game got them to the Warriors' ten-yard line. The crowd rose to its feet and the air crackled with energy.

The worst thing about playing defense was sitting out moments like this. They could still stage a comeback if they scored here. Jack wanted another chance to flow.

The center snapped and the quarterback stepped into his pocket, scanning receivers. He pumped the ball once, twice... and fired to a wide receiver on the far side of the field. The receiver caught the pass, spun, and evaded a defender. He sprinted towards the far corner of the field, but two Central defenders closed in fast and tripped him. The Scout player stretched out as far as possible and fell like a plank. The referee called it down on the one-yard line.

Noah grabbed Jack's pads at the neck and shook him as they howled at each other. The players lined up after a quick huddle and he knew they were going for it, fourth down or not. He wanted more than anything to be out there right now. The call rang out, and both lines collapsed into a giant mass as if the ball had become a tiny black hole.

Apparently, the sidelines and bleachers were also affected by the black hole because everyone leaned in to get a better view. As players peeled off the pile, it became clear that the Scouts were seven points closer to tying the game. The crowd erupted and Jack steeled himself. It was up to his squad now to hold Central from scoring again.

As Jack pulled on his helmet and put in his mouth guard, Coach Kelley walked over with a clipboard. "Henderson," he bellowed, "you up for this? I can give you a rest."

"No way, Coach. I'm good."

Coach regarded him with steely eyes for another two seconds.

"I'm good, Coach."

"That's what I like to hear. Get in there."

* * *

Renn pulled a small Maglite from her pocket and tested it against the hedge that divided Owen's yard from his neighbor's. Owen's house stood dark and gray, like a two-story tombstone. The night was clear, and the moon just bright enough to resolve ghostly shapes into focus.

It didn't look like anyone was home, and she wondered, for the first time, whether Owen had a family. Were they out bowling and eating pizza, or was there a toddler tucked into bed up on the second floor? Renn might be the scariest one here. After all, she was the intruder. She took several deep breaths and crept onto the lawn.

All the windows in front had curtains or blinds except for the largest one, a bay window that must look into the living room. The darkness was impenetrable. The Maglite clicked on, but the majority of its light reflected off the glass into her face, blinding her. She staggered back a step and clicked it off.

She crept around the sides of the house, first to the right. There were no first-story windows here, just an air conditioning unit and a short section of chain-link fence barricading the backyard. Like a ghost, Renn glided back across the house to the left side, only to find more dark windows and another fence. But this section had a gate.

Leaning over the gate, she strained to get a picture of the backyard. Renn saw a smaller structure stuck up against the back of the house, probably a shed. She could make out a couple of trees and bush-like shapes at the back of the yard.

Renn stilled herself and tried to fade into the darkness. Crickets chirped and a dog barked in the distance. What was she doing? Was she going to break into Owen Sutherland's house and search it? She hadn't studied how to pick a lock. She'd completely forgotten to research home security systems. Wait, didn't they put a sign in your yard if you were protected? There was no sign in Owen's front yard. Great, Adrienne, feel free to break and enter!

She was here for a reason, and that was Stella. There weren't many people who even knew Stella existed, much less cared she was missing. Renn cared, and Ranger Scott cared. Owen committed a felony, and he was going to get away with it unless someone did something. All she needed was some shred of evidence to give the police, enough for a search warrant.

The gate was not locked. Maybe the shed wasn't either; it would be easy to check. Renn lifted the latch and swung open the fence gate, closing it behind her as she slipped into the inky darkness of the backyard.

She walked around the shed. It looked large enough to hold a riding lawn mower. Even in the darkness, Renn saw that it was ventilated through a little fake chimney on its top. She tested its double doors. There was a latch, but no lock. Folks in Black Hawk Bend were very trusting. Ever so slowly, she undid the latch and swung the doors open. From the black interior, she could just make out the outline of the riding mower. Shelving units stood against the back wall, lined with cans, bottles, and tools of all sizes.

Renn's hopes for saving the day fell. A disappointed sigh threatened to turn into a frustrated sob before she steeled herself. This was not the time or place to lose it. She swung one door closed and reached for the other one when a faint rustling came from the shed. It was the first sign of life she'd encountered.

Renn swung the doors back open to let in maximum light from the moon. On the floor, next to the right wall of the shed, sat two rectangular shapes. She stepped inside and kneeled to isolate the sound. They were aquariums. One held a few small mice, and the other something a little bigger—rats.

This was it. It had to be eagle food. A voice at the back of her mind reminded her it was more likely snake food, but she suppressed it. What were the chances that Owen Sutherland, her prime suspect in Stella's abduction, just happened to need eagle food for a completely innocent purpose? That's what she told her inner voice, anyway.

With renewed hope, Renn scurried around the shed, looking for more clues. A light clicked on somewhere and filtered in through the ventilation slats. The sound of a door opening reached her, along with the realization that the door and the light had to belong to this house. Owen was home.

Renn froze, immobilized by fear and indecision. The door closed. Had she been discovered? Should she run, or close up the shed and hide? Before a plan had time to form in her mind, a low dark shape padded out to the middle of the yard, lifted its leg, and did its business. She couldn't quite tell, but she thought it looked lean and powerful, a Pit bull or a Rottweiler. The dog turned its head towards her. Two eyes glowed in the darkness and met her own. It stood there, frozen, and she dared not move.

Strange. Her normal inclination would be to make friends with it and scratch it behind its ear. But she realized the dog would understand her true status as an intruder, just as clearly as she did.

Renn considered her situation for a full five seconds and then took action. She stepped forward and reached out with both hands to pull the double doors shut. The moment she moved, a snarl came from the dog that erupted into a full-throated bark. It launched itself towards the shed like a missile. Renn focused on making one fluid motion without fumbling. She didn't have a second to spare. Fortunately, the doors had interior handles to grab onto. She took a step back and pulled the doors shut on herself. As the opening to the yard grew narrower, the barking dog jumped. Its arc would have it land right on her. She saw its bared teeth sailing towards her like the tip of a spear. Renn heard a loud thud as the dog's mass collided with the shed, and she let out a shriek.

The entire structure shook and threatened to vibrate apart. Tools thudded to the floor. Snarling and barking assaulted her through the too-thin doors.

She was safe. The doors were shut; she held them shut. She was safe.

Renn looked around for a broom or something to shove through the inside handles and jam the door. There was nothing within reach.

She was so dead. There was nothing to do but wait for Owen to come open the shed.

Panic overwhelmed her.

Renn breathed. Once, twice, three times she forced air into

her lungs before a sensible thought passed through her brain. Trying to keep both doors shut with one hand, she unbuckled her belt and slid it out of her jeans, wrapped it around the handles, and buckled it again.

Renn's hands hovered over the handles until she was sure the door wouldn't be jarred open by the frantic beast. Then she sunk down to sit against the front of the riding mower. Her hands shook. She wondered if this was what shock felt like. Why hadn't she waited until tomorrow for Jack to come with her? Sitting there in the dark with the shed doors thundering and the dog barking, Renn wondered how the game was going.

* * *

Jack rested his fist against the grass, feeling every blade. The smell of hot dogs hit him with the breeze. All around him, other players crouched into similar stances. Beyond them was the glare of bright lights and a swarm of fans that buzzed and roiled at the edge of his vision. In front of him was a large and nasty fellow. He knew this because of the snarl that distorted his opponent's face like a mask. Also, because he had been beaten up by this guy all night.

Beaten up enough to learn some of his patterns and tells.

For instance, Jack was too quick on the fake. His opponent's momentum, or perhaps slow reflexes, allowed him to miss the fake completely and respond to Jack's true intent.

The call came down the line and his universe narrowed to include only him and Mr. Nasty. Jack shifted his mindset. He was no longer a defender; he was on offense, and his target was the guy with the ball. Jack lunged left but didn't commit his weight behind it. Then he forced himself to slow down and

84

wait for the tackle to shift. There it was. Jack danced back, letting his nemesis lurch forward even further. He felt the moment that he'd been too hasty to let happen before, when he knew he could dart around to the right unopposed. The action gave Jack a spike of energy, which he used to draw a bead on the quarterback and launch into a sprint.

Two steps away from victory, the quarterback threw the ball. Jack slowed and gently bumped him anyway. Time sped back up and he scanned the field. The pass had resulted in a short completion followed by a quick tackle. He ran to his huddle, grinning. He had his counterpart's number, and he would exploit it for the rest of the game.

His next chance didn't come for a while. Central switched to their ground game and had been making short advances, reliably and efficiently. The Scouts had been pushed back to their own twenty-five-yard line, already in field goal territory. Central was on the verge of scoring yet again, dashing Black Hawk Bend's hopes for a state championship. Almost as disturbing, it would prove Bernie right. They would have let Central roll right over them.

This drive had to stop right here.

Third down, and the Warriors were sitting pretty. If they got a touchdown, it was game over. If they scored a field goal, the Scouts would have to score again just to tie the game. At least that wasn't game over.

Jack sensed the play by the way the offensive line sat. Their wide receiver looked a bit too pumped up. When the quarterback danced back into his pocket, Jack knew for sure. He did his own dance, and the tackle followed him just as before. He arced around the line. The quarterback hadn't seen him yet. He lowered his shoulder for a clean tackle and the quarterback's head turned, his eyes becoming wide.

Only then did Jack catch a blob of green in his own peripheral vision. In midair, another player's helmet crashed into his own. He spun around before landing on his stomach. His head exploded with a sharp pain. The cacophony of the crowd faded. His world became blurry and grew dark. Someone knelt down beside him and shouted something, but it was dim, as if from the other end of a long tunnel. Then the blackness took over, and he knew no more.

Chapter 12

A sound, muffled and distant, rumbled at the end of a long tunnel. It was joined by a point of light, inviting. He moved down the tunnel. The light darted around in time with the sound, like some mechanism. It might have been the head of a 3D printer zipping back and forth, laying down material. What was it making? He approached.

He found he could control the mechanism with a force of will. Under his careful guidance, the printer spun a round shape of blue and green, the world. Cracks appeared on the surface of the earth, dividing it into pieces, and the pieces turned until the continents and oceans were hopelessly mixed up. There was some key to putting it back together, but he could not will it whole.

The world exploded. Sound and light assaulted him, and he knew he'd made a terrible mistake. A train hurled down the tunnel, its whistle screaming.

"Shh, it's okay, Jack. Wake up, honey."

Jack bolted awake and sat up, but tight sheets attached him to the bed like a spring. The world was full of light and it hurt, so he clamped his eyes shut.

"Turn the lights off, please," a voice said. Then the light dimmed and the voice continued, "Sorry, honey, light sensitivity is pretty common. Is that better?"

Jack cracked his eyelids open. He could resolve the figures in the room and assign names: Mom, Dad, Timmy.

"Hey, Bud, how you feeling?" his dad said.

He had a splitting headache. "Like I got hit by a train."

His dad laughed and his mom continued to look concerned.

Jack brushed away a few more mental cobwebs and asked, "Is it just Saturday?"

"Yes, sweetie," said his mom. "They put you on a stretcher right there on the field. We were so scared for you, Jack."

"It was so cool," interjected Timmy. "You got a standing oblation."

Jack tried to laugh, but quickly aborted the attempt. "I think you mean ovation, kiddo. But that's pretty cool." He pushed his hands against the bed and tried to slide back and sit up more. His mom rushed to fluff his pillow and prop it behind his back. "Say, did we win or what?"

Now Timmy couldn't contain himself. "Oh boy, you should have seen it! They got another field goal, and then there was only one minute left and our quarterback ran the ball right into the end zone and we got a touchdown!" On the last word, he made the universal gesture for a touchdown with his arms.

Jack's dad added, "The team really pulled together, Jack, and beat them in overtime. We're just glad you're okay, though."

"When can we get out of here?" Jack asked.

His mom said, "Later today, sweetie, after you can walk up and down the hall and get checked over by Dr. Cutty."

He nodded and settled back into the pillow. He didn't feel up to taking that walk right now, so this was going to be home for a few hours at least.

A large sliding glass door opened and a nurse with red hair

and green scrubs came in. She held a little paper cup and a glass of water. She looked familiar.

"I'm so glad you're awake, Jack. How are you feeling?"

Jack used the train analogy again, and the nurse smiled.

"What's your level of pain on a scale of one to ten?"

Seeing the water made him realize his mouth was dry. He swallowed and said, "Uh, six, I guess."

"That's fine, perfectly normal. I've brought you some pain pills. Why don't you see if you can drink some water and swallow them?" She rolled a table over the bed and put the medication on it.

He tossed back the pills and took a long drink of water. "You're Renn's aunt, right?"

"That's right. I'm Jamie. I've been looking in on you since about midnight. We've been waking you up every couple of hours just to make sure you could, but you might not remember."

The next time Jack woke up, his room was empty. The dim light didn't bother him and his head didn't ache as much. He drank some more water and channel surfed, stopping on a golf tournament. He thought he should be doing something today, but he couldn't put his finger on it.

The sliding door opened, and Nurse Jamie rolled in a cart with food.

"Hi, Jack. I'm going off shift, but I wanted to bring you some lunch first."

"Thanks, I'm starving."

"That's very good. I think you'll be sleeping in your own bed tonight. There are some more pain meds on your tray."

The tray had something that looked like meatloaf, green beans, orange Jell-O, a bun, and water and juice. *Just what the doctor ordered*, he thought. He scooted back and sat up straight, this time without help. A knock sounded on the glass door. Jamie walked to the door and looked back at him.

"Feel like a visitor?"

"Sure, I guess. Who is it?"

Jamie slid open the door and gestured for the visitor to enter. Renn offered a tentative wave and stepped closer. "Hi, how are you feeling?"

The train had been downgraded into a small car, maybe a large motorcycle.

"Have a seat, but I'm not sharing my lunch with you."

She laughed and pulled up a chair beside his bed. "You must be getting a little better."

Jack slurped a cube of Jell-O and said, "I guess." Another memory clicked into place. "Hey, were we supposed to get together today? If so, sorry."

Renn shifted in her seat and looked uncomfortable. "Yeah, you were going to come with me over to Owen Sutherland's house."

Jack froze, and a piece of orange Jell-O jiggled in mid-trip on his spoon. His eyes grew large. "Oh my God, I'm so sorry. I can't do it today. I'm a little tied up."

Renn laughed again. "No problem." She gave him a sheepish look and continued, "Actually, I've kind of been there already."

He studied his friend. She seemed tired, and there were little bags under her eyes, which were mildly bloodshot. Jack reviewed his fractured memory, but nothing came to mind explaining why Renn would have gone over to that guy's house by herself. There must be a story behind it.

Jack wolfed down the rest of his lunch and Renn seemed content to sit in silence until pressed for more information. He wiped his mouth and tossed the napkin down with a flourish. "Hey, I'm supposed to walk around the halls for a while to prove that I'm not an invalid or something. Want to come?"

Renn nodded. "Okay, as long as your butt's not hanging out the back of your gown."

It was Jack's turn to laugh, and he nodded at a robe hanging on the bathroom door. "Hand me that and I'll be good to go."

A moment later Renn, Jack, and Jack's rolling IV stand emerged from his room. He took things easy, setting a slow pace. There was no cool way to push his stand down the hall, so he shuffled along like an old man. "So, what happened with Owen?"

Renn caught Jack up on the events of Friday night, leading up to her sneaking into Owen's backyard, and getting trapped in the shed.

"God, Renn, you must have been terrified. Then what happened?"

* * *

The incessant, thunderous barking of the dog beat against Renn's consciousness. It was going to wake the whole neighborhood up, not to mention Owen. She felt like such an idiot for getting herself into this mess. One step after another, she overcame every barrier set up by common sense and put herself right in this shed. She touched her cheeks, found they were wet, and wiped the tears away.

A voice called out from the house. "Rosco! What on earth is your problem, boy? Shut your trap and come here!"

The door shook, and the barking continued unabated. Renn counted the seconds until Rosco's owner would try to open the shed and discover its jury-rigged doors. Time to face the music.

Owen shouted again. "Rosco! Here boy, come!"

By some miracle, the door stopped shaking and the barking did, too. She didn't know what magic Owen had used to distract Rosco, but she thanked her lucky stars for it. She thought about what would have worked with Bear, his favorite treat, or some peanut butter. Maybe a leash? Definitely a leash would have drawn her big lug of a dog. She strained to listen, her ears still ringing from Rosco's assault.

"Good boy, that's a good boy. You want to walk a little? I bet you didn't even do your business, did you?" Owen's voice moved from the house into the yard. "You'd love to get a hold of those rats, I bet. Yes, you would. You know they're not for you, no they're not for you." Now his voice emanated from the other side of the shed by the fence gate. "It's like I'm running a zoo or something. What a menagerie. Well, it won't be for much longer, Rosco, I promise."

Renn heard the gate open and the sounds of dog and owner faded away. She sat there, counting off another thirty seconds in the silence, scarcely daring to believe her luck. Finally, she stood up, unhooked her belt, and fastened it once again where it belonged. She pushed the shed doors open, and when no one and nothing were there to greet her, she stepped out and closed up the shed.

The fence gate stood open, and she ran through it to the front edge of the house, hiding in its shadows. No sign of Owen and Rosco. With a little luck, they had gone the opposite direction of her parked car.

Seconds ticked by and her heart pounded in her ears.

What a rush. How long would Rosco's walk take? She had

to walk Bear around the block at least; anything less was a rip-off.

She jogged up to the corner of the hedge and peeked up and down the sidewalk. There was no sign of man or beast. The house and street were quiet as a graveyard once again.

Renn clenched her fists and walked a tight circle in the yard. "Wasting time," she muttered as she ran to the backyard, around the shed, and to the back door of Owen's house. Not caring about stealth anymore, she tried the door and found it open.

If Stella were being kept here, she guessed Owen had to keep her separated from Rosco, or there'd be no peace to be had. That meant she needed to look for some place shut off from the rest of the house, like a closed-off room or a basement. She ran around the house testing doors, opening them as quietly as possible just in case there was someone else around. She discovered stairs leading down and descended at speed.

The basement was mostly unfinished, with one walled off section. It turned out to hold the washer and dryer, and some cleaning supplies. The water heater and furnace sat off to the side, surrounded by the skeletal frame of the house. Fat pads of insulation were tucked in between wooden bones. The absence of walls created a visual clutter that made it hard to understand the layout.

Renn found a chain dangling from the ceiling attached to a bare bulb. She pulled it and the bulb bathed the room in a harsh light. Now she could see into the back corner of the basement. A chicken-wire cage with large pieces of plywood resting over it looked like it had been hastily constructed. Stella stood inside the cage on sheets of dirty newspaper. Her head swiveled, surveying now-visible surroundings.

Renn rushed to the cage, dropped to her knees, and let out a sob. She had hoped for this, but not really expected it. Finding Stella, alive and well, was almost more than she could take. Renn tried to remember the rest of her plan. She couldn't do anything for Stella right away. She needed to get out and call the police.

"Hang in there, girl," she said to the bird, still majestic even in these humble surroundings. "I'll be back with help as soon I can."

Renn jumped up and started for the stairs, before stopping and cursing. "Evidence!" she whispered as she reached for her phone. She needed proof, or she'd have nothing to take to the police. Her hand shook, and she fumbled the pin pattern on her phone twice before unlocking it.

Renn was in the belly of the beast, but her straining ears picked up no sounds. How many clicks and swipes did it take to open the dang camera? She could take a selfie with the best of them, but when she held the phone up to snap Stella, it slipped from her shaking hands and clattered onto the floor. She cursed again and snatched it up, this time holding it with both hands. Stella regarded her with head cocked to the side. "You must think I've lost it," Renn told her as she snapped several pictures.

She tried to reverse her steps as quickly as possible, turning off the single light, taking the stairs by two, turning down the hallway and bursting through the door into the backyard.

All was quiet except her pounding heart. Almost home. Just run to the car and call the police.

She rounded the shed and saw Owen. His back was to her. He was closing the fence gate. Renn stopped, turned, and fled the other direction. Owen picked up his one-way conversation with Rosco.

"Stop yanking on my arm, boy, it still hurts like the dickens. If I didn't have such a soft spot for animals, we wouldn't be in this mess."

Renn ran across the yard to the other side of the house with the short stretch of fence. Gripping its top with both hands, she stepped up with one foot and swung the other one over. As she threw her weight to the other side, her windbreaker got hung up on the top of the chain link. She landed okay, but her jacket tugged at her, tying her to the fence. She heard the gate close. Rosco, clever boy that he was, raced directly to her.

The barking began all over again.

Renn was face to face with his bared fangs, and she panicked. She pulled back harder, but her jacket kept her from escaping. She yanked mindlessly until her brain caught up. Then she paused and unzipped it as much as she could. That allowed her to drop her body straight down until the jacket was over her head and she was pulling the sleeves inside out.

Owen found her in this awkward position when he came to check on Rosco. "What the... who is that? What are you doing?"

Renn tugged harder, freed her hands from the sleeves, and landed on her rear end on the grass. She had gained several feet of distance between herself and the fence, but she now looked directly at Owen, and he at her. Even in her fear, she almost broke into laughter at his surprised expression.

Owen sputtered, "You! It's you. What... what are you doing at my house?"

She crab-walked back a few feet, then scrambled to her feet and sprinted to her car as fast as her legs would carry her.

* * *

Jack gripped the rolling stand and tried to keep from doubling over.

"Ow, don't make me laugh. I can't stand it."

Renn crossed her arms and puckered. "Laugh? I could have *died*, Jack. It's not funny!"

"Well, whose fault would that have been?" He managed to stand up straight and start shuffling along the hallway again. "I'm happy you made it—for you, as well as for Stella. But, God Almighty, you are stubborn."

"I had to go, Jack. I didn't have a choice." Renn separated half a step from him, arms still crossed.

A few smart replies flitted through Jack's mind, but he stuffed them all down and merely asked, "What did the police do?"

"Oh, they showed up fast. They probably thought Owen tried to kidnap me, the way I sounded."

Renn dropped her arms and stuck her hands in her front pockets. Her Aunt Jamie was off, but the desk nurse wave cheerfully at them. Renn seemed lost in thought, and Jack let her be.

"Anyway," she said, "they found Stella and called animal control. I had to go to the police station and answer a bunch of questions on how I ended up at, and in, his house. I think I was there until one in the morning. And I had our car, so two of the officers had to drive it home so Mom could come get me."

Jack glanced over at his friend. Her watery eyes stared ahead, unblinking. He saw embarrassment with a tinge of guilt, but overshadowed by steely determination that was the hallmark of Adrienne Chao. After the shock of the thing wore off, she'd look back on last night with the righteous conviction that justice was on her side.

He couldn't even disagree with that part. But she acted stupidly going over there by herself. He'd promised to go with her. A wave of nausea rolled over him and pain lanced behind his eyes. He put his weight on the IV stand and felt, rather than saw, Renn add her hands on it for stability. "Come on, let's get back to the room," he whispered.

Safe in bed, he lay with eyes shut until the episode passed. Only after the worst of it did he notice that Renn still sat by the bed, a furrowed brow over widely spaced, dark eyes. Light punched into the gray room between the curtains and in cubic shafts from the hallway.

After some time she said, "I'm going to go, Jack. Want me to ask the nurse for anything?"

He shook his head, let her almost reach the door before calling her name. "Renn, things don't always work out. You don't always get a happy ending. Just look at what happened to me. You have to be smart as well as brave."

Renn stood by the door, fragmented by light and shadow. He imagined her coming back with some comment about his intelligence, but she simply said, "I'm glad you're okay."

She slipped out of the room, leaving him alone with the shadows.

Chapter 13

Jack reclined in the hard waiting room chair, his planked body touching the top of the backrest, the front of the seat, and the floor. He flipped through an old edition of *Entertainment Weekly* and absorbed none of it. His mom sat against the adjacent wall, and they shared a corner table. A grade school kid sat with his mom on the other side of the room, picking his nose. Maybe it was time to lose the pediatrician.

A TV was mounted near the ceiling, kitty-corner across the room. The local news anchor started talking about Silver Labs. Jack tossed the magazine and rolled his head to face the screen.

"The billionaire Jason Silver has come under increasing criticism from investors for moving part of his company to the small Midwestern town of Black Hawk Bend. Silver, who was born in Muscatine, Iowa, has alienated investors with his embrace of small-town America."

Jack scoffed and muttered, "We're not that small."

A nurse stepped out from the office area and called his name. He and his mom rose to follow her to an examination room, where his mom answered the nurse's questions. An old steel examination table took up the room's center like some torture device. They even lined it with paper for easy cleanup; like it never happened—smart.

"How's your pain today, Jack, on a scale of one to ten?" the nurse asked.

"Uh, three, I guess."

She took his blood pressure and reviewed symptoms: Headache, dizziness, sensitivity to light. Check, check, and check. On her way out, she promised a brief wait for Dr. Cutty.

The pictures on the walls featured Looney Tunes characters and glow stickers of the moon and stars were arrayed on the ceiling. Jack invented constellations to stave off boredom. He wondered whether he'd have to miss the game this Friday, tried to prepare for the worst.

A knock rapped against the exam room door, and it immediately opened to reveal Dr. Cutty, making Jack wonder why he had knocked at all. He wore his white doctor's coat with a stethoscope hanging around his neck. He had a ring of gray hair crowned by a shining bald head. His belly protruded from the front of his coat. He smiled amiably and shook Jack's hand.

"Well, Jack, you're looking much better today. How do you feel?"

"Fine, I guess. A little headache, but not bad."

"I'd think so after the hit you took." He shined a light in Jack's eyes. "Headache is one symptom of a concussion. But there can be others, including balance problems and cognitive deficits."

His mom, who'd had resting worry face all morning, stepped it up another level.

"Now, these are most often temporary," Dr. Cutty continued, holding his palm up to fend off concerns. "Today we're going to get an idea of how you're doing in these other areas, and it will tell us where you are in the healing process, okay?"

He had Jack do a few puzzles with pen and paper. Then the

nurse brought in one of those exercise balls, but the kind with only half a ball against a flat platform. He developed a bad feeling about it even before it thudded onto the floor.

"Jack, I'd like you to take off your shoes and stand on this balance ball."

* * *

In the parking lot after the appointment, Jack vented at his mother. "Six weeks? I'll be out for six weeks?" His sullen mood after the pronouncement had turned into hot anger. "I'm fine! I mean, other than some headaches. There's no way I'm sitting on my butt for six weeks! Just because I fell off the stupid ball? That doesn't mean anything." His head pounded as he got in the car and his mom pulled out of the lot.

She used her best peacemaker's voice. "He said up to six weeks, Honey. It probably won't be that long. We just have to monitor your symptoms. When your headaches and dizziness are completely gone, then you'll be able to resume normal activities within a few days. But it *could* take as long as six weeks."

Six weeks was enough to miss state, not to mention the games leading up to it. He had expected a few days off, but this was insane. "Can I go to school at least, or am I confined to my bed?"

His mother ignored the sarcasm and pointed the car towards Black Hawk High. When the car stopped in front of the school, he clambered out gloomily. She managed a cheerful, "Have a great day, Honey!"

Jack slammed the door, took two steps, turned around, marched back to the car and opened the door. "And I want a new doctor!" He slammed the car door again and felt a tiny bit better.

Everyone at school was happy to see Jack and inundated him with stories about the game. Central's drive had been stopped on the play that took Jack out. That it wasn't Jack who stopped it didn't seem to matter. His injury turned out to be the most memorable thing about the game.

As the day wore on, he drifted from class to class, rudderless. Without the next game to look forward to, what was the point? He needed to be right there in the thick of it, or he was nowhere, cast out to sea.

A couple texts came in from Renn, but he didn't feel ready to deal with them.

Mrs. Anderson tossed him a lifesaver in Chemistry. They worked in groups of four on an ideal gas law problem set. With increased pressure, volume gets smaller and temperature goes up. Jack's cranium could testify. She caught his eye and waved him up to her desk. He sat in the spare wooden chair placed by her desk for just such occasions.

"Jack, I just wanted to ask you how you're doing. I wasn't at the game, but I heard you were hit pretty hard." She spoke just a hair over a whisper but still conveyed a full range of emotions. Now, she sounded genuinely concerned.

"I'm okay. Sometimes I get headaches but the nurse's office has Tylenol," he trailed off, ran out of words.

"That's good, dear, I'm happy to hear it. Now, how are you doing?" Somehow, he realized she was asking a completely different question this time.

"I'm not sure. I..."

"I was just watching you in the small group. Normally, you'd be leading it, making the others laugh, and still manage to finish first. So, what's wrong?

"Yeah, I guess. It's just that I won't be able to play football, for up to six weeks. I might miss the rest of the season."

Crinkles deepened at the corners of her eyes and her double chin manifested as she looked down at her desk. She laced her fingers and her rings clinked together. A few heartbeats passed before she looked back at Jack. "What are you planning to major in? In college, I mean."

The change in topic took Jack off guard. "Mechanical Engineering. Well, probably."

"Are you planning on playing football there? Getting a scholarship?"

Aha, he saw where this was going. "I don't know. The chances are low, I guess."

She nodded. "It's good to love football. I don't want you to misunderstand me. But you have so much more going for you. While you have this down time, take the opportunity to indulge some other interests. Find a project to occupy your time. I think you'll find it very rewarding."

He could tell she was going out of her way to be sensitive to his situation. Jack didn't want to be done moping, though. He wanted to kick and scream and throw a temper tantrum about the unfairness of life. He wanted people to, what, feel sorry for him? No way. Folding his arms on the desk, he leaned in and said, "Like what?"

Mrs. Anderson smiled encouragement. "Oh, it could be anything. Think about what you love to do. Your hobbies. Anything come to mind?"

Jack tried to think about something other than football and his inability to play it for a moment. He loved video games, but his attempts to play on Sunday had just caused massive headaches and nausea. Thanks for that reminder. His hand went to his pocket and returned to the desk holding the blue cryptex. He'd shown it to her already, and Mrs. A's eyes lit up when she saw it again.

"Oh marvelous, Jack."

"Can I use the printer this week? There are some designs on here I'd like to print."

They worked out a schedule that would get Jack all seven pieces of the tangram by the end of the week. Each one was simple, a triangle, square, or parallelogram, and one of four solid colors: red, green, yellow, or blue. He started printing the first piece at the end of class.

At the end of the day, he stopped by the chemistry lab to pick up his first piece, a blue square. On one side, a number was printed next to each edge, running from one to four, but not in any specific order.

The other side was interesting. There were more numbers engraved at various angles, but not integers. Each number ran to six significant digits. Some were positive, and some negative—another mystery.

Okay, this might distract him from football for a little while.

* * *

Renn held her jet black hair to one side as she drank from the cool stream of water. The bustle of hallway traffic pressed up against her. She had a moment to spare in between classes, so she leaned against the wall by the fountain and braced one sneakered foot against it.

Bonehead had still not texted her back all week. She had soccer friends who'd had concussions. She wondered if his personality had changed. Maybe her friend was no longer the same Jack she knew and tolerated. He was keeping his distance and that meant something.

Renn's phone rang from an unknown number. On a whim, she decided not to screen it.

"Hello?"

"Hello. I'm trying to reach Adrienne Chao. Is this she?"

The voice was female and sounded young, but very formal.

"Yes."

"Hi, Adrienne. This is Amanda Hastings from Channel Nine. We're doing a story on the missing bald eagle, Stella. I understand you were involved in her recovery?"

Involved. You could say she was involved, like a surgeon is involved in your appendectomy. "Yes, that's right."

"Great, I'd love to come out with a cameraman this afternoon and get your story for the five o'clock news. Would that be alright with you and your mother?"

Renn scanned her clothing situation. Mom could bring her an outfit from home over lunch. "I guess so."

"Great. Thanks so much, Adrienne. You sound like a brave young woman and I look forward to talking with you."

"Yeah, I am a brave person," she said to herself after the line clicked dead. "What do you think of that, Jack?"

At this rate, she would never know what Jack thought of it. She ought to be done with hard luck cases for a while. She hadn't studied for her ACT in days, and she didn't have the time to save any more lost animals or stray football players. Renn tired of seeing the same face whenever she closed her eyes. Owen stepping out of the shadows, pointing an accusatory finger, indicting her with his words. "You. It's you."

Jack stepped out of the boys' bathroom and turned to walk

in front of her. He focused on his phone, and she wasn't sure if he'd seen her or not. She could let him roll right on by. Instead, she called, "Hey, Jack."

He lifted his sandy blond head from his phone and stopped in the middle of the hall.

"You've been ignoring my texts."

"Sorry, still trying to catch up with stuff."

Weak. He didn't seem hostile or angry, but she couldn't tell if he was her Jack. He didn't seem like himself. She pushed away from the painted brick wall with her foot and guided Jack to a patch of closed lockers on the other side of the hall.

"How are you feeling?" she asked.

Jack looked amused by some private joke, and said, "On a scale of one to ten, I'd say I'm a seven."

She met his gaze, icy blue with no humor behind it. "Seven is pretty good. So, what's up with you?"

He told her about the doctor's appointment, being benched, the possibility of missing the rest of the season. She heard his frustration, his anger, and some bitterness in his voice. She didn't begrudge him any of it, only wanted to know if it sounded like Jack.

"God, sorry. That's rough."

It didn't seem like the right time to tell him about her TV interview.

He dropped his backpack on the floor between them. It was unzipped, because that's how he rolled, and fell open when it hit the floor. Renn could not help but notice two colored plastic pieces poking out.

"Are those...?"

"Yup."

"Why are you messing with that stupid puzzle, Jack? You

should be home resting." The words had more bite than she intended.

"Thanks, doc, but I'm not an invalid. And your bedside manner sucks."

Renn leaned her shoulder against a locker and tried to calm down. She idly spun one of the combination locks, then tried again in a gentle tone, "You know, you might heal faster if you took it easy. Why push yourself?"

"Oh, you're one to talk. Why are you pushing yourself to take the ACT? We're only sophomores."

"Don't turn this around on me. You know why, Jack." Renn stopped playing with the lock and planted her hand on her hip. "It's important for you to give your body time to heal. Why are you on this wild goose chase?"

"Because I..."

They had to step out to unblock the lockers. Jack hoisted his backpack and started to turn. Renn grabbed the strap of the pack and urged him to continue with a nod.

He bowed his head and pushed two fingers against his temple, as if in pain. "Because it's all I have now," he whispered bitterly.

All he had? What the heck was he talking about? He had friends. Wasn't she standing right in front of him? She released the strap. "Okay, Jack, I hope you know what you're doing." Stepping around him, she raced to biology.

Bonehead.

Chapter 14

Dom studied the test lying on his desk, turning its pages and recalling the problems and how he had solved them. Mr. Harvey had meant for number seventeen to be tricky, but it wasn't. There was very little red ink until he got to the end and saw the word 'good!' with a big circle around it. He flipped it over and checked the other red mark again: A+, also circled.

Dom hung his head until the desk became his entire world. He imagined its glossy tan surface as the land, a No. 2 pencil in a groove near the top its sun, the test paper a house built with his own hands, the rich brown soil of his skin supporting it at the bottom. He wondered what effect he could have on this little world, a pocket universe of his own creation. Dom ought to be its master. With thumb and forefinger, he pinched his arm hard and let go. His skin became ever so paler. Hardly any change at all. He pinched harder and harder until his eyes watered. His little experiment had proven one thing. He could make trivial changes in his world, but only at a great cost. Not worth it.

A similar scene had played out every morning this week. He would wake up with a bad stomachache, turn off his alarm, and roll over into the fetal position. Sometime later, his mom would come, an irresistible force. She'd rub his back, hit the highlights on the all-importance of school, and make him tea with honey. He hadn't missed a day all semester. Great pain to little effect; it was the story of his life.

"Dominic."

His world snapped back to full scale. Other kids joked and compared test scores. Someone's test floated across the room in the form of an airplane. Mr. Harvey sat behind his desk, nonplussed. He was looking at Dom, must have called his name.

"Could I talk to you, please?"

Dom walked up to Mr. Harvey's desk and stood awkwardly beside it. He felt the eyes of the class drilling into him.

"Hi, Dominic, you were pretty quiet in class today."

"I'm just a little tired. I didn't feel well this morning."

Mr. Harvey leaned in to listen, a cue to Dom that he was mumbling again.

"I'm sorry to hear that. I must be giving you too much homework." He chuckled a little at his own joke, and Dom shifted uncomfortably.

"Anyway, I wanted to ask you if you've given any more thought to Math Club. We could use your help this year."

"Oh, thanks. I thought about it, but I need to take the bus home after school 'cause my mom can't pick me up when club gets out. I don't know—"

"I'm sure we can work something out. The competition season only lasts a few weeks. Maybe I can drop you off at home after practice. Where do you live?"

"Um, you know where High Tower Apartments are? Over by—"

"I know it. It's only a few minutes out of my way. Why don't you check with your mom whether that arrangement would be alright? We're going to have a strong team. We even have a shot at beating Regina."

Mr. Harvey had a gleam in his eye when he talked about beating their perennial rival, their Math Quiz nemesis.

"I'll ask her."

"Thank you, Dom. Will you let me know this week?"

The bell rang, and the chaos in the room increased and flowed towards the door. Dom felt like he had to shout his answer.

"Okay, I will."

Waiting for the turbulence to die down, Dom collected his test and backpack from his desk and prepared for the journey from class to class, from safe zone to safe zone.

Maybe Math Club would be good for him. Math was the one thing he'd gotten any positive recognition for. Perhaps it could help him have an effect on his world.

He turned the idea over and over in his head as he walked to his next class, thought about the best way to present it to his mother. He did not see Bernie leaning against the wall as he turned a corner.

"Well, if it isn't DominEEK. You know you're going to be late to class?" Bernie had a smile on his face as though he were doling out friendly advice.

Glancing at his watch, Dom replied, "I have plenty of time."

Bernie's smile faded. "I said you're going to be late. To. Class." As he said this, he kicked off the wall and approached Dom, walking right through the invisible line that defined a person's private space.

Dom backed up but felt his backpack bump up against something, knowing instinctively that it was a someone.

"Hey, watch where you're going. You're going to take

109

someone out," said Ryan. He felt a shove from behind that sent him, chest first, right into Bernie, who now stood much too close.

"Jeez, watch it Marshall. You really are a klutz, aren't you?" Bernie motioned to Ryan, who yanked Dom's backpack to the floor and kicked it to the wall.

Dom felt naked without it, like it was some kind of armor. He could not run away now without leaving all his possessions behind, likely never to be seen again. It had become an anchor. He lowered his eyes and said to no one in particular, "I don't want any trouble."

"Then why do you have to go banging around into everyone you meet, Marshall?" Bernie had become openly aggressive. "You owe me an apology for trying to lay me out, and you owe my friend an apology for bashing him with that bag of bricks."

Ryan piped in with, "Hey, maybe he should be on the football team, Bern. He could take out the whole line, right?"

Bernie's brow raised, and he looked like he had come up with the most brilliant idea in the world. "Ha, maybe you're on to something there. Thing is, we don't know if he can take a hit. What do you say, DominEEK? Can you take a hit?"

Dom shuffled sideways in his best attempt to bump neither Ryan nor Bernie. "Uh, we're late to class now guys, we'd better get going."

But Bernie, now intent on following through with his brilliant idea, grabbed Dom's upper arm. "Line up right here, Marshall. Ryan, you line up right next to him like you're an offensive line. I'll be the defense."

"Hear that, Marshall? You're offensive." Ryan guffawed and Bernie slapped his knee in exaggerated hilarity.

It felt like a dream. How could this happen again? He wasn't paying attention. He let himself get caught daydreaming about Math club. Stupid, he was so stupid. He was not safe in this place. Why did he have to be here? He stood limply while Ryan faced off against Bernie in football crouches. Ryan counted off like a quarterback. Then he heard the words, "Hut, hut, Hike!" He thought he might faint.

A few things happened at that moment. Ryan stood up and jogged backwards, pumping his arm with a pretend ball in search of an imaginary receiver. Bernie shifted his weight and propelled himself towards Dom. A small group of students rounded the corner at the far end of the hallway to witness the play. At the near end of the hallway, behind Bernie, another student entered the field of view. Dom felt himself falling, but not before the full weight of Bernie hit his chest, knocking him back. He sprawled out and slid on his back on the polished hallway floor. His eyes were clamped shut. He heard another impact between two bodies and felt someone go down on the floor next to him.

Shouts. Footsteps. Other voices emerged from nearby classrooms.

Dom realized he was not breathing. When he tried to take a breath, he could not. His chest refused to expand. He panicked. He sensed someone leaning over him. A forearm gripped his own and started to tug him up.

"You're okay, you just had the wind knocked out of you. Come on, sit up now, sit up."

Dom opened his eyes and did his best to comply. To his shock, he found himself looking into the face of the other football player, the popular one. At last he got his air back and gulped it in like a fish out of water. Jack helped him to his feet and collected his backpack for him.

"I'm sorry.   I'm sorry that happened to you," he said. "They're gone and I'll do my best to make sure they don't bother you anymore."

Dom stood weakly, still gulping in fresh air, but nodded his head in wishful agreement.

* * *

At the far end of the hall, a crowd of onlookers gathered, and in the front stood a petite figure with curly brown hair and chocolate brown eyes. They'd all seen the two football players attack the other kid. Her entire body tensed and she leaned forward onto the balls of her feet. Her hands clenched into tiny fists. A fourth character, also a football player, dove in and broke up the fight. It wasn't much of a fight, though.

Clara drew up her hoodie and cinched it tight. She couldn't do anything at the moment, so she watched and remembered.

Chapter 15

The football player had Dom's backpack flung over his broad left shoulder. His right arm wrapped behind Dom, supporting him. They headed to the nurse's office. He'd never had the wind knocked out of him. An involuntary biological function that he'd relied on his whole life had just stopped working. It was like having your heart grind to a halt and resist all efforts to shock it back into action.

"Your name is Dominic, right? Dominic Marshall?"

"Yeah," he coughed out the word, then caught his breath. "But everyone calls me Dom. Almost."

"My name is Jack. We're in the same math class."

"I know. I saw you." Dom stepped out of Jack's support and away. His breath still came hard, so he bent over and braced his hands against his knees. Jack towered over him a few steps away. "I mean, I've seen you around. You're a football player, like them. Why would you help me?"

"Not like them," Jack said, and took a step towards him, arms spread in a show of peace.

Dom waved him off and stood up straight. His balance was okay, so he started a slow pace down the hall. Jack fell into step beside him and they walked in silence for almost a minute.

"I know they've been bothering you," said Jack. "I saw it. It really sucks."

"You saw it, but you didn't do anything. Why now? Just leave me be. And gimme my backpack." Dom felt vulnerable and shaky, and he hated that he might owe this jock something. But an involuntary response compelled him to add, "Please."

Jack complied, hefting the loaded backpack behind Dom, waiting for him to get his arms through the straps.

"Look, I'm sorry about that," Jack said. "I was in a hurry. I don't know what I was thinking." He paused. "There's no excuse. By doing nothing, I let it happen. I'm sorry and I'd like to help you out."

"Forget it, man," Dom said as he marched on. He'd tried to narrow his world so it excluded all football players, all bullies, all people. He had to get out of this place. He didn't feel safe or welcome, just stress and heaviness. His mom wouldn't let him stay home and study for the GED. Dom wondered what she'd think after this. He reached and felt the back of his head where it hit the floor. He'd bet money there'd be a bump, and also a bruise on his chest where Bernie had hit him.

Dom glanced over to see if Jack still shadowed him. There he was, half a step behind. He rubbed his temples and his eyes alternated between squeezed shut and stretched wide open.

"You get hit, too?" Dom didn't want to owe this white football player anything, but he didn't want him to be hurt either. He wouldn't wish that on anyone.

Jack nodded and said, "No. Well, not today. I just have a headache, that's all."

When they arrived at the nurse's office, Jack asked for some Tylenol. The nurse fussed over him like he was the one who needed attention. Dom wanted to scream, *Don't you know I'm the injured one here?* He bit off the spiteful words and silently dared the nurse to keep ignoring him.

But then Jack told her about the bullying and introduced Dom. She asked him to sit down and gave him her undivided attention.

"Hey, Dom," said Jack. "I'm going to go report this in the principal's office." Jack stood in the office doorway, filling it up.

Dom waved him away. "Don't do me any favors," he muttered.

At dinner that evening, Dom's mother was unmoved by the events of the day. She provided ice, aspirin, and motherly affection, but she would not see reason. He didn't have it in him to disobey her, to disappoint her. She'd had enough of that.

The next day he was late to school on account of his stomachache, which had grown worse. Dom wanted nothing more than to shut the world out and ignore all the kids at school. There were only two kinds: those that hurt you and those that turned a blind eye. But he couldn't afford to let his guard down, even for a minute. So he planned each trip through the blackboard jungle like he was on safari, keeping the predators at a safe distance.

Something weird struck him halfway into the morning. Dom had seen Jack around, more than usual. He'd be hurrying from class to class and there was the football player, hard to miss, sneaking glances his way. He took out-of-the-way routes to verify it. There might have been the added bonus of shaking Bernie and Ryan off his tail, because they were nowhere to be seen.

Dom felt a little like James Bond sneaking around a mansion—until his arch villains stepped into the lunch line, two people behind him. Brief eye contact confirmed that they meant to target him again. He broke into a cold sweat and his left hand started to shake. What was he going to do?

He'd almost decided to yell "fire" at the top of his lungs when Jack cut into line behind him. An athletic boy sporting long hair twists slipped into line with him.

"Dom, this is Noah. Want some company?"

"What are you doing?" Dom demanded. "I said I didn't want your help. I just want everyone to leave me alone."

Jack grabbed a tray and started loading it with spaghetti and toasted bread. "I'm sorry you're dealing with this, I truly am. But Bernie's out for blood and you need help. You don't have to like it, but I'm asking you to trust me. Give me a chance."

They explained the situation over lunch. Coach Kelley was pissed when he heard about the incident. He often turned a blind eye to a little trouble from his guys, but the tackling scenario in the hallway was over the top and the principal had called him about it. Coach kicked Bernie off the team and benched Ryan for two games.

Noah talked to him some more and vouched for Jack's intentions. More than anything, it was Noah's testimony that convinced him to accept Jack's help. Dom sighed and relented.

The next day Jack, Noah, or one of a handful of other football players personally escorted him between classes. It was like a waking steroid-fueled nightmare, only turned on its head in a way he never imagined.

Another surprise awaited him after school. His obstinate mother, unswayed by two football players with death wishes, had encouraged Dom to join Math Club, even insisted on it. So he slipped into Mr. Harvey's classroom after last bell and took a seat at the back of the class.

"Ah, Mr. Marshall, great to have you here. Gang, this is Dominic Marshall. I've asked him to join our team. I think he can be a great asset."

Dom sunk lower in his desk as everyone's heads turned to stare at him. He prepared himself for faces covered with derision and disdain. But everyone smiled and greeted him warmly. Not one threatening face in the bunch.

After a time, he grudgingly admitted that he enjoyed the meeting, too. Mr. Harvey taught them some rules for integration, and Dom looked at it like a puzzle. His mind turned every new equation over, this way and that, as he searched for the right rule to apply.

The next morning he was halfway through a shower before realizing there had been no stomachache.

Chapter 16

The image on the TV screen in Renn's homeroom was none other than herself. Renn was talking to a female reporter in a smart suit holding a huge microphone which she alternately jabbed into Renn's face and pulled back to hers.

Reporter: "Adrienne, when did you first know that Stella was being held captive in the basement of Owen Sutherland's house?"

Renn: "Well, uh, I *suspected* when I saw him. I happened to see him with an injured arm in a truck reported to be at the scene of the, er, at the Raptor Center."

Reporter: "Who reported the truck?"

Renn: "Um, the ranger in charge of the center."

Reporter: "How did you rescue Stella, Adrienne?"

Renn: "Well, I just, I just got very lucky. I was able to collect enough evidence to give to the police. They're the ones who rescued—"

Reporter: "There you have it. The brave actions of one young woman to save a raptor in distress bagged a bird-napper red-handed."

Mercifully, the interview wrapped up and Renn breathed again. The class erupted in claps, cheers, and a few whoops. Her flush deepened and she thought her entire face must be cherry red. She hid it in her hands and shook her head back and forth. Nearby friends patted her back and shoulders. The cheers transitioned into laughter and she dropped her hands and laughed with them. The situation was so much easier to handle as a big joke.

Except she knew it wasn't a joke. Stella had returned home, but Ranger Scott installed a security camera and better locks on the cages. The police really didn't think it was a joke, and Renn felt like as much of a criminal as Owen after they got done with her. As for Owen, the FBI was going to question him—no joke. Least funny of all the not-a-jokes was how Owen knew Renn. He'd recognized her face. How?

The bell rang and Renn hurried on to her next class, pausing to give a little curtsy to her most vocal fans. She managed to get through the morning in relative anonymity. On the way to lunch, a reporter for the school paper insisted on a picture and a quick interview. Great, she was on her way to fame and fortune, only without the fortune part.

Renn claimed an empty table with her tray, hoping for a little quiet time.

"Mind if I join you?"

She turned her head towards the familiar voice, then back to her veggie lasagna. "It's a free country. But I thought you wanted to be left alone."

Jack sat down at the table opposite her. "Yeah, I guess I've had enough alone time." He sounded a little sheepish. "Sorry, it was just a combination of everything, the concussion, getting benched, arguing about the cryptex, my headaches. I'm sorry I yelled at you."

He had an earnest expression with puppy-dog eyes. Absolutely ridiculous, yet somehow effective.

119

"Apology accepted. How are you feeling?"

"I still get a few headaches every day. I'm trying to keep busy."

Renn regarded him coolly for a moment before shaking her head. "Men!" she said with some exasperation. "I swear, you hit your head or any little thing and your whole lives fall to pieces."

Jack sat up a little straighter. "What are you talking about? I got a concussion. Brain damage!"

"Ha, I wouldn't just blame the concussion for that." Her lips curled up as she tore a piece from her bread. "Remember when you were sick a couple of months ago? You hobbled around like you were about to die. It's the man-cold all over again!"

"The, what? You're crazy," Jack protested. "Girls get sick, too, and they're no better."

Renn shook her head. "Uh-uh, Jack-o. You are mistaken, sir. The man-cold is real, and I think it extends to injuries as well. I'm going to do a paper on it when I get to med school."

"Okay. Good luck with that." Jack cut his meat lasagna and shoved large pieces into his mouth. His appetite had returned, if it was ever gone.

"By the way," he added, "I saw your interview this morning. It was inspirational. I want to grow up to be just like you."

"Jerk," said Renn, as she threw the piece of bread heading for her mouth at Jack instead.

"One thing, though," Jack said, ignoring the bread attack. "This guy Owen works, or worked, at Silver Labs. Do you think that's coincidental to our finding your last cache right there? And the cryptex?"

Renn hadn't told him about being recognized by Owen. "I don't know. But it has to be, doesn't it?"

"Hmmm," said Jack as he stuffed the last of his food into his mouth. After wiping his face with the napkin and crumpling it on his tray, he looked again at Renn. "Listen, I'm going to keep working on the puzzle. It helps me keep my mind off things. And it's pretty interesting."

Renn shoved her tray back and folded her arms on the table. "I know. But I hope you're not too disappointed if it doesn't lead anywhere."

"Don't worry, I won't be. I'll have all the pieces printed this week. And I've been thinking about asking for some help with it."

"Help? Who from?"

"You heard about the thing with Bernie and Ryan? The one I helped break up?"

Renn repositioned her arms on either side of her tray and leaned in some more. "Of course, the entire school heard about it. You're practically a hero. Almost as much a hero as moi." She fluttered her eyelashes.

Jack, bless his heart, looked a little embarrassed about the hero talk. "No, you can keep that title. But I am trying to make things better. So, I knew that Dom was really good at math, but I found out he also likes puzzles. I thought he might be as interested in it as I... Oh, there he is now." Jack waved his arm and raised his voice. "Hey, Dom, over here!" he called.

Renn followed Jack's wave and saw a boy who must be Dom shuffling along with his tray of food. She knew him by face from around school. He looked up from his feet, saw Jack waving, and looked back down. But he made his way to their table and sat down, sparing only the briefest of glances towards her.

"Dominic Marshall," Jack said, "this is my friend, Adrienne

Chao."

"Nice to meet you," Dom mumbled while fidgeting with his hands.

"Nice to meet you, Dom. You can call me Renn. I'm sorry about those terrible bullies giving you trouble. I hope you're feeling better."

He mumbled something. Dom didn't present very well. You could tell with a glance that his self-esteem was in the dumps. He sat slumped at the table and glanced furtively around the room without ever making eye contact with anyone. He was probably on the lookout for that awful Bernie. Poor guy. She did feel sorry for him.

She tried a little humor. "You're not thinking of going out for football now, are you?" she asked in a friendly tease.

But Dom only looked surprised and a little confused. "Why would I do that?"

"Oh, I guess that's probably not the best idea." She checked the time and said, "Well, I've got to get to class. See you 'round, Jack. Nice to meet you, Dom." Renn got up from the table and picked up her tray. As an afterthought, she added, "Don't let Jack sell you any bridges." She smiled and stuck her tongue out at Jack, who waved her away.

Dom seemed like a nice enough guy, and if anybody could draw him out of his shell, it would be Jack. She hoped he was ready to step out of his comfort zone, though. As she walked away from the table, she heard Jack's animated enthusiasm. "Listen, Dom, I've got this thing, and I think you could help me out with it."

Chapter 17

Dom huffed up four flights of stairs, pausing to rest on each landing to catch his breath and curse the broken elevator. It was like he was living out all the worst parts of *The Big Bang Theory*. His backpack felt like one of those massive barbell plates he saw at school.

"Nice to meet you, Adrienne," he said the words a few times, almost spitting them out of his mouth just to prove he could. They echoed around the stairwell and eventually returned to him. He walked up to the next landing where he paused again. "I've heard so much about you." No, that wasn't true, but he did look forward to using that line someday. "Your reputation precedes you." Man, that was a little creepy. No one in his family talked like that. But people in movies never talked like his family did. Wrong words, wrong time.

At his front door, he pulled out his keys and undid two deadbolts and the knob lock. He shouldered the door open, entered, and dropped his backpack onto one of the dining table chairs. Boots lazily lifted her head from her paws and deigned to favor him with a disapproving glance.

He filled a glass with water at the kitchenette sink, gulped half of it, topped it off, and set it down on the dining room table. Then he went to his bedroom to look for his tangram. It was on the bottom shelf under his chess set and an old book of Sudoku. He wanted to bone up on some shapes.

Dom still couldn't believe the recent turn of events. Why had Jack stopped Bernie and Ryan? Why would he choose Dom over them, his own teammates? It didn't make any sense, and he had entertained the idea that it might all be an elaborate practical joke. Or maybe it was a new and subtle form of bullying raised to another level. Jack was no slouch intellectually, but Dom didn't think that he, or the football team as a whole, had the ability to pull off such a clever scheme. He wanted to believe that Jack was helping him out.

He shuffled the colorful pieces on the table and assembled them to form a single square. After reviewing the basic tangram solution, he jumbled them again and resumed a childhood pastime, putting the pieces together to form as many shapes as possible. An animal, a house, a bird, a sailing ship. A memory tickled, something about some paradox and two monks, both using all seven pieces, but one missing a foot.

Jack had told him about how he and Renn had found the cryptex, how he had unlocked it, and about the designs for 3D printing a tangram that were on a thumb drive. It all sounded very intriguing. He didn't quite understand the part about a riddle and some numbers, but Jack was so enthusiastic that it was hard to ignore him.

The intercom buzzed and buzzed again. Dom pushed off the table and almost knocked his chair over. At the door, he pressed the button and said, "Who is it?"

"Hey, it's Jack, can I come up?"

"Okay," Dom said, buzzing him in. "Apartment four oh two." With a snap of his fingers, he turned back to the button and pressed it again. "You'll have to take the stairs. The elevator's broken." Jack didn't seem to be there.

No sooner had the kitchen table chair creaked in complaint at accepting his weight than the doorbell rang, a full minute too early by his reckoning. He almost knocked the chair over on his way up to let Jack in.

"Oh, cool, you have one too!" Jack exclaimed upon seeing Dom's tangram.

"I got it when I was a kid," said Dom, settling back into his seat.

Jack pulled out the adjacent chair and sat down. "Excellent, I knew you'd be the right person to talk to."

Dom steeled himself. "I have some questions."

"Cool," said Jack. "Wait 'till you get a load of this." He reached into his backpack, which he had laid on the dining room table, and pulled out a large Ziploc bag. He dumped its contents onto the grainy oak surface of the table. It was larger than Dom's and the colors didn't match piece for piece. In every other respect, it was a similar tangram puzzle. Jack reached back into the backpack, pulled out a piece of paper, and handed it to Dom. "This will answer all your questions."

Dom read the short riddle between glances at Jack's tangram.

"The tangram is an ancient Chinese dissection puzzle. Well over six thousand different configurations are known from just seven simple pieces. But in order to reveal its secret, you'll have to put it together in a very specific way. Print the pieces in their specified colors. Put the puzzle together in its standard configuration while simultaneously satisfying the four-color theorem as well as the number matching problem. Only then will the riddle be understood."

Dom considered the riddle for a moment and was drawn back to one part. He asked, "What's a number matching problem?"

Jack looked blank and said, "I was hoping you'd know. You're better at math than I am."

Dom pulled out his phone and began typing in queries. After several minutes of this, he studied the pieces. He held each one and studied the numbers on both sides before setting it aside and taking up the next one. Then he went back to his phone and typed and read some more.

* * *

Jack's attention waned as Dom did research on his phone. He wandered over to the sofa where a Tabby cat was posted as a sentry, monitoring the stranger in its domain.

"What's your cat's name?" Jack asked as his hand approached the feline form.

"Mmm? Oh. Boots."

"Here, kitty." Jack purred as he reached to pet the cat. Boots' right paw shot out and swiped the air twice as it hissed and showed its fangs. "Not so nice kitty." Jack murmured and returned to his seat at the table.

"Don't pet her, she doesn't like strangers," Dom said, without looking up. Finally, he put his phone away and looked at Jack. "I can find several references to matching problems that have something to do with graphs. I'm not sure what those are, but I think I understand what we're supposed to do." Dom picked up two pieces, one in each hand, and continued. "Each edge of a piece has a unique number, and most pieces use the same numbering scheme."

"Right, except that one piece starts its numbering at two."

"Yeah, I noticed that," Dom agreed. "So, what if we're restricted in how we put the pieces together? What if we can only match edges that have the same numbers? A one with a one, a two with a two, and so on."

"Yeah, I thought that might be it." Jack spun a piece on the table, causing the numbered edges to blur. "I'm glad you came to the same conclusion. What about the other parts?"

Dom was quick with an answer and sounded almost confident. "I also looked up the four-color theorem. It's a famous problem in Computer Science. It says that any map, like the pieces in the tangram or the U.S. states map or whatever, can be filled in using no more than four colors so that no adjacent regions have the same color. In other words, no two pieces of the same color can ever touch."

Jack counted four distinct colors of the tangram pieces. "That seems easy enough. Most of these pieces are different colors already. We just can't let same-colored pieces touch, right?"

Dom did not look quite so confident as he explained further. "True, but we're constrained by these three conditions. Very constrained."

Jack only remembered two conditions listed in the riddle. "What do you mean three?"

Dom pulled over his toy tangram and used it to make his point. "Look, with the normal puzzle here, we can flip most of the pieces over or rotate them and it won't make any difference." He flipped and rotated the squares and triangles as he spoke, and Jack agreed with his claim. Dom continued, "Also, in my puzzle you can swap the triangles that are the same size for one another. There are two pairs of them like that."

"Oh, I see that."

"In your puzzle, because there are different kinds of engraving on each side, we can't flip the pieces. The number matching problem prevents us from rotating the pieces how we like. And the four-color theorem might mean that each piece has one and only one correct position in the puzzle."

Jack conceded the point, but his experience with the cryptex made him optimistic. "Yeah, I get all that, but there must be a solution. They wouldn't have made the puzzle in the first place if they didn't want it to be solved."

"Okay, I guess," said Dom. "Do you have a piece of paper?"

Jack pulled some paper and a mechanical pencil from his backpack and slid them over to Dom, who quickly became engrossed with writing down rows of numbers. Bored once again, Jack stood and wandered over to Dom's open bedroom door, giving Boots a wide berth. He saw the Einstein poster, the chess set and other puzzles, and the rows of novels. Dom was obviously a very smart guy. He could do with some more socialization, though. He was a prime target for people like Bernie, who liked to pick off the slowest gazelle from the herd.

"How's it going?" he asked Dom, who had not made a sound.

"Good." And after a couple beats "Working through permutations."

Jack chuckled inside. He would go about it in the nerdiest way possible. While glad for Dom's help, Jack wasn't one to hand over all the heavy lifting to someone else. He took his seat at the table and studied the tangram again. It was a small puzzle, no matter how complicated.

"Let's just try some things," he said.

Dom looked up from his half-filled paper, glassy-eyed from concentration. Jack flipped all the pieces of his tangram so the numbers on the edges faced up. Then Dom assembled them into the square shape, what they assume was the 'standard' shape.

They were both studying the result when Jack heard the thunk of the door lock retracting and the apartment door swung open. An older lady who must be Dom's mother came in with a bag of groceries in one arm, and mail and keys in her free hand.

Dom said, "Hi, Mama," without looking up. He failed to introduce Jack.

Jack said, "Hi, Mrs. Marshall, I'm Jack. I just stopped by to get Dom's help with something."

Dom's mom squeezed her way around the dining room table into the kitchenette and set her load on the counter. "Well, nice to meet you Jack, I didn't know Dominic had any friends at school, leastwise he never had none of 'em visit before." As she unpacked the groceries she asked, "Jack, you staying for dinner? We ain't fancy, but we have plenty to go 'round." She scanned her bags as if verifying to herself that she really did have enough for an extra person. "Yes, yes, we do."

"Oh, no thank you. I have to get home soon. Thank you for the invitation, though." Jack glanced at the puzzle and at Dom. "What do you think, Dom?"

Dom stirred from his concentration, looked at Jack, then over to where his mother was busy preparing dinner. "Hi, Mama. This is Jack," and then added for good measure, "from school."

Mrs. Marshall chuckled and remarked to Jack, "That's my baby, always got his head in the clouds."

Dom returned his attention to the puzzle and pointed out the problems. "Look here, the numbers aren't matching and we've got two of the same colors touching here."

Jack, feeling some time pressure now to wrap up and get

home to his own dinner, plowed ahead. "Okay, let's fix the color problem first." He picked up one pair of triangles and swapped their positions, then the other, then put the first pair back in their original order. "That might work. Now let's rotate pieces to match the numbers."

It took them only a few minutes to discover that there was indeed a solution to the puzzle, perhaps only one. Jack held out his fist for a fist bump and Dom awkwardly slapped it with his open palm. Realizing his faux pas, Dom closed his fist and completed the bump. Jack left his own hand in place long enough for the exchange to be completed.

"Great. Now what?" Jack asked.

"What do you mean? We solved the puzzle," said Dom, apparently satisfied with their progress.

"The message said the riddle would be understood. I don't understand anything from this."

It was Dom's turn to wear the blank stare. Jack continued studying the puzzle with a furrowed brow until he finally hit the heel of his hand to his forehead. "Oh, stupid!" He looked at Dom and revealed his insight. "What's on the other side? Help me turn the puzzle over."

They flipped over each piece, being careful to keep the puzzle in its solved configuration. Jack studied it eagerly, as if expecting the Magna Carta writ in plastic. Real numbers printed at various angles and locations on the pieces. They seemed almost random in their position and orientation, except for one pair of numbers that now seemed to have the same orientation and form a single line of text. A number sentence that read "41.467481 -90.570330". Jack took a notebook from his backpack and scribbled down the two numbers. "Yup. Clear as mud. Well, I've got to get home,

Dom. Thanks for the help. I really appreciate it."

"No problem." Dom took a drink of water, his eyes never leaving the colorful puzzle.

Jack put the tangram pieces back into their baggie and packed up his backpack. At the door of the apartment, he paused and looked back. "Hey, Dom. Would you be interested in following this through to the end with me? Seeing where it leads?"

Dom pushed pieces of his own tangram around the table. He looked up at Jack, then his mom, then Jack. Finally he said, "Uh, I guess."

"Great, talk to you tomorrow. See you later, Mrs. Marshall," he said, letting the apartment door swing closed behind him.

Chapter 18

Renn whistled to herself as she strolled down the halls of Black Hawk High, holding her dog-eared copy of Kaplan's ACT study guide to her chest. Things were finally getting back to normal. Her fifteen minutes of fame had died down, as had Jack's. ACTs were in a week and a half. Her scores were improving, but she still had time to study and bump them up a little more. She was going through one section of a practice test every couple of days, training herself on the types of questions she was likely to encounter on the actual test.

Jack and Noah rounded the corner ahead of her and she gave them a wave, clutching her tome in one arm. They stopped to talk in the open area that was part of the school library. Friday's football game would be the first one Jack missed. She wondered how he was doing. The boys glanced across the space every so often, their attention divided. Renn followed their glances and saw Dom studying at a table.

"You're doing a good deed there," she said.

"Well, no one's bothered him yet. I think people know we've been looking out for him," said Jack.

Noah added, "There are about six of us from the team who keep an eye out, just in case."

"I'm proud of you," said Renn, squeezing their arms with

her free hand.

The bell for lunch rang, and Noah disappeared to find his girlfriend.

"I feel like getting fast food today. Want to come?" Jack said with a burst of cheerfulness.

"Sure, we deserve a treat."

Jack raised his voice to catch Dom's attention. "Hey, Dom, wanna get some food?"

Dom waved and collected his books and papers.

They loaded themselves into Jack's forest green hand-me-down Jetta they called his Green Machine. Renn was glad to see he didn't have to wear sunglasses anymore to shield his eyes from the sun; his light sensitivity must be getting better. He still winced from time to time, and she knew he was not over his headaches.

Twenty minutes later, after she had failed to draw Dom out of his shell during the excursion, they sat together on the wide front steps of the high school munching on burgers, fries, and Cokes. Renn took a bite of her chicken sandwich and studied Jack. "So, you find any buried treasure yet?"

Dom, all ears now asked, "Is there buried treasure?"

Jack laughed. "No, there's not buried treasure. That is Ms. Rennie teasing, but we won't let it bother us." He returned his attention to his burger.

Dom shrugged his shoulders and dipped three French fries into ketchup.

Jack, undeterred by Renn's teases, shared their progress. "I'm pleased to report that we've solved the tangram, and we're close to figuring out its message. We're hot on the trail."

"Is that so?" Renn responded. "It's not as simple as X marks the spot?"

"Well, I wouldn't expect you to understand. These things are more subtle than that. Highly complex and mathematical. Isn't that right, Dom?"

"We don't have a clue," Dom chimed in helpfully through a mouthful of burger. Renn snorted soda through her nose, and Jack shot a mock glare at the boy of few words.

After she had regained her composure and wiped her nose, Renn said approvingly to Dom, "You're funny!"

This appeared to please Dom immensely, and he sat up a little straighter.

Jack polished off his burger and pulled the tangram pieces from his backpack. "See, Renn, we had to put these pieces together in a very special way. We had to obey the four-color theorem."

"The what?" said Renn. She knew she was inviting the geekery now, but she was game.

"Four... maybe Dom can explain. Dom?"

Dom scanned the expansive green lawn in front of the school for a time, as if lost in thought. He pointed at a large tree near them that was in the middle of turning color and losing leaves. "Look at the leaves on that tree."

Renn looked, and Jack joined her to study the tree, a large maple not unlike the one where they found the cryptex. It was gorgeous this time of year, a jigsaw of bright yellow, blazing red, and orange leaves, gnarly brown branches, and patches of sky peeking through the bare spots. "I love the fall colors," she said.

Dom appeared unaffected by its beauty and continued his object lesson. "Red, yellow, and orange. The four-color theorem says that no matter how much you arrange the leaves of those three colors, you're always going to have an overlap with the same color. But, if you add a fourth colored leaf, then you should be able to position the leaves so they only touch leaves of different colors."

She tried to arrange the leaves in her mind, but they swirled together in a jumble. "Even with twenty colors there would still be yellow leaves overlapping," Renn said.

Dom nodded. "True. It won't happen automatically. You'd have to be able to paint each leaf the color you want to make it work."

Jack assembled the tangram on the concrete steps and continued the lecture. "See, highly mathematical and complex. I don't blame you for not getting it." He pointed to the completed puzzle. "We just have to figure out this code thing on the back and we'll be in business. Dom has some ideas."

Renn's lips curled up at the corners and she checked Dom's expression. It seemed to say that he did not have any ideas on the matter. She turned to Jack and her smile widened.

"What?" he asked.

She knew her smile had grown into that of a Cheshire cat, but she couldn't help it. "Well, well, isn't this interesting?"

"What?" Jack asked. "What is it?"

Renn flipped her ponytail behind her shoulder and took a long drink. "Oh, nothing," she said. "It's just that little ole' Renn seems to know something that the great code-breakers don't."

"Spill it, freckles, or I'll have to coerce you."

Renn tightened her lips together, pulled an imaginary zipper across them and tossed it behind her back. She shrieked as Jack rocked forward and pulled her into a fireman's carry, causing Dom to scooch over on the steps a few feet. Jack carried her over to a large pile of dead leaves below the tree they had all been contemplating.

"Jack, no, don't you dare!" she protested.

Jack unceremoniously dumped Renn on her back on top of the pile and started covering her with leaves. She squirmed and squealed but continued to be buried.

Jack turned to shout to Dom. "Dom, need you over here, buddy."

Dom looked around, meekly stood up, and walked over to the pair. He kicked his foot through the pile of leaves and one drifted upwards before landing on Renn's sweater.

She glared at him and proclaimed, "You're on my list, mister."

This sent Dom scurrying back to the steps.

Jack paused his attack and held up two fingers to his left temple, then lowered them so fast Renn almost missed it. He wouldn't want sympathy or pity, so she ignored it and said, "Okay, I give up. Help me up, please."

Jack extended a hand, pulled her to her feet, and she brushed off leaves as they sauntered back to the steps. Both boys looked at her expectantly.

She squinted at them each in turn, wondering if she could prolong the anticipation any further. "What you don't seem to have figured out, my math geek friends," she paused for dramatic effect and glanced between them again, "is that those are GPS coordinates. X marks the spot."

Jack grabbed his head, and Renn hoped it was the good kind of blown mind. "That makes so much sense," he said. "Why didn't we think of that? Why didn't we think of that, Dom?"

Dom shrugged and said nothing.

Renn took her phone out, opened her geocaching app, and typed in the coordinates. A pin appeared on the screen and she zoomed out to get a sense of where it was. "Oh, my God," she said, her breath hitching and the words sticking in her throat.

"What?" said Jack and Dom together.

"This says that those coordinates are in the woods right by the Raptor center."

Jack became quiet and Dom watched them contemplate this twist of fate in peace. The satisfaction Renn felt about getting one over on Jack suddenly faded as a realization came upon her. She had found every geocache in Black Hawk Bend; she was done. Now, she wasn't.

They finished their food in relative silence, cleaned up their litter, and hiked up the steps back to class.

* * *

Clara sat on the school's front steps, eating her PB&J, when Adrienne, Jack, and the bullied boy stationed themselves at the other end. She heard strange talk about leaves and buried treasure. She heard mention of the Raptor Center. That was where Stella lived. She heard all this but avoided looking in their direction at all costs. Instead, she focused out across the wide yard to the street that bordered the school, even as the voices receded up the steps and were cut off by the large entry doors. A sleek navy-blue car, she could swear it was a Tesla, was parked illegally at the curb. And it was facing the wrong way. It might have been her imagination, but just as the three disappeared into the school, the driver's window rose and snapped shut.

Chapter 19

Jack's Green Machine crunched the gravel of the parking lot, pulling into the Raptor Center. The reddish glow of the sun was already starting to dip towards the western horizon. Renn licked her greasy fingers and crumpled the food wrapper, dropping it into the empty fast food bag. The boys had been kind enough to bring her dinner after soccer practice, so she could hardly say no to joining them on this cache hunt.

She wouldn't tell Jack she had an inner compulsion to find this cache, anyway. Once they had it, she'd check it off her list (again) and get back to her other goals. Renn hopped out of Jack's car and disposed of the bag in the trash can near the ranger's station. The lights were off, meaning Ranger Scott was gone for the day.

Two more car doors shut, and Jack and Dom joined her.

"So, want to meet Stella?" Renn said.

"Absolutely," said Jack, and Dom nodded in agreement.

She led them behind the small building to where the cages stood in isolation, like stones at Stonehenge. The new security camera was easy to spot under the station's roof overhang. Renn looked at it and waved, then greeted her girl.

"Hi, Stella, sorry I don't have any food for you." She put her hand on the cage and let the tips of her fingers cross the chicken-wire boundary between her world and Stella's.

If the majestic bird was any more nervous around people than she used to be, Renn couldn't tell. She probably wasn't nervous enough. It was such a shame that this beautiful creature would never be able to have a normal life in the wild.

"Dom, this is Stella."

Dom stared at the stoic creature.

"Stella's been through an ordeal, haven't you Stella?"

"What kind of bird is she?" Dom asked.

"She's a bald eagle. You can tell by the white head. Haven't you ever seen one before?"

Dom shook his head and shrugged. "Never in real life. Looks like the pictures, though."

Jack stood on Dom's far side. "Hi, Stella, good to see you again." He turned to Renn and said, "Daylight's burning. Can you do your geo-thang?"

Reluctantly, Renn gave Stella a parting wave and stepped away from the cage. "Sure, let's do this thang."

This cache differed from any other she'd searched for. It wasn't on her app. It was like an unlisted phone number, though not a problem since they had the coordinates. Renn opened her app and brought up the last cache she and Jack had found. Then she added a new waypoint. It brought up a screen where she typed in the latitude and longitude. Then they could navigate to it, just like any other cache.

"Let's try that trailhead over there and see how close it gets us."

They marched into the woods, following the trail before them. Jack fell into step beside her. Dom was content to follow in their wake. The trail was clearly marked at the wood's edge, but it soon narrowed and began to wind around, side-to-side as well as up and down. Fallen tree trunks were arranged to form loose borders for the trail. They passed maple and oak trees and the occasional stand of birch. Renn could still name more than half the trees and plants in these woods. They were as familiar and comfortable to her as her flannel pajamas.

She stopped and held up her right hand, palm open. With her left, she pointed at the deer she had spotted a hundred feet ahead just off the trail. She looked over at Jack and back at Dom and mouthed "deer" until they saw it, too. Its head was down and it was munching on some undergrowth. Raising its head, the deer continued chewing, turned its head, and looked at them. Renn swiped and clicked, trying to bring up her camera. The deer was still as a statue. A ray from the waning sun broke through the trees at just the right angle to highlight the animal. It was a fawn.

Suddenly there was a loud crack of a branch snapping. The fawn bolted, exposing its white tail before disappearing into the undergrowth.

Renn looked around in annoyance. What scared her away? "Let's get moving." After a few more minutes on the trail, she halted them again and scanned the area with her phone. Pointing with her straightened arm, she said, "Okay, I think we should leave the trail here. It looks like it bends the wrong way up ahead."

"How much farther is it?" asked Dom, panting from the exertion.

"Hmmm, less than half a mile. Hang in there, Dom."

Once off the trail, they had to hike down one side of a large ravine and up the other. The ground was clear of undergrowth, but they had to go around, or over, a few fallen trees. Renn stood at the top on the far side with Jack and they shouted encouragement to Dom, who had paused to rest halfway up.

The quiet of the darkening woods was beautiful to Renn, but it also felt a little foreboding. Everyone in the woods was prey or predator, hunted or hunter. A feeling had been creeping into her belly and up the back of her neck that they might not be the only predators around.

"Hey, Jack," she whispered, "I've got a funny feeling."

"Me, too," he said softly. "Something or someone is making a racket on the trail behind us."

"We should have seen them by now if they're hikers."

"Well, let's keep our eyes open,"

Dom had begun climbing again and had almost closed the distance to the top of the hill. Renn and Jack each extended a hand to hoist him the last few feet. He thanked them, panting. Renn checked her geocaching app again and led them on into the lengthening shadows.

They were descending in elevation once more and heard running, bubbling water. The creek was shallow at this time of year and they could walk along its banks and even inside them without getting wet. Renn found a narrow section and jumped across. Instead of leading them on, however, she walked parallel to the creek, scanning around her with her phone.

"It ought to be right around here, guys. I'm not sure what else to tell you. The coordinates look to me like they're centered right in the stream. Look for anything out of the ordinary, I guess."

They scoured the area, Renn and Jack hopping over the water every once in a while. Dom found a large stick and used it to poke around in the stream. The growing gloom, both in the woods and in Renn's mind, was interrupted by a loud sound over the crest of the hill they had climbed down. She exchanged a meaningful look with Jack.

Jack leaped across the stream to stand with Renn and said, "You guys stay here. I'll go check it out."

"Okay. Be careful, Jack."

"Always. Back soon."

Renn watched her friend climb the hill, picking a path with larger trees that he could hide behind. She looked for Dom and smiled when she found him. He was still poking around in the stream with not a care in the world. She wondered if he had even heard the sound.

"You spend a lot of time in the woods, Dom?"

"No. I've never been in the woods."

"What?" Renn exclaimed in disbelief. "That's so sad. There's so much to see and listen to out here."

"There was a ravine near where I used to live," said Dom. "My mom didn't want us to go near it because they found a dead body there once. No, twice."

"Yikes," was Renn's first reaction. Her second was, "You said us. Do you have any brothers or sisters?"

"Um, yeah," he stopped poking with his stick and looked thoughtful and a little sad. "He's older, still in Detroit. He's not what you'd call a productive member of society."

"Oh, sorry. You don't have to talk about it if you don't want to."

Dom said nothing more, and an awkward silence fell about them.

"Dom, will you try something with me?"

"Okay."

"Close your eyes and listen. Try to relax and breathe slowly."

He leaned on his branch with both hands and eyes shut. Renn

let her eyelids close and the bubbling water of the shallow creek rushed in. But there were other sounds, too.

"What do you hear?"

"Water."

"Good. What else?"

"I don't know. Birds?"

"Yup, those are grackles. They're working their way south, stopping for a while to rest in the trees."

"What's that high-pitched sound, like a whistle?"

"Those are crickets. They make chirps by rubbing their wings together."

"Do you hear the wind?" said Dom.

"It's blowing through the trees. You're hearing branches sway, the sound of trees."

Renn opened her eyes and saw that Dom was looking around him with a new level of interest and awareness. She tried to remember when this was new and fresh, and envied him a little. Some taller trees cast shadows across the creek. "It looks like the cache hunt is a bust. That's the way it goes sometimes."

Dom resumed walking along the water, poking it with his stick. "That's okay. Renn?"

"Yeah?"

"Are rectangles out of the ordinary?"

That was an odd question. "Huh?"

"You said to look for anything out of the ordinary. I've noticed that pure shapes are not so common in the woods: squares, circles, rectangles, and so on."

"Okay, I guess," said Renn. He must be thinking about another math theorem. And where was Jack? It was getting dark, and she didn't want to be hiking through the woods at night.

"Here."

She walked over to stand next to Dom. He held out a dripping wet, white rectangle with rounded corners. Renn accepted the gift and shook excess water off it.

"You found it, Dom. Good eyes!"

"After I opened my eyes, it was like everything was high-lighted, like it was more real."

Renn said, "Yes. I know exactly what you mean, but I guess I had forgotten."

From up the hill where Jack had gone, there came sounds of some commotion. People had a real knack for stomping all over things. It sounded like a bush had come to life and was waving all its branches around wildly. Renn heard a high-pitched "Eeek!" That was no bush.

Renn didn't think of running, or hiding, or investigating. She just stood there with the cache, looking up the hill, Dom by her side. Gradually, the sound of a person's voice, a girl's voice, grew louder and closer. "Is that cursing?"

"Cursing in Spanish, I think," said Dom.

There was a crescendo of commotion followed by a conspic-uous silence. A few seconds later, Jack crested the hill next to a short figure wearing a hoodie. He both supported the figure and prodded it onward with his hand on her arm.

"Ouch. Get your hands off me. And get these things off me. I've had enough nature for one lifetime." She swiped unseen horrors from her face and picked things off her shirt and pants.

Renn could not contain her amusement as they were joined on the bank of the creek. The poor thing had obviously gotten stuck in a bush and was covered with big, brown, sticky burrs. If she hadn't had a hood, they'd be all up in her hair, too. Renn covered her mouth with her hand and stifled a giggle.

* * *

"Ow, let me go!" The girl in the hoodie was thrashing her arm, trying to break Jack's grip, but to no avail. She'd hurt herself if she wasn't careful. This girl had spunk.

"Let her go, Jack," said Renn, more curious than alarmed by the appearance of this diminutive stalker.

Jack released his grip and the girl almost tumbled to the ground from her effort to pull away, combined with the mass of the backpack she wore. "She was trying to sneak up on us. I hid behind a tree and watched her get closer. Then she got caught in a bush and that was the end of her sneaking."

The four teens stood facing one another. Renn held the cache down at her side, trying to be casual, yet hide it behind her leg. The girl might be harmless, but they didn't know what her goal here was.

Jack, a hard edge in his voice, pressed her on it. "Why are you following us? What are you doing out here?"

"I'm not," she began defensively. "I mean, I am, but it's not what you think."

"Oh, so you didn't follow us into the woods and try to spy on us?"

"No, I mean I'm not trying to spy, or steal your treasure, or whatever." She deflated as if the admission had drained her.

Renn stepped over to stand in between the girl and Jack and rested a hand on his arm. "It's okay, Jack. I don't think she's a threat, let's just listen to her story."

She turned back to the girl and asked, "What's your name?" Renn recognized her from school, but her name was just past the tip of her tongue.

The short girl pulled back her hood to reveal a cascade of

curls. She had brown eyes and a clear, olive complexion. Her struggle to hold back tears played out across her face. Finally, she regained her composure and said, "Clara Flores. I go to school with you."

Tumblers clicked into place in Renn's mind.

"You're a dancer, right?" she asked. "I tried dancing for about two minutes."

Jack shoved his way back into the exchange. "Why would you think we have any treasure? Why are you here?"

Clara stiffened, then met Jack's gaze full on. She had turned some mental corner. "You're Jack Henderson. I saw you stop those bullies from messing with Dominic." She shifted her gaze to Renn after sparing Dom a quick glance. "And I saw you on TV, how you saved that eagle." She studied her feet for a moment. "I saw you all having lunch outside the school. I was sitting there eating and you showed up. I wasn't trying to eavesdrop, but I heard you talking about buried treasure and X marks the spot."

Words bubbled up and flowed out of her. When she finished, she raised her head and looked sheepishly around the group. "I want to help. I can help."

They all looked a little shocked when Renn threw her head back and let out a sardonic laugh. "Another one. Jeez, Jack, you converted another crazy person to your quest, and you weren't even trying. Un.Be.Lievable."

Jack's face softened a hair. "What can I say? I'm charismatic."

Renn lifted the cache container had Dom found and popped open the lid. Inside was a Ziploc baggie. She unzipped it only to find another baggie. She opened it and turned it upside down over her open hand. Out fell two thumb drives. This time, they were not hidden behind combination locks.

"Well, there's your buried treasure, Clara. What do you think now?"

Clara peered at the thumb drives with something like wonder on her face. "Wow, do you have any idea what's on them?"

Renn had regained much of her jaded attitude towards the puzzle, but she looked at Jack to see what he was thinking.

The drives had shifted his attention from the new girl back to their mission for the evening. He said with some excitement, "Maybe there's another puzzle."

Dom stepped forward with interest. "Another puzzle?"

"Un.Be.Lievable," said Renn.

"Listen," Clara said, "I have my laptop with me. Let's find out right now."

"Why not?" said Renn, dripping sarcasm. "It's not like I have homework or anything."

"Tell you what," Jack said. "Why don't we stop by the Village Inn on the way home. We'll check it there."

"Cool, let's go," said Clara, turning to leave. She turned back after a couple steps. "Uh, how do we get out of here?"

Renn's head spun. What was even happening right now? Jack had totally forgotten his animosity towards Clara and was completely focused on the cache. Had he accepted her just like that? Was he so easily distracted? Dom seemed nonplussed on the whole, but he snuck an occasional glance at the thumb drives. His curiosity was piqued. There was no point in fighting it.

"Fine. Let's go." They hiked back through the ravine to the trail. Jack was quiet. They'd both been through a lot. Who knew, maybe this would lead to something good—a reward for all their troubles. Renn glanced over her shoulder at Dom and Clara. Dom was telling Clara the story of how they had gotten here, to the best of his knowledge.

Clara, a look of concentration plastered across her face, said, "Cool." She drew out the word, so it took a few seconds for it to die away. She said, "Just a couple things. What's a geocache? And what's a tangram?"

Chapter 20

Jack ran up to the Village Inn door like a kid going to recess. With a flourish befitting a Musketeer, he held open the door and ushered the others into the restaurant. The mystery surrounding the new cache was too delicious to wait, even more delicious than the coconut creme pie here. A few days ago he'd been alone; Renn clearly convinced he was going nuts. Now he felt vindicated, and he was joined by three friends. Well, more like one friend, one new acquaintance, and a complete stranger. But Jack made friends quickly. He was willing to forgive Clara for her poor first impression—if she really wanted to help.

They found a booth near the back of the restaurant and Clara tossed her backpack into the seat against the wall.

"How did you even get to the park?" Jack asked her as they settled into the booth.

Clara unzipped the pack. "I hitched a ride with a friend. We followed you into the park and she dropped me off. I was going to call her later." From the recesses of the backpack, she pulled a massive laptop. It had a bug-eyed bald head emblazoned on its lid.

Jack ogled the machine. "Alienware, nice."

Clara smiled sweetly and held out her hand for the thumb

drives. Renn handed them over and she plugged one into a USB port. Her tiny fingers danced over the keyboard. It struck Jack how different this version of Clara was from the helpless waif he had rescued in the woods. A Silver Lab's logo showed on the drive Clara had plugged into her computer. The other one was unmarked.

"Okay, let's see what we've got here," Clara said, her face illuminated by the computer's digital glow. She frowned and let out a frustrated, "Meh."

"What is it?" asked Renn.

Clara turned the computer around for them to see. "There's just a README file on here. One lousy text file on this entire thumb drive. What a waste of space."

This news didn't surprise Jack much, though it would have been cool to find more. "I bet it's another puzzle. May I?"

Clara shrugged her consent.

Jack pulled the laptop closer and clicked open the text file. "Want to hear it?"

Dom and Clara nodded.

He read aloud the four lines of text. "There are thirteen ways to convexity / thirteen shapes of complexity / But only one is a rectangle you see / And the four colors must be separately."

Renn giggled and began beat boxing while Jack glared her into silence.

"So what?" he said. "It's another puzzle. Obviously involving our tangram, right, Dom?"

"I guess," said Dom, taking a sip from a Coke their server had dropped off after taking their orders for pie.

Clara, still pouting, said, "Let's see what's on the other one. It can't be any more disappointing than this." She swiveled the computer back around to face her and swapped the drives.

A few clicks later, her eyes widened, and her face became a mask of concentration.

After much scrolling and clicking, Jack demanded, "What is it?"

Clara lowered her laptop screen enough to see over it. "There are dozens of files on here. I don't know, maybe more than a hundred. They look like diagrams, schematics, design documents, and papers. I don't know what this stuff is." She lifted the screen and read from it. "'The 3D printing of gelatin methacrylamide cell-laden tissue-engineered constructs with high cell viability.' That make any sense?"

Renn snorted, "Oh sure, perfectly clear."

One phrase jumped out at Jack above the noise. It was about 3D printing. He knew that Silver Labs made 3D printers. Maybe this was their tech.

Dom said, "Can I see it, too?"

Clara slid the computer over and Dom scanned his eyes up and down the list of files.

"I want to see it next," said Renn.

While they all studied the contents of the second thumb drive, their server delivered pieces of pie, coconut creme for Jack, apple for Dom, and cherry for Renn and Clara. Renn pushed aside the laptop and dug into her pie. Jack wasn't sure whether the silence that ensued was due to the pie or the strangeness of their discoveries.

It was Dom who spoke up first. "If this is from Silver Labs, we could get in trouble. It could be intellectual property or something."

Renn swallowed a piece of pie and washed it down with Coke. "Okay, let's say that it's Silver Lab's IP. Why was it sitting out in the woods? It doesn't make sense."

"Is there a theme to the files? Something that connects them all together?" asked Jack.

Renn said, "I noticed several references to 3D printing and various mentions of tissue."

"What does it mean?" said Clara.

Jack wondered the same thing. It seemed like Renn had an idea.

"Living tissue," she said, holding her hand out for the others to inspect. "Like skin, for one thing. Imagine being able to print skin grafts for burn patients without having to take skin from other parts of their body. Or what if you could print a new kidney? Organ transplants might be a thing of the past. And if the material comes from the person's own DNA, there would be no rejections." Excitement shone through in her voice.

"I've never heard of that," Dom said.

"Me either," said Renn. "At least, not for real. If Silver Labs is developing this tech, it will be amazing. It could change the world."

"It could be worth billions," said Clara.

They returned to their food and cleaned their plates in silence. Jack tried a subject change. "Dom, any ideas about the puzzle?"

Dom shifted in his seat and opened his mouth a few times before words came out. "No, I mean, yes. I haven't solved it or anything. Convexity is a geometrical property of shapes, but I don't know what the number thirteen is about. I assume the reference to four colors implies the same constraint we had before."

"I'm glad at least one of us understands what the heck it means," said Clara.

Dom shifted and looked uncomfortable, though his lips

curled up a hair.

Renn pushed her plate back and looked pointedly at Jack. "Does that mean you're going to keep following this?"

"Why not?" he said.

"Why not?" she echoed. "Because this might be stolen property. You should take it in to the police or drop it off at Silver Labs. Who knows, they might give you a reward."

"I don't think we're hurting anything," Jack said. "And if there are more of these caches out there, don't you think they'd appreciate it even more if we found them?"

They were quiet again, but it fell upon them with an air of awkwardness. No one wanted to be the first to break it.

Changing the subject hadn't worked, so Jack tried another tack to lighten the mood. He lifted his glass and said, "I'd like to propose a toast."

The other three looked at him and waited.

"For my friend, Adrienne. She saw an injustice and didn't give up until Stella was home safe and sound." He lifted his glass in her direction. "You're one of the bravest people I know."

"Not this hero stuff again," Renn protested, wiping a fake tear out of her eye.

He meant it, too. Of the challenges Renn had faced in her life, this one was not even close to the top. She'd always been a champion for the vulnerable and wounded. Until the bad years, when she'd been the vulnerable one.

They all raised their plastic glasses and clinked them together. Renn, trying to shift the attention away from herself, said, "And here's to our new adventure, as weird and possibly illegal as it is."

"Here, here," said Jack. What puzzled him at this moment

though was Clara's reaction to the toast. She looked a little like a kid who'd been passed over for kickball, or the guy on special teams who was jealous of the star quarterback.

His thoughts were interrupted by the server who returned to the table with a giant ice cream sundae with four spoons.

"This is your lucky day, darlins. You got your check paid for and this here dessert to boot."

"Paid for? By whom?" Jack said, seeing that they were all confused.

The waitress turned and pointed to a table halfway across the restaurant. There sat an Indian man with closely cropped dark hair, wearing a maroon sweatshirt. He offered them a friendly wave, wiped his mouth, stood up from his chair, and approached their table.

Renn looked at Jack and mouthed, "Who?"

Jack shrugged and shook his head.

"Greetings, my young friends. Please, allow me to beg your indulgence for a moment. May I sit?" The man spoke with a mild British accent and met the gaze of each person at the table as he spoke.

"I guess." Jack was off balance, as much as if he'd been pushed by an offensive lineman. "For a minute. Why'd you pay our bill?" He snuck a glance at Clara, was relieved that she'd closed the laptop and hidden the thumb drives.

The man pulled a chair over from a nearby table and sat on it backwards so he could rest his arms on its high back. He grinned at Jack, but Jack thought it showed enough of the man's teeth to seem more predatory than friendly.

"My name is Sam. Please do accept it as a small kindness. It really is the least I can do for the favor I must ask of you. I understand you have come into possession of a cache of information." He smiled and waited.

Renn, who looked spooked, replied a little too quickly, "I don't know who you think you are, or what information you're talking about."

The man's smile flickered for the briefest moment before he continued silkily, "Tsk tsk, hush now. I'm not upset in the slightest. It just so happens that a colleague of mine stored the cache at the very spot you found it. He was going to retrieve it for me soon. But, by an unfortunate turn of events this colleague is now, let's say he's otherwise indisposed." Sam glanced at Renn before continuing. "And the tragedy of it all, my friends, is that there are still more such caches with additional information, and only my colleague knew where they were located." Sam frowned and adopted an expression sort of like his dog had died.

Jack spoke up with some impatience. "I'm sorry, Mr., uh, Sam. I don't know why you think we have these caches or how we can help you."

Sam's smile was solid as a rock. "Again, no need to apologize, Jack. It's quite simple. You see, you were recorded trespassing in the woods on Silver Labs' property. On top of that, I overheard you talking about the information I was alluding to just tonight in this very restaurant."

Jack reeled. Sam had used his name. How did Sam know his name?

An apologetic expression crossed Sam's face when he disclosed his eavesdropping. "Ah, I find this whole affair quite unfortunate, and so needlessly complicated. My associate chose to hide these caches at places he knew of and thought no one else would check. It was used originally for a team building exercise or something. I guess the game was some kind of scavenger hunt to follow clues and win a prize. Jason always liked a good competition. Apparently, security is getting quite strict over there these days. There have even been spot searches in people's homes."

In Jack's mind, clouds parted and a beam of sunlight pierced his confusion. "A team building exercise."

Clara said, "So, you have some video of kids trespassing in the woods, so what? Happens all the time."

Sam swiveled his head to face her. "You must be Clara."

Clara sat back as if struck, and Jack understood how she must feel. She had only joined this gang tonight. She must be wondering what she'd gotten herself into.

Sam's grin only widened at the reactions he was getting. He shifted to face Dom and said, "And you must be Dominic. You've been most helpful to young Jack. You might come to wish that he hadn't dragged you into this." He turned his attention to Renn last. "And Adrienne, I'm sure I don't need to point out the risk that trafficking in stolen property could pose to your future."

Renn turned as white as Stella's bald head. Her jaw worked as if she had something to say, but nothing came out of her mouth.

Jack's voice rang out in anger. "Look, I don't know how you know us, but if you're threatening—"

Sam interrupted, "Calm down, Mr. Henderson. I wish you all to know that this is not a game, not a team building exercise. If I had access to my associate, I assure you I would not entrust the retrieval of my data to... children." His smile was gone. "But things are as they are, and for several reasons, it is better that the four of you continue on your little journey of discovery. All I require is the information." He paused and looked at each of them in turn. "All of it. Every last bit. And I have deadlines. You don't even need to turn over the one you have in your possession. Let's meet again a week from Sunday, shall we? Then we can put the whole sordid mess behind us."

Renn's voice was hoarse and weak. "Or what?"

Sam gave Renn a wise, sad smile. "My friends, I know that each of you will go on to do great things in your lives. But to do that, you'll need to get through university. And to get there, you have to graduate high school. Please let me assure each of you that the trouble I can cause you—with your teachers, with Uni admissions, with potential employers—is considerable." He sat there with his arms dangling over the back of the chair, as comfortable as he could be. Suddenly, he stood up, the smile plastered back into place. "I'll be in touch. Good night to you, and good luck." He turned and strode out of the restaurant without looking back.

Jack only needed to look at the faces around the table to know how he must have looked. They were all stunned.

Renn spun sideways at the end of the booth bench and doubled over. "I have to throw up." She ran and disappeared into the bathroom.

Clara, who had been blocked in by Renn, slid out and ran to the front door. She opened it and peered out into the parking lot.

Jack rested his elbow on the table and his head in his hand. "I wouldn't blame you for being mad."

"For what?" asked Dom.

"For dragging you into this. I did kind of talk you into it."

"It's okay. It's been... interesting."

Jack almost laughed at the understatement.

Clara returned to the booth. "He drives a Tesla. That day at school, when we ate lunch on the steps? I saw a Tesla on the street. He was watching you then."

Renn skulked back to the table and collapsed into the booth. She snatched a napkin off the table and wiped her mouth with it. Her eyes were red and wet.

Jack moved to the chair Sam had used and squeezed Renn's shoulder. "What's going on?" he asked.

Another moment passed before she could face them. "He meant Owen. Don't you see? Owen is his associate, and I got him locked up." Her eyes grew so large, the whites showed all around. "Owen recognized me when I was at his house. He knew me, Jack. He probably knows you, too. This is all my fault!"

Chapter 21

The alarm jarred Renn into consciousness. *Wake up*, it screeched. *Time for school! This is the end of your short life!* She punched snooze with such force that the clock clattered off the nightstand. When it woke her a second time, she slapped the nightstand ineffectually and groaned in annoyance. This, at least, was a solvable problem. Renn pulled the covers up over her head, curled into a fetal position, and squeezed her eyes shut.

It was all too much for her to process. Sam's threats had eaten into her mind like a cancer, infecting her dreams and every waking thought. All it would take was the snap of some stranger's fingers and her whole future would go up in smoke.

A knock sounded on her door and she sensed her mom's presence. "Good morning, my heart. Time to get up. Were you up late studying? You're going to be late."

"What's so good about it?" Renn growled.

Her mom sat at the end of the bed and squeezed Renn's toes through the comforter and sheets. She hadn't done that for a long time. "Well, even if it's not good, it's a new day. Yesterday is a memory, tomorrow a dream, and today a blank page."

Renn growled again, but threw off the sheets and flung her flannel-clad legs over the edge of the bed. In the end, it was another stupid goal that got her out of bed. She hadn't missed a day of high school, ever.

"See you at breakfast, sunshine," her mother said, closing the door behind her.

Thirty minutes later, she sat at the breakfast table munching on a piece of toast and finishing her second cup of coffee.

"I wish you wouldn't drink so much caffeine. Your brain is still developing."

"My brain will be developing until I'm twenty-five, Mom. And I promise you I'm going to need coffee to get through college and..." Renn wasn't able to finish and almost threw up. It took all her effort to keep new tears at bay.

"I know, sweetheart, just take care of yourself. Promise?"

"Promise. Gotta run." She threw her backpack over her shoulder and lathered hazelnut spread on a piece of toast before rushing out the front door. When the bus pulled up to the stop at the corner, she wiped her eyes and waved it on, giving some excuse about forgetting an assignment. Then she placed a call. "Hey, can you give me a ride? I can't deal with the bus today. Thanks."

Renn dabbed her eyes with a Kleenex and dragged her feet back towards the house. What was she going to do? They had to go to the police and hope they could get protection. Then Sam would carry through on his threats, or not, when it became clear he wouldn't get what he wanted. She didn't know how spiteful a person he was, and she couldn't imagine ruining someone's life on purpose.

Renn didn't have to wait long before the Green Machine pulled into the driveway. She collapsed into the passenger seat and let her head roll against the headrest until she faced Jack. He looked better than she felt. But extra lines on his knitted brow told of his worry. The radio was off and she spoke softly. "I've got to tell you something. The bravest person you know is a royal mess."

"Yeah," said Jack. "I'm not doing so hot, either."

He backed out of the driveway and pointed the car towards Black Hawk High.

"Let's stop by Java Jive," Renn said. "I need a drink."

Jack saluted and stepped on the gas. "Let me check this with you to make sure I understand everything. We were caught on some security camera that day in the woods where we found the cryptex."

"Apparently," said Renn.

"And Owen, who works, or worked, at Silver Labs, recognized you at his house."

"He did."

"And this Sam guy knows all about us, and Owen, and the caches, and Silver Labs."

"Seems like it."

"And, weirdest of all, Owen grabs Stella and just takes her from the Raptor Center?"

"I know, right? It doesn't make any sense."

"Pretty much nothing about this makes sense, but everybody seems to know more about it than we do."

"Except," said Renn as she pointed out the turn to get coffee, "we have this cache of secret stuff they want."

"Right," said Jack, "and the guy who knows how to find them is in jail."

"Speaking of which, how are we going to avoid going to jail? And how are we going to keep Sam from wrecking our lives?"

"I don't know," Jack admitted. "But this information we have is our only leverage. The minute we give it up, we have nothing anybody wants."

Jack pulled into the drive-through and ordered a latte.

Renn leaned over and yelled at the speaker, "Pumpkin spice almond milk latte with an extra shot." Then she added, "Thank you."

She fell back into her seat. "We have to go to the police. Don't you think?"

"I don't think they can protect us from Sam, Renn. There's a lot of money at stake. It could be worth billions, right?"

"Yeah." Renn mulled it over in silence until Jack passed over her drink. She took a long sip and tried to lose herself in its bliss. "Okay, not the police, then. What if we took it to Silver Labs? There's got to be someone over there who will be pretty happy to get it back, right?"

"I think that's true," Jack started, "But who do we talk to? How many Owens are hiding over there? If we talk to the wrong person, we're toast."

"Yeah," Renn took another long sip. "We're in trouble." They needed more information. Everything Renn thought of was a long shot, what Jack would call a Hail Mary. Lacking any other good ideas, she punched out a quick email to the TacoCat on her phone. Could he look for any employees of Silver Labs named Sam? Were there Facebook accounts with pictures, anything like that?

Jack pulled into the school's parking lot, already full, and took a lonely spot in a far corner. He turned off the car and unbuckled but made no move to get out. Instead, he sipped his latte and scanned the world out of his front windshield. His sense of serenity and availability was one of Renn's favorite qualities of his.

"If only I had left Owen alone."

"Then Stella would be dead or gone," Jack said. "You stood up for what you thought was right. You can't second guess that."

"You clearly underestimate my second-guessing abilities."

They finished their coffees and walked into school, fifteen minutes late but much better prepared to take on the day.

Renn met Jack for lunch, but they had no new ideas for how to resolve their situation. Dom shuffled over to join them. He was unreadable, but must have been affected by the events of yesterday. Renn was a little surprised he even wanted to be seen with them.

Jack and Dom ate the mystery meat while Renn stuck with a light salad. "You hanging in there, Dom?"

He shrugged, chewed, and generally avoided eye contact. Not much different from the first time she met him, so it was hard to tell how he was doing.

Clara approached and asked if she could join, and Jack waved her in. She sat next to Renn, across from Dom, and offered them a sunny smile. "Hey guys, what's up? Have you figured out how we're gonna get ahead of this Sam guy yet?"

"Not yet," said Jack.

Renn fixed a stare on Clara. "I guess you're part of our little group now, whether you like it or not."

Clara shrugged.

"There are so many questions," said Renn. "My God, we don't even know if Sam is his real name. Why would he give us his real name, right? Anyway, I'm trying to find out more."

Clara grinned. "Come on, guys. It's going to be okay. We'll find the other caches and just give him what he wants. Or we can run a sting and send him right into the arms of the police. No, it would be the FBI, wouldn't it?"

Renn studied Clara for any sign of fear or nervousness, but saw none. Either she'd drunk more caffeine than Renn that morning, or she was actually having fun.

"You know we're in big trouble here, right?" said Renn. "We didn't plan for this to happen, and I'm sorry you got involved."

Clara looked at Renn, then at Jack and Dom. "Listen, Sam is going to get what's coming to him. I for one want to be part of making that happen, don't you?"

Renn caught a gleam in Jack's eye.

"More than anything," he said, crushing an empty milk carton and dropping it on his tray. "Dom," he said, turning to the quiet boy, "any ideas on the puzzle?"

Dom reached into his backpack and pulled out his toy tangram. "As a matter of fact, I think I might have."

"You want to go after the next cache?" Renn said. "We don't need to go looking for even more trouble."

"Yes, we do," Jack answered. "Our only way out is forward. It's like that Chinese finger puzzle you showed me once. You have to stop fighting it to escape."

Renn forced her reply through clenched teeth. "Don't get philosophical with me. I'm not in the mood."

Dom had constructed the standard square with his tangram. "I did some research last night. I found out that there are exactly thirteen different convex shapes you can make with the tangram."

"What's a convex shape?" Clara asked.

Dom opened his mouth, then shut it. He tried drawing something on the table with his finger but aborted the attempt. "Can I borrow your earbuds for a minute?" he said to Clara.

She shrugged, unwrapped a long white wire from around her neck, and handed it across the table.

He still looked uncertain of how to explain and, despite herself, Renn was intrigued. "It's okay, Dom, take your time."

He made a claw with his left hand and rested the tips of his fingers and thumb on the table, creating five points of contact. With his right hand, he laid out Clara's earbud wire around the outline of his left hand's digits. He pulled the wire tight, so it stretched around his fingers rather than making a loose circle.

"You'll have to imagine that the wire makes straight lines between my fingers. You see how it kind of makes a five-sided shape?"

"A pentagram!" blurted Clara.

Dom smiled and shook his head.

Jack said, "No, that's, like, Wiccan or something. It's a pentagon."

"Right," said Dom. "It's one example of a convex shape. In fact, I've shown you a general procedure to make one. We all put a finger on the table and wrap the wire around them until it's tight. That's called a convex hull. Make sense?"

Renn followed, urged him to continue.

"But it might happen that one of our fingers ends up in the hull's interior, not touched by the wire. Then you'd have to push the edge in to touch it, and that would make the shape look more like a star. That's non-convex. See?"

"Yes!" said Renn. "You explained it better than Mr. Harvey could."

"Ugh," said Clara. "I can't understand anything Mr. Harvey says."

Dom lifted his hand, leaving the earbud wires on the table in a loose pentagon. "The square solution of the tangram is one of the convex shapes. There's also a triangle, some five-sided shapes, and a six-sided one. Turns out, one and only one is a rectangle."

He disassembled the tangram and started rearranging the pieces. It took half a minute and a false start, but soon a rectangle emerged. Dom looked up in triumph and smiled shyly.

"So, what's the answer?" Renn asked.

"I don't know," Dom said. "I haven't done it with Jack's tangram yet."

Jack dived into his backpack to retrieve his 3D printed version of the puzzle. He dumped the pieces onto the table, and he and Dom flipped them so that the edge numbering faced up. Together they set about recreating the rectangle. Dom studied it a moment and switched around a couple of the pieces so like colors didn't touch.

"Here we go again," Renn muttered.

Beside her, Clara paid rapt attention.

The boys seemed satisfied with the shape and started systematically flipping the puzzle over piece by piece, being careful to not mess up their work. They all leaned in to look at the result. Renn squeezed her eyes shut after seeing a clear number sentence. Two numbers were aligned along an imaginary line. It popped out from among all the randomly oriented numbers.

"Can you check those coordinates, Renn?" Jack asked.

Renn sighed and pulled out her phone. She typed the coordinates into her geocaching app and waited for a location to appear. When it did, she felt herself drawn in, the same as every other cache she had hunted. It was an involuntary response.

"I've got a location," she reported. "It's over at Wappoke Zoo somewhere."

Renn saw Jack and Clara exchange excited looks. Dom appeared calm and receptive to the next development, whatever it would be.

"Crap," said Renn. "Listen, if we're going to do this, it has to be on the condition that Sam doesn't get the caches. We take them to the authorities, either the police or someone we trust at Silver Labs. Okay?"

They agreed.

The afternoon went surprisingly well for Renn. She was able to concentrate in her classes and do some ACT prep in study hall. She received an unexpected email from TacoCat during last period. Had he dug something up already? It told her to go to their secret locker. She had only emailed him that morning. Was she supposed to bring more payment? The email hadn't mentioned it.

After school, Renn walked the lonely hall on the third floor to its dead end. It was deserted except for the occasional student running out of a classroom towards the stairwell. She found the locker, spun its combination, and popped the latch. The interior was stark and almost empty. On the top shelf sat an envelope. She worked the flap open with her finger and flexed the ends together to widen the slit. What she saw made her gape, and she stole glances left and right to make sure she wasn't being watched.

She pulled out several crisp bills, adding to fifty dollars, the same amount she had paid TacoCat for the information about Owen. Behind the money was a folded piece of paper. She pocketed the bills, unfolded the note and read: "I know what you did. TacoCat has your back. Will contact you with info on Silver Labs employees."

This message shocked her almost as much as Sam's appearance. What did TacoCat know? He'd probably heard that she found Stella, but everyone knew that. Something about the caches, then? But how?

Whatever, he had her back, and he'd returned her money as a show of good faith. That meant something. Renn clutched the note to her face and dared to smile behind it. A single tear rolled down her cheek. It wasn't from despair this time, but hope.

Chapter 22

Renn sat on her front stoop and sipped coffee, hands cupped around an insulated travel mug. The air was crisp and cool on her face, and the coffee radiated heat from within her. Leaves swirled in eddies around the Japanese Maple in her front yard.

This adventure, or fiasco—she wasn't sure what to label it—took Renn on a tour of childhood memories. She'd spent many a Saturday morning skipping through the zoo, trying to crawl between fence posts to pet the animals. She remembered swinging by her arms between Mom and Dad, and Dad calling her his little monkey.

Jack pulled into the driveway, and Renn shook off the memories. She saw Dom and Clara already in the car. She noted, with approval, that Jack had saved her shotgun. He had on his leather jacket with silvered aviators.

"You are too cool for school, Jack-o," she said.

He ran a hand through his hair and grunted in reply.

Renn looked over her shoulder and flashed a peace sign at the duo in the back seat. They both looked catatonic. Pretty sad for 8:45 on a Saturday morning. She contented herself with sipping her coffee and watching the town roll by out the passenger window.

On the way out of town, in between the suburban strip

malls and new housing developments, they passed through her favorite neighborhood. Old-growth trees and Victorian homes with wrap-around porches and jutting towers lined the streets. She could picture herself living in one of those, lounging on the front porch with Bear at her side.

Jack turned on the radio and tuned it to the first good station. Country music blared. He turned it down, but not off. The Green Machine was pre-Bluetooth. Still no signs of life from the back seat.

As they left town, they passed the big Presbyterian church, Casey's gas station, and a Farm and Fleet. Cornfields, cow pasture, and pig farms dominated the land outside Black Hawk Bend. They occasionally passed grazing horses, and one farmer kept a small herd of buffalo for some reason.

Renn cracked her window and smelled the fresh country air, almost tasted it. Corn, grass, hay, and animals were all mixed up in it. They passed a pig farm and a new scent took over.

"Shut the window," Jack said.

"Ew, that is gross," Clara said.

"What's that smell?" Dom said.

Renn smiled and rolled up the window. "Good morning everyone!"

Ten minutes later, Jack pulled into the zoo parking lot, comprised of gravel and grass. The small paved parts had grass growing up through cracks. Two other cars were parked at the far side of the lot. The only buildings in view were a small gift shop and an arched entry with two ticket booths on either side. Renn couldn't see anyone staffing the shop or booths.

"Are we going to break in?" asked Dom.

He asked it so innocently that Renn had to laugh, but inside she sighed.

"We are not going to break in, Dominic. We're going to buy tickets like everyone else." Under her breath she added, "Looks like they need the business."

"I was here two or three times," Jack said. "Once for your birthday party. Remember?"

"Of course I remember," said Renn. "On a different birthday, I stayed overnight here with some friends."

Clara wrapped her arms around her chest as if to ward off the cold—and maybe the "nature", too. "Is it haunted?"

Renn sighed. She hoped the zoo hadn't gone downhill too much. "Come on. Let's go."

The four bought tickets, grabbed zoo maps, and wandered into a wide area with concession stands, picnic tables, and restrooms. Renn checked the cache location on her app and compared it to the zoo map. The layout was basically a big oval with habitats and exhibits on both its inside and outside.

"Hey, look!" Clara pointed at her map. "They have one of those walk-in cages where you can feed the birds. I want to do that."

"Huh, I don't remember that one," said Jack. "It must be new."

Renn looked up from her map. "Not what we're here for, people. But I'm sure we'll have time for it. It looks like the cache is on the far side of the zoo, halfway around the path."

"They have a lion?" Dom said. "I've never seen a lion."

"We'll check it out on the way," said Renn. "Let's go."

She struck out on the path to the right, leading them counterclockwise around the oval. They passed some emu, a few gazelle, and pens with lemurs. Renn had always thought their huge eyes made them look like little aliens.

Clara ran over to check out a small building on the outside of the path. After a brief scan, she scurried back and reported, "Reptile House, ew."

They continued down the path and passed monkeys, vultures, and a habitat with black bears. The larger animal habitats all lived at the back of the zoo: wolves, lions, giraffes, and zebras.

Renn paused when they reached the farthest tip of the oval, checked the coordinates, and scratched her head. "Something's not right here."

Jack looked over her shoulder. "What is it?"

"The cache coordinates are still a ways off," she said, pointing through the lion habitat. "I don't get it. Are we supposed to climb the fence?"

Dom and Clara joined the huddle.

Jack said, "How do the zoo workers access the habitats? Do we have to sneak in through tunnels or something?"

"Ay, Dios mio," said Clara. "We're going to get eaten."

"Can I go see the lions?" asked Dom.

"Let's all go," said Jack.

They walked over to the very tall fence and looked around the grassy habitat. There were fallen logs, large rocks good for catching some rays, and plenty of shady spots, but no lions in view.

"These caches were meant to be found," Jack said. "This was some corporate retreat game for Silver Labs. I don't see how they could be expected to jump in the lion's den."

"You're right," agreed Renn.

Dom scanned the habitat over and over, trying to find some evidence of a lion. Almost to himself, he said, "Now, eventually you might have lions on your lion tour, right?"

Jack clapped him on the shoulder and laughed. "Jurassic Park. Nice."

This quiet, gentle boy surprised Renn. He was so introverted and shy, but every once in a while, he came out of left field with something amazing. "Why don't we go feed the birds and finish walking around. Maybe something will come to us."

They were admiring a herd of zebras when Clara said, "Look at that guy. Who does he remind you of?"

Back by the giraffes, Renn saw a tall, muscular man with closely cropped blond hair.

Jack whistled. "He could play in the NFL, no problem."

"Captain America?" said Dom with a tilt of his head.

"I was thinking Thor," said Clara.

Renn snapped her fingers. "Of course. Short-haired Thor."

"Whatever. I could take him," Jack said nonchalantly.

They walked and laughed and chatted. It was a beautiful day, Renn told herself, regardless of whether they found the stupid cache. But she could not forget about Sam, or Owen, or Stella.

Wappoke Zoo had changed from her memories. The animals were there, mostly. But everywhere she looked, she saw worn, gray wood and weathered, rusted pens. The whole place needed a fresh coat of paint and a landscaping crew. But more than anything, at the heart of the dissonance between memory and reality, was one particular detail.

They used to have an elephant.

Elephants were expensive. When their star attraction, already old when Renn was a kid, had passed away, they had quietly remodeled the whole enclosure.

Renn was not prone to bouts of melancholy, but she grew pensive and quiet as they entered the tropical bird cage. Even the sight of Clara holding up her cup of sugar water and shrieking when a tiny bird alighted on her arm, couldn't snap her out of her mood.

She held up her own arm to allow several colorful birds to feed while she looked around, past the confines of their cage. Next on their tour would be the pond with the koi and turtles, and a dock you could drop fish food from. After that, there wasn't much before they arrived back at the food court.

Silver Labs was a big-time Silicon Valley company. They could have rented out the entire zoo for their retreat. So why not put the cache be in some private area? Maybe they would have to sneak around a bit. Renn remembered being given a behind-the-scenes tour during her sleepover, many years ago. She knew there were hidden access routes behind or under the habitats. How committed were they to this venture?

A sound attracted Renn's attention. A low rumble emanated from beyond the koi pond. It had a rhythm to it that brought another memory to life. A piercing whistle blew over the rumble and Renn pumped her arms, causing an explosion of colored feathers around her. "That's it!" she yelled, which scared the birds off her friends, too. Clara cast an annoyed glance her way.

"Come on, guys. This way." Renn hurried out of the cage and ran past the pond, not waiting for the others. When they joined her, Renn read the confusion on their faces. There was nothing here except a set of train tracks. Then understanding dawned on Jack's face.

"We're taking the train, guys," he said. "Yeah!"

"There's a train?" asked Dom.

"We walked over the tracks when we left the food court, but I didn't notice them. If we'd gone left instead of right, we would have come to this spot first."

Clara still looked confused and annoyed, and Dom's face was blank.

"Okay," Renn said. "This train goes all around the zoo. On the far side, it goes around the outside of the habitats. Get it?"

They got it.

Chapter 23

The shrill whistle sounded again as the train rumbled into view. It had about ten red and gold cars, and they all bounced in different directions. Clicking and clacking its way to the loading zone, the train's engine gasped with relief before quieting. A mom and two kids clambered out the other side. Renn and the others claimed the front car.

"I can't believe I forgot about the train." Renn reached out with both arms to embrace the open track in front of them. "Isn't this great?"

"Are you sure it's safe?" asked Dom.

Renn patted the enclosure in front of her. "This is how we're going to find the cache," she said in a hushed whisper.

"I've got a good feeling about it," said Jack. "I believe."

Clara leaned in from the second row and whispered, "Uh, guys, don't look now, but Thor is on the train."

Renn started to turn around, and Clara shoved her shoulder. "I said don't look!"

"So what," said Jack, "it's a free zoo, right?"

"Yeah, but why is he here? Where's his family? Don't you think it's a big coincidence we keep seeing him?"

"You're paranoid," said Renn.

"I am not," Clara insisted. "But even if I were, it wouldn't mean he's innocent."

"Oh, boy," said Dom, who stared back in the direction of the man they called Thor. He turned to face the group. "He was looking at me."

"Well, you looked at him, right?" said Jack.

"He *smiled* at me."

Renn snuck a quick glance back and saw the man examining his phone.

Dom rubbed the back of his neck and studied his shoes. "It was weird."

The train lurched and chugged as they began rolling down the tracks. The rhythmic motion and oily smell brought back memories of riding it with her family long ago. She slid down until she could lean her head against the hard back of the seat. "Fine. Here's what we'll do. We won't get off the train. We'll ride it back to this spot and wait for him to get off."

She didn't hear any replies, so she assumed her plan had met with approval. Like a game of chess, which she didn't even like to play, the next move grew in her mind. "If he doesn't get off, Jack and Dom can hop off. We'll see if he sticks with the girls or follows the boys."

"That's good," said Jack. "Just act natural."

Renn's gaze drifted to the scenery rolling by. She hadn't experienced this much peace for a long time. She could almost imagine it was her dad sitting beside her. Wappoke Zoo might be run down, but it still retained its charm. Kids still visited and experienced everything for the first time, dragging their parents from animal to animal. And she had forgotten how nice it was to ride the train, to not have to think or drive. Maybe that was a new pleasure of the zoo, a thing for grown-up Renn to enjoy.

She must have drifted off because the whistle jolted Renn awake and upright in her seat. They approached the loading zone, having completed a circuit around the zoo. She kicked herself for not checking on the cache's location.

Jack pulled out his phone and said, "Lean in guys. Let's get a selfie."

Once the train stopped bouncing, the four of them clumped together and Jack held up his phone. Only then did Renn recognize his brilliance. Jack angled the phone, not for the best group shot, but so he could see the cars behind them. Thor didn't budge.

Jack snapped a photo and lowered the phone. "Dom and I will head over to the bathroom and get a water or something. That should be enough time for the train to start again."

"What do we do if he follows us?" asked Dom.

"You be as boring as possible while we get the *thing*," said Renn, snapping another selfie with her phone. "Hang on. He's getting off." Relief washed over Renn as she watched Thor climb out of the train and wander away. Of course, he wasn't following them. Clara was paranoid.

The train started up again with all four aboard, and this time Renn felt free to enjoy the scenery. They passed the koi pond and the tropical bird enclosure. She opened up her geocaching app and monitored the cache location. "Okay, guys, here we go." The coordinates were on the far side of the lion's habitat. "We're on the right track now." She smiled as the others groaned at her pun.

It was going to be a little tricky. They decided that Jack would lower Renn off the side of the train, while Dom lowered Clara. The boys would have to jump off themselves. By the giraffes, Renn gripped Jack's forearm while he gripped hers. "Don't you dare drop me."

"I won't. Trust me."

And he was as good as his word. He lowered her until her feet brushed the ground. Renn pumped her legs to match their speed and let go of Jack's arm. She underestimated the speed a bit and had to put on a short sprint to avoid ending up in the tall prairie grass. She looked behind her and saw Clara picking herself up from the tall grass. Poor girl had short little legs.

It looked like Jack and Dom had decided to disembark on opposite sides of the train. Renn couldn't see Jack, but Dom hesitated, not willing to commit to the jump. She caught up to the train and offered encouragement. "Come on, Dom. You can do it. It's okay if you fall. Just tuck and roll."

"You're not helping," said Jack, who had crossed the tracks behind the train and caught up to her. He extended his arm out to Dom. "Grab my hand."

Renn stopped jogging and watched between split fingers as Dom hung suspended between a moving train and a running Jack. Suddenly, Dom let go of the train and both of them disappeared. She and Clara ran to check on them and found them sprawled out in the prairie grass.

"We're okay," said Jack, and he gave a thumbs up.

Dom patted himself all over, verifying whether Jack had told the truth.

Renn suppressed a laugh and offered Dom a hand up. "Come on, let's find that cache." She led them back the way they had come, about a hundred feet, then turned left. There, at the base of a three-trunk birch, sat a white paint pail. Renn popped its lid and pulled out a familiar Ziploc baggie with two thumb drives. "Got it. Let's go."

"Well, that was anticlimactic," said Jack.

"Why try to hide it? It's already hidden by virtue of its location,"

"Now how are we going to get back onto the stupid train?" said Clara. She sounded like she just now thought about that inevitability.

Jack tried to reassure her. "It'll be easier getting back on, I promise. It's easier to jump onto a moving object than to jump off it. And I'll get on first and help you in."

"Hey, what do you say we start walking along the tracks?" Renn suggested.

"If it will get us back sooner, why not?" said Clara.

They hiked for a minute with their prize before Jack asked, "Where's Dom?"

Renn realized with a start that he was missing. What could have happened to him? He had fallen into weeds, but she didn't think he was hurt. She turned around and ran back towards the cache site.

Past the birch, she glimpsed him. After drawing closer, she stopped and held out her arms to halt Jack and Clara.

They joined her and stared.

Dom stood by the tall outer fence of the lion habitat. He was motionless, transfixed. About ten or fifteen feet beyond it stood another fence. On the other side of the inner fence, Renn saw a lion. It was a male, his mane framing an enormous head, eyes fixed on Dom. Boy and lion, like statues, regarded each other.

Wappoke Zoo was the best.

Chapter 24

Dom bounced and shook with the train. Their day at the zoo was drawing to a close, and he was a little sad about it. He'd had fun exploring the deserted place with his new friends, imagining they were being followed, jumping off the train, then back on. It was the best day he'd had in forever.

And the lion—the lion was different from what he'd expected. He'd seen *The Lion King* and *The Chronicles of Narnia*, and he'd been impressed by the regal stature and nobility of the movie versions. But his preconceptions were also colored by *The Wizard of Oz* and the Bible. This lion didn't seem particularly brave, and it certainly didn't prowl around roaring at everything.

Above all, Dom got the sense of *serenity*. It accepted all things without being changed by them. Dom imagined the beast was the same as if he'd encountered it on the open savanna. Its stature spoke volumes. "You can capture me and lock me in this cage, but you can't force me to go on parade for the kiddies, and you can't take away my dignity." Nelson Mandela must have had a lion's heart.

Dom tried to be serene as he shook around on the old train. He found that if he relaxed and stayed centered, he could filter out most of the shocks from the seat through his body, allowing his head to remain basically level and fixed. He was on the cusp of understanding something important, something about acceptance and overcoming, humiliation and nobility.

The train whistle blew, interrupting his thoughts, and soon it shuddered to a stop at the loading zone. They all hopped off and debated whether to get some food here or go back to town before deciding to drive into town. Dom had arrived thinking the zoo broken down, wondering if it was even open. He left with a whole new picture. His mom would like it; he'd have to bring her next season.

Content to bring up the rear, he looked around the concessions area with new eyes. The zoo exit was through the gift shop. Jack led the way into the shop. As the door opened, out of nowhere, a hulking shape appeared.

It was Thor.

With a low and menacing voice, Thor grabbed Jack's arm and said, "Hand it over, kid."

Dom screamed and ran.

Chapter 25

Someone screamed, Jack never found out who—no one would admit to it later. It might have even been him. This guy was huge, and built from solid muscle. Jack was at eye level with Thor's Adam's apple. So he jabbed it with his free hand and kneed him in the groin. It kind of worked. Thor let go of Jack's arm and tried to protect his parts. But he still blocked their escape.

Jack turned and yelled, "Run!"

The others, who had already taken a few steps back, also turned away from their attacker. They headed back in the zoo, racing towards the path they had started on this morning. Jack heard, or felt, the blood rush through his head, and his headache was ramping up, threatening to make him nauseous. He drove the feeling back and raced on. He soon passed Dom, who now brought up the rear, even though he'd had a head start on the running.

Jack slowed to meet Dom's pace. The boy huffed, trying to keep up.

"Come on, Dom, just a little farther, don't slow down yet."

Jack looked up ahead and saw Renn in the lead. He yelled her name. When she turned her head, Jack motioned towards the small building approaching on their right. Renn nodded and diverted her path towards it.

"Keep going, Dom. Just to that building. You can do it."

Jack kept encouraging Dom, even though his own head pounded. The headache was a one-way trip, like the train. It would only get worse until he had a chance to take some Tylenol and rest.

He saw the girls go into the reptile house and risked a quick glance back. Thor had recovered and lumbered after them. "Let's go, Dom."

Jack made it to the house and held open the door for Dom, who took precious additional seconds to arrive and fall through the doorway. Thor was still far back, but he had built up momentum into a full run. Jack slipped inside and pulled the door shut.

He plunged into darkness and for a few seconds he only heard the sounds of his friends breathing hard. Gradually, his night vision kicked in and he looked around. It wasn't that dark inside, but the sudden transition from bright daylight, and the fact the walls were all black gave it an otherworldly quality. Dim lights glowed softly from behind plastic ceiling panels. The walls contained a grid of rectangles that shone with an eerie blue-green light. As his eyes adapted, he realized they were aquariums, all filled with tree branches, rocks, sand, and, presumably, reptiles.

He had to take stock and they had very little time. A hallway lead behind the wall of exhibits and ran the length of the building. Renn darted into it and reappeared on the far side of the house, a scant fifty feet away.

"No way out back there," she said, continuing until she stood opposite Jack. "But there's another door at this end." She tried it and a crack of light pierced the dark.

"Is he following us?" Dom wheezed.

"I slowed him down a little," said Jack, "but he's coming. He'll be here in half a minute, at most." He pressed on his temples and fell back against the wall.

"Come on," urged Renn. "Let's slip out this door and double back. We can get a head start on him."

"Yes, let's get out of here," said Clara.

Jack knew instinctively that it wouldn't work, the same way he knew when a play was going south, or when he had an opening to the quarterback. He needed to stop and rest, and Dom couldn't keep running. "Who has the cache?" he asked.

Renn said, "I have it."

"Good. Do you remember the gas station we passed about a mile back?"

"Jack, no," Renn began.

Jack interrupted, made her listen through sheer force of will. "I want you three to leave through the other door right now. Sneak around the back of the building. As soon as he gets inside, you head for the exit and get to the station. I'll meet you there." He looked at Renn. "I'll be all right, I promise. If I'm not there in an hour, you can call the police."

Renn stared thin-lipped at Jack for a tense moment, then nodded curtly. "Come on, let's go."

Dom and Clara stood looking back and forth between Jack, who gripped the lever of his door, and Renn, who stood by the other door.

With his free hand, Jack dug his car keys out of his pocket and tossed them to Dom. He was about to tell them to get going when he felt the lever turn. He gripped harder and tried to resist it. The force on the door lever eased up, and he risked a quick glance over his shoulder. Good, the others had slipped out. He rested his forehead against the heavy door. Layers of black paint and some condensation in the cool room made it sticky and damp. The lever tried to turn in his hand again and every muscle in his body tensed.

"Let me in, kid." Thor's deep voice boomed through the door.

Jack tried to come up with a plan. But unless he could break open an aquarium and use a python as a weapon, he didn't have much to work with. "What do you want from us?"

"You know what I want, kid. Give me the flash drives and no one has to get hurt."

The lever pulled up, down, and up again in Jack's hands. Jeez, this guy was strong. "Uh, what's your name? Mine's Jack."

The torque on the lever became more random, trying to catch him off guard.

"Nice to meet you, Jack. Let me in."

How to keep this guy off balance? Maybe a little truth. "Listen, we don't know what's going on here. Are you with Sam? He's already talked to us."

The lever went still, but then the door boomed and shuddered from an impact. Okay, that was the wrong thing to say. The handle suddenly turned all the way and an irresistible force yanked the door back, almost right out of his hand. A wedge of daylight blinded him. He braced his left foot against the door frame and pulled with all his might. The door slammed shut again. "Who do you work for?"

The door was silent. He braced for the next attack. "Hello?" He heard nothing but the rush of blood pounding in his own head.

"Where are your friends, Jack?"

Jack turned on Jell-O legs and saw the god man's silhouette

filling the other doorway. He'd slipped around the building and come in on the opposite side. Jack leaned back against the damp door. Panic threatened to rise in him, and his lizard brain urged him to run towards freedom. It was on the other side of his door, mere inches behind him. But then his rational mind took over. Renn and the others needed more time to escape.

Jack dashed into the hallway. He could play keep-away with this guy for a long time. He braced his hands against glass and looked right, left, right, for any signs of Thor rounding a corner. Jack glanced into the aquarium in front of him. Eight beady eyes stared back. They were mounted on a gigantic black and brown spider, its front two legs also braced against the glass wall in a mirror of Jack's pose.

"Holy crap on a stick." Jack leaped back.

Low laughter rang through the room. "It's not that bad, Jack. We can make a deal, right?"

"Uh, I mean, yes. I have what you want. But who do you work for? Silver?" said Jack to, or through, the spider.

"You're flying blind here, aren't you?"

Strange that he hadn't tried chasing Jack. His voice came from the other side of the wall, not moving. He just sat there, spinning his web.

Jack reckoned the others had enough time by now, and he needed to get out of here. He fished in his pocket, finding a few coins and his pocketknife. He pulled out two quarters, hefted their slight weight in his hand, and shrugged.

"Okay, I'm going to toss them to my left, your right, okay? Then you let me go. That's the deal." He tossed, and the coins tinkled against concrete. Jack crept right. He peeked around the corner and a meaty fist shot out, grabbed around his neck, and spun him into a headlock.

Jack barely choked out, "Sorry, confusing, I know, you were supposed to go to your right."

"You think I'm stupid, Jack? That's a bad way to start."

He shoved Jack from behind and forced him out the far door, the door the others had left through, into the bright sunlight. He was blind again. Thor held him there until they didn't have to squint. Then they turned and the man scanned up and down the path. There were more people around than there had been this morning, but it wasn't busy. Thor turned Jack and marched him towards the rear of the reptile house.

Jack protested and fought, but the man was too strong. The brute pacified him by tightening his arm around Jack's neck, causing pain to lance through his head. He only hoped the others had gotten away. They cleared the corner and saw no one there. Jack let out the breath he had been holding. "You're never going to get them. They're long gone."

"I may not have them, but I got you, kid. I suppose that's worth something. Maybe the thumb drives?"

Jack was silent. He looked around, trying to spot some new opportunity. He could scream bloody murder and hope someone came to the rescue, but all the people in sight were moms and kids. No wonder Clara was suspicious of a man wandering the zoo by himself. He should have listened to her.

"Don't make a sound," Thor hissed into his ear. "We are going to call your friends and make a deal."

Chapter 26

Thor led Jack back to the concessions area. He had loosened his boa constrictor embrace enough to allow walking. People passing by would only see an affectionate father and his son, flush from horse play. Jack didn't think yelling for help would accomplish anything at this point. He had to be smart and bide his time. He would get an opening, and he needed to be ready to take advantage of it. All he knew for sure was he wouldn't win any direct fights with this guy.

How long had it been since the others left? Fifteen minutes? He didn't want them to have to call the police. He thought about what he had on him. His phone was tucked securely in the front left pocket of his jeans, wallet in the back right and a little pocketknife in the front right. He wasn't even sure why he'd started carrying it. Maybe it was his recent outdoor lifestyle instigated by Renn and geocaches. It wasn't much of a weapon, but Jack knew he could inflict a lot of damage with it. He could elbow the taller man in his solar plexus and stomp on his instep. That might give him enough time to ready the knife and stab at eyes or throat. *Jeez, listen to yourself, Jack*, he thought. Was he considering violence against this stranger? For all he knew, Thor was one of the good guys. What if he was police or FBI? They might already be investigating the theft of trade secrets from Silver Labs. What was the right move in this situation?

"Keep walking, son," said Thor. The way he emphasized "son" did not make it sound like a term of endearment.

"Listen," Jack improvised. "We don't like Sam. He's kind of making us do this. If you can protect us from him, maybe we can work together."

"Kid," said Thor. "I'll give you points for bravery. But you're in over your head with Sameer."

Jack couldn't disagree. He fumbled the little knife in his pocket, trying to get it open and ready for any opportunity. He didn't want to hurt this man and guessed he would find out how far he was willing to go pretty soon. Wait, *Sameer*? That was new.

It must have been close to lunch time because several families sat at picnic tables eating hot dogs and nachos. Jack's head still hurt, and he wasn't making any progress with the knife. "I'm thirsty. Do you think we could stop for some water?"

"Sure, kid, I'll get you some water. We'll sit right here and call your friends."

"You don't want to, uh, leave the park for that?"

"Nah, you'll behave yourself, won't you? Tell you what. Unlock your phone for me and hand it over. Then I'll have most of what I need."

The walls were closing in fast. This guy wasn't giving anything away about his identity or his employer. The more he thought about it, the more Jack doubted the man was police. Police or FBI would identify themselves, right? There was no reason to go undercover just to fool some kids. That left Sameer and Silver Labs, assuming the two weren't somehow linked.

Not seeing other options, Jack pulled out his phone, unlocked it blind, and handed it to Thor. The big man never gave up his grip on Jack, but accepted the phone with his left hand. They ordered a bottle of water at the concession stand and Jack witnessed some graceful choreography as Thor transferred the phone to his mouth, pulled out some bills, and reversed the steps after pocketing the change, all without giving Jack his opportunity.

They sat at an empty picnic table. Jack drank water while Thor navigated to the contacts list on the phone. Jack felt the man's steel grip around the back of his neck. What would Coach Kelley do in this situation? What would MacGyver do? He looked around at the families eating in the dining area and went stiff.

"What's up, kid? Need some nachos, too?"

Jack tried to relax and glanced at Thor, still focused on the phone. He had only caught a glimpse but was sure of what he had seen. Sitting at a picnic table with an Asian family was Renn. She had untied her ponytail, letting her long straight hair fall over her ears. And she wore a Wappoke Zoo cap. But she had on the same quilted vest. It was her. What was she thinking? She was going to try something stupid, of that Jack was sure. Which meant he had to do something stupid first.

Thor had his contact list open and scrolled through it. Jack tried to catch Renn's eye, managed a quick connection. She gestured with her head back into the park. Were Dom and Clara still stuck in the zoo somewhere? What had gone wrong? He was so distracted that he almost missed Thor looking up and following his gaze. Fortunately, Renn had turned her head and was talking to her fake family.

He took a swig of water and tried again to tease out a blade of the pocketknife with his thumbnail. A last resort.

"You were with a black kid, an Asian girl, and a little Mexican girl. I'm pretty sure Adrienne Chao is the Asian. Am I right, Jack?"

For crying out loud, did he not have any other Asian friends? No, probably not. Walls closed in some more. The funny thing about it was that Thor didn't seem to know their names, whereas Sam, or Sameer, knew all about them. He risked another glance in Renn's direction. He wanted to warn her, to tell her to get out. Jack jutted his chin towards the zoo exit. She shook her head.

When his attention snapped back to their table, he noticed Thor had Jack's phone up to his ear.

"No, wait!"

Thor shoved him down harder into his seat with his powerful arm. Jack took another risk and slipped the open knife from his pocket. He heard the faint sound of ringing from his phone's speaker. A heartbeat later he heard Renn's phone play a digital rendering of the *Grey's Anatomy* theme. He looked straight at her, trying to warn her, screaming with his eyes.

It took a few seconds to pick up on the coincidence of the singing phone nearby, but when he did, Thor looked over and saw Renn's open-mouthed stare.

"Well, well. Look who we have here."

Jack clutched the small knife and pressed his thumb against its end, as if clicking a pen. A small bit of blade poked out from the bottom of his fist. He wouldn't go for an eye, but he could try to distract. "You know my offer to cooperate?"

"I don't need you, kid, just what you have."

"Good, because it's expired." Jack raised his arm and

pounded the man's hand with his meager weapon.

It had the desired effect. Thor yelled and jerked back his wounded hand. Jack just needed to create a couple more seconds to get away. He grabbed his water bottle and squirted it into Thor's eyes. Not very effective, but maybe just enough. He jumped up and snatched his phone back. Thor let out a few choice curses and wiped his eyes. Jack ran over to Renn and took her hand. "Come on, let's get out of here." He dragged her towards the exit.

She resisted and said, "No, he's already after us, Jack. Look!"

Jack looked back and saw the truth of her words.

"We have to go back into the zoo and lose him."

For the third time today, they ran around the main zoo path. They sprinted, and the big man could not match their speed. Both Jack and Renn were athletes—and teenagers. After they lost sight of him, they slowed to a more sustainable running pace. Jack's head already pounded from the effort and he had to stop.

"Where are the others?"

"They're out. Dom drove your car to the gas station."

Jack looked up and stared at Renn in disbelief. "Then why on earth did we run back into the zoo?" His speech became a roar. "I'm sick of this zoo."

Renn, who wasn't even breathing hard, gave him a look flavored with annoyance and pity. "I know you're hurting, Jack. I know that's why you told us to get out while you stayed behind. You saved us, and now I'm saving you."

She looked over his shoulder to the path behind them, causing him to check for Thor's pursuit. He was nowhere in sight.

"Do you really think we could outrun him all the way to the

gas station? He'd just hop in his car and run us down. Or worse, he would follow us to the others and get the drives."

Jack hadn't thought it through. His own pain and frustration had gotten in the way. She was right.

They were near the giraffe habitat. Jack walked over to a recycling bin and tossed in his empty water bottle. "Okay, so what do we do now?"

Renn at last looked less than certain. "I'm open to suggestions."

Jack rubbed a hand over his unkempt hair. "If we swim across the koi pond, we could get out on the service road."

Renn's look was disapproving. "I don't feel like getting wet."

Jack's head was clearing, and he replayed his encounter with Thor in his mind. He reached into the bin and retrieved the water bottle. "I have an idea."

"Great, what?" asked Renn.

"Nachos."

Chapter 27

Renn scanned the open dining area, looking for any sign of their large blond friend. She saw none. He wasn't lurking around the restrooms or the gift shop as far as she could tell, which made her nervous.

Where was Thor?

Renn stepped back behind the tree that served as cover and wrapped her arms around her torso. She had given her quilted vest and new cap to Jack and pinned up her hair. He might recognize her like this, but he probably wouldn't expect her to do what she was about to do.

Jack could have been an evil genius in another life. His plan was sound, but it had some risk, and she was taking that risk. She took a deep breath and scanned the entire area one more time. Gripping the refilled water bottle, Renn stepped out into the open, lowered her head, and marched straight towards the concessions stand.

She knew Jack watched from some hidden vantage point, but feared that Thor might be watching too. She felt naked and vulnerable, and her heart raced. By the time Renn made it to the back of the concessions line, she panted from lack of breath.

They had staked their futures on finding some hidden

geocaches and retrieving some stolen intellectual property. But new players kept getting in the game. And this one seemed perfectly willing to hurt, kidnap, and threaten them. She still had no idea who were the good guys and who were the bad guys.

And now she was going to order nachos.

Renn glanced over to where Jack should be hiding but couldn't see him. Four people stood ahead of her in line. She willed herself to become invisible. It occurred to her that she hadn't only visited old childhood haunts lately; she had experienced traumatic events she would forever associate with them. Stella's abduction. Thor's assault. The zoo was where her love for animals and for biology had taken root and blossomed. Ranger Scott had taught her to respect life and nurture it. She was having some non-nurturing thoughts right now.

The front two people in line walked away carrying a tray heaped with zoo food. As Renn stepped up, she sensed a presence behind her. Rationally, she knew it was just the next person in line. Panic rose in her and she squeezed her eyes shut. Jack was watching. If Thor was standing right behind her, Jack would see and save her. He would do something.

A tap on her shoulder made her scream.

"Can I help you?"

The voice came not from behind but from in front. The next people in line were gone, and a chubby teen with greasy hair covered by a net looked at her expectantly. Renn turned towards the shoulder tap and saw an old man behind her. She apologized with a nervous laugh and stepped up to the counter. "Um, nachos, please."

The boy punched a screen and said, "That'll be six dollars."

Renn handed over her debit card, then kicked herself for almost forgetting the whole point of the exercise. "Oh, with a side of jalapenos please."

The boy's boredom took on a hint of annoyance. "That's fifty cents extra."

"Okay, okay. Actually, would you make it two sides and add a bunch of yummy jalapeno juice too?"

The boy's hands froze on the screen, and he stared at her.

"I just love jalapenos!" said Renn with forced cheerfulness.

He rang up the nachos with extra-extra jalapenos and grabbed two small black plastic cups with his gloved hands. He spooned jalapenos into each cup and shot a suspicious glance at Renn.

"Oh, more please, and more juice," Renn cooed at the boy.

He shrugged and added another spoonful to each cup, then spooned on some juice.

Renn thanked him profusely and took her food and water to the nearest table, sneaking a glance around for signs of Thor. She worked with urgency, setting the ingredients on the bench beside her to mask her intent. She opened the bottle and started jamming jalapenos into the water. After emptying one black cup, she poured in the remaining juice too. She wondered if the boy would have given her a pair of his food service gloves if she'd fluttered her eyelashes. After all the jalapenos and their juice were mixed in with the water, she sealed the bottle and shook it.

Renn let out a long breath. That job was done. She treated herself with a nacho covered in creamy golden cheese, then waved the bottle in Jack's general direction. He emerged from his hiding spot and strolled over to join her. Here's where it got real. If Thor lay in wait for them, they had to draw him out and incapacitate him long enough to get away.

Jack helped himself to some nachos. "Oh, man, these are so good."

"Do you ever not think of food?"

"Well, it's sitting right in front of me. I'm only human," he said while crunching chips.

Renn took back her vest and cap. There was no reason to hide anymore.

They decided to walk leisurely along the perimeter of the area. As they passed the entrance to the restrooms, Jack took a drink from the water fountain while Renn kept lookout. Next, they passed by the gift shop. They peered in through the window but didn't catch any sight of Thor. Nevertheless, after they passed the shop door, Renn heard it open and shut behind them. She turned to see him with his muscled arm around Jack's neck. Renn noticed a red wound on the back of his hand.

"Hello again, Jack. Hi, Adrienne. Let's talk," he said.

After the day they'd had, Renn didn't want to talk. She unscrewed her weaponized water and said, "Hi, meatloaf." Then she squirted him in the face.

"Missy, Jack tried that before and all it did was piss me off. Which is what I am now."

He must have squeezed on Jack's neck because Renn heard a gurgle from her friend. Why wasn't it working? Had she missed his eyes? Jack raised his eyebrows at her insistently, and she widened her own eyes in an exasperated retort. What did he want her to do? It wasn't working. She stepped closer and squirted him again.

"Would you stop that? I'm gonna..." He wiped his eyes with his free hand. "I'm gonna... what the? What did you do?"

Renn took the man's sudden inability to finish his sentences as a good sign. Thor let out a yell of pain, let go of Jack, and put his hands to his eyes. He tried to wipe the pain away, but ended up getting more of the jalapeno water in. He moaned and flailed around a little.

Renn and Jack backed away cautiously, but he didn't even notice them anymore. They were free to go. They ran past him to the gift shop entrance. Before going in, Renn turned back and said, "I hear milk helps." They ran wildly into the parking lot and towards the road.

Chapter 28

Adrenaline pumping through them, Renn and Jack ran. They kept to the side of the road by the woods, since the other side had no cover, only a big ditch and a fence bounding farmland. Renn slowed and stopped when she noticed Jack was no longer by her side. She saw him, doubled over a ways back, vomiting. She paced in a small circle, giving him some privacy. He'd pushed himself way beyond his limits today. Not his normal limits, of course, but the new ones imposed by his concussion.

Renn felt sorry for him, and a little guilty. Only a few days ago she reprimanded him for not taking it easy. She should have looked out for him better than this. If she'd had a medical degree, someone would show up right about now to take it away. The good news was that they shouldn't have to run anymore. If they stayed close to the tree line, they could duck into the shadows whenever a car passed.

Jack spit, wiped his mouth, and slowly caught back up with Renn. "Sorry, I'm about done."

"No, I'm sorry, Jack. I've made you run all over the zoo today. Come on, let's walk slower for a while."

They adopted a slower pace, no longer trying to outrun Thor, just evade him. They stepped behind trees, too small to hide them whenever the sound of approaching cars reached their ears.

"Everything will get back to normal," Renn said, unsure of whom she was trying to convince. "You'll feel better and start playing football again, and I'll take my ACT. It will all be fine."

Jack spit into the woods.

Renn, struck with a sudden realization, pulled the water bottle from her vest pocket. "I'm sorry, I forgot about this. Do you want to try some jalapeno water?"

Jack waved her off. "Are you kidding? No, thanks."

They walked for a while before Jack broke the silence. "Things are not going back to normal. This thing, whatever it is, is already so much bigger than us." More quiet. "Anyway, who knows if I'll even play football again?"

"What are you talking about?" said Renn. Jack was normally an optimistic guy.

"I don't know if I want to put myself in the way of more hits like the one I took last week. I'm not expecting a football scholarship, so high school is it. Why should I kill myself for a sport I'm giving up in a few years?"

"Because you're not a quitter, Jack. You don't have to give up. We both know there's a lot more to sports than getting scholarships."

"I think life might be telling me something here," Jack said with a hint of bitterness.

Jack had sometimes played the class clown and sometimes the heartthrob jock, but he had always been filled with boyish optimism. Renn had never seen him like this. She also felt out of control after recent events. She'd been on the verge of losing it many times, had let her own tears come, alone in her bedroom. But she had to believe that they would find their way through this. Otherwise she'd lose it.

They stepped out from behind cover after a cluster of cars passed. The wind grew colder and Renn pulled the zipper of her vest up as high as it would go. She tried to lighten Jack's mood. "I can't believe your crazy plan worked."

"It was all I could think of," he said, shrugging. He stopped, as if remembering something, and smiled. "Hey, meatloaf?"

She blushed. "It was all I could think of!"

"It was great," he said. "You were awesome."

She wanted to tell him again that everything would be okay. Instead, she stepped forward and gave him a hug. "I don't think," she said, taking a step back, "that I need to go to the zoo anytime soon."

"My friends, what a coincidence!"

Startled, Renn looked towards the road for the source of the voice. A dark blue car sat parked a few yards behind them. Sam stood behind the shield of his open door. He beckoned to them with his arm.

"What the?" she started, wondering how they had failed to hear him.

Jack answered her spoken question by muttering, "Stupid Tesla."

Of, course. Sam's car had no engine, just their luck.

Renn sighed and turned back to the Tesla. There was no outrunning or escaping anymore.

"I'm so glad I ran into you. It looks like you could use a ride." Sam closed his door and opened the stealth car's rear door. "Come on, hop in. I'll drop you wherever you want to go."

Renn looked back at Jack, questions in her eyes. Jack shrugged and started walking towards the car. He was out of steam and needed to get home and lie down. But Sam was definitely not trustworthy. He was like a Venus flytrap, drawing you in with a bit of color and sweetness, then grabbing hold. But he'd sprung his trap at the Village Inn. They were already his prey.

Talking to him might yield some clues as to who he represented and how to get away. Renn shot him a defiant glare before climbing into the back seat. Jack followed. The black-stitched leather seats still carried that new car smell. The Tesla glided onto the road and threw them against the back seat with a quick acceleration. Then he came to a stop at a point where the road stretched out in front of them like a ribbon.

"Hey, have you heard of ludicrous mode?" said Sam, turning his head and grinning at them.

Jack half raised one hand, and Renn glared. What was he up to now?

"Great, you've got to experience this." He tapped on the large digital console, looking for some setting.

Renn saw a starfield on the screen, like warp speed or something.

He tapped once more and grinned again with child-like excitement. "Okay, are you ready for this?"

"I doubt it," Renn said.

"Ah, of course not," said Sam with a frown after scanning his passengers. "Put your seatbelts on. You young people are so risky. You think you're going to live forever." A hint of impatience leaked through his excitement as he waited.

Renn and Jack complied, and she pressed her head against the headrest, not knowing what to expect.

"Here we go," said Sam as he jammed on the gas pedal.

The acceleration flattened Renn against her seat like a pancake. She'd never experienced anything like it, except maybe on some roller coasters. Her eyes snapped shut, and when they opened, the scenery flew by them. She glanced over at Jack. He appeared to be somewhere between ecstasy and nausea.

"Stop the car," she shouted. Renn felt like she was going to be sick. Sam had shown them once again and in a new and innovative way that he had total control.

He pulled into the gas station, parked, and looked back at them with a satisfied expression. "Amazing, isn't it? Zero to sixty in 2.8 seconds. This baby drew 1500 amps during that little maneuver."

"What do you want? Your coming along was no coincidence, right?" Renn's glare could have drawn 1500 amps, whatever that meant.

Sam turned to business, but his tone remained conversational. "I assume you were out this way on a cache hunt. Any luck?"

Renn's mind raced. Sam knew how to find them out here. How much more did he know?

"Sorry, we don't have it. You can search us if you want."

"Oh, no need for that, Adrienne. We're associates." He leaned in a bit and added in a low voice, "Collaborators, if you will." He scanned the parking lot of the station and continued speaking, his eyes fixed in the distance. "I wanted to make sure you're on track. We have deadlines, you know."

Deadlines, right. "We walked all around the zoo but came up short." Renn fixed her gaze on the big screen. She didn't think she could make eye contact with Sam and lie. "We can try again tomorrow."

"Well," Sam paused as if contemplating this disappointing news. "You know what will happen if you miss your deadline. But I hate to operate by punishment alone. So let me assure you that if you do deliver a complete set of information on time, you'll be handsomely rewarded. All four of you."

Sam's promise only thinly veiled his threat. She felt vaguely insulted.

"Who are you, Sameer?" Jack asked suddenly.

Sam regarded him and the corners of his mouth turned upwards. "Ah, you have been busy. You know, I'm just a guy with a dream, in the heartland of America, trying to retrieve some lost property. Everyone needs a dream, don't they, Jack?" He laid on the American accent, leaning on the r's in 'heartland' and 'America'.

"Why use the caches to store this stuff. Isn't that a bit convoluted? Why not have someone keep it for you?"

"Ah, now you're asking good questions. After the failed attempt with the intern, his replacement got a bit *too* clever—paranoid if you ask me."

Renn, who had been staring at Jack during this exchange, opened her door. "We'll get out here. My mom's on her way to pick us up." She climbed out and slammed the door.

Jack followed suit and they stood there, arms crossed, until Sam waved amiably and pulled away. The Tesla's tires screeched on the country highway as he accelerated and disappeared around the bend.

Renn turned to Jack and demanded, "What was that about?"

Jack rubbed the side of his head. "I almost forgot. When I asked Thor about Sam, he used the name Sameer. That's his real name."

Useful, for sure, if they could learn more. "Didn't get a last name, did you?"

Jack shook his head.

Renn removed her new hat, pulled the band off her ponytail,

combed out the tangles from her flowing ebony hair, and tied it up again. She brushed dirt and twigs from her vest and jeans. Renn put the cap back on and fed her ponytail through the hole in the back. She started towards the gas station. "Let's go find the others."

* * *

Clara sipped Diet Dr. Pepper from a straw poking through a large lid and followed it up with a bite from a half-eaten slice of greasy cheese pizza. Her laptop sat open in front of her. She had been studying the files on the cache drive for half an hour but couldn't come up with a unifying theme. This bunch wasn't about 3D printing at all.

"Forty-seven."

Dom's voice carried from the large front window where he stood looking out into the parking lot around posters and display stands. He had taken to announcing the time by the minute, starting seven minutes ago. In thirteen minutes, if Renn and Jack didn't show up, they were supposed to call the police.

Clara didn't want to call the cops. Two teenagers, minorities at that, didn't need that kind of attention. They wouldn't be taken seriously, anyway.

"They'll be here, Dom. Take it easy."

Dom paced back to the table and plucked a small, powdered doughnut from a half-empty package. "They'd better, or we're all in trouble." He shoved the whole thing into his mouth and returned to his post.

The mix of document types was similar to the last cache: papers, spreadsheets, presentations, schematics, reports.

But the topics seemed all over the place. There was stuff about unmanned aerial vehicles, but that was only one part. There were also a lot of statistics about world poverty. She had found documents about miniaturized electronics, high efficiency communications, and more reports about access to the internet. Clara scanned over an engineering drawing of a solar panel concept. She could tell it was all valuable, but it seemed kind of random.

"Forty-eight."

She'd like to take this home and work on it in depth. She'd start by listing the authors on every document and seeing if they all belonged to Silver Labs. Maybe one mentioned Sam. It was unlikely Renn would let her take the thumb drives home with her, and she didn't want to copy the files to her laptop. If they were captured by Silver Labs, or the police, she didn't want to be caught red-handed.

"Forty-nine."

Clara took another bite of her lukewarm pizza and a sip of soda. She took quite a risk in letting her new friends see her with her laptop. If she wasn't careful, Renn might connect her to TacoCat. Clara wasn't even sure why that mattered, but it did. TacoCat was a persona she had cultivated, part shadowy hacker and part hero for hire. Neither part jived with her public image as a delicate ballerina. She didn't even have any computer friends at school. She couldn't see how the two halves of her identity fit together. Her mother would never allow it.

"Fifty."

"Dominic, come here and sit down. You're stressing me out."

Dom reluctantly took his seat at the table and tapped his

fingers on its smooth, gray surface. "I don't think they're gonna make it. What if they don't get back in time?"

"They'll be here, you'll see. And if they're not, we can give them a few extra minutes, right?"

"Extra minutes... how many?"

"I don't know. How about ten? But you have to promise not to count them out."

Dom had an app on his phone that showed an old-fashioned watch with ticking hands, which he consulted frequently. "Ten extra minutes. Okay."

Clara, who faced the window, glimpsed Jack and Renn in the parking lot and murmured thanks under her breath.

Dom popped in another doughnut, eyes on his phone. The door of the gas station opened, causing a bell to ring. When Dom saw the missing duo, he leapt from the table and tried to say something. What came out was a muffled sound and a puff of white powder.

"Whoa, there, what was that?" asked Renn.

"He said fifty-one," said Clara. "He's been counting the time until we'd have to call the police. You know you only have nine minutes to spare?"

"Sorry," said Jack. "We were delayed."

"You don't say," said Clara.

Renn took a seat at the table and set down a bottle of water. Jack bought himself another water and a pack of chocolate doughnuts before joining them. He and Renn took turns recounting their adventures since Renn had turned over the cache and car keys, and they had parted ways. Clara cheered at the harrowing bits and Dom apologized for being a nervous eater, while he finished his last doughnut.

"So Sam is really Sameer," said Clara. "What do you think

his history is with Silver? They've got to know each other at least." TacoCat might have better luck tracking him now.

"I don't know," said Jack, "but it didn't sound as though Thor liked him much."

Renn threw a quick glance out the window before crossing her arms on the table. "I'd bet that Sameer is working against Silver Labs somehow, and that Thor works for them. It's just a hunch."

"How do we find out?" asked Jack.

Renn shook her head. "I guess I can ask TacoCat to do some more investigating."

Clara did a little dance on the inside. TacoCat to the rescue.

Renn smacked the table with one palm. "God, there's another one. How did so many people drop into our lives who we know so little about? I'm sick of it."

Clara wilted behind her laptop. "I'm sure she—er, I mean he—I'm sure that he or she will find out more about them." She dropped her gaze and took a long, noisy sip of soda.

"Did you get a picture of the guy?" Dom asked. "I bet a hacker could use that."

Jack snapped his fingers and pulled out his phone. "The selfie on the train." He brought the picture up, frowned and showed it to them. "No good. He was looking down."

Clara's mood brightened a bit. They might not have gotten a picture, but she already knew what Thor looked like. She wondered if it might be time to come clean about the TacoCat. Renn was tired of secrets, and Clara was getting her identities tangled up.

"So, what have you two found out?" Renn asked. "What was in the cache?"

"Clara's been looking through all the stuff in one of the

thumb drives," Dom replied.

Clara described what she'd found while Jack perused the files.

"The last cache had a bunch of papers about 3D printing with organic materials," Renn said. "This one is about robot planes and poverty. Is it possible that Silver Labs is doing all this?"

Dom, who appeared to be calming down now that they had reunited, said, "Sure. I've been watching some of Jason Silver's speeches online. He talks about a whole range of technologies. He even wants to go to space."

"This is interesting," said Jack, who had a file open on the laptop. "This looks like plans for a scheme to provide internet access to poor areas using solar-powered UAVs."

"What's a UAV?" asked Renn.

"Unmanned aerial vehicle," replied Jack, still distracted by the documents.

"Of course," Clara said, "*that's* the theme of this cache."

"Wow, ambitious," said Renn.

"Hey, Dom," Jack said, "Have you looked at the puzzle yet?"

Dom looked chagrined and apologized, "Sorry, I haven't."

"I haven't given him the chance," said Clara. "I've been hogging the computer. And he's been preoccupied with calling the police for you two."

She reclaimed the laptop from Jack and swapped out the drives, shaking her head in disgust at the lone file. When its contents came up on the screen, she clapped her hands and laughed. "Here you go, Dominic," she said. Then she read the puzzle aloud, "Congratulations, you got this far / Score a point and run to base / Form the shape, the heart is there / Down the stretch to end the chase / Now to unlock the final clue / Get out free and win the race"

Renn chortled and Jack looked intrigued, but poor Dom looked confused. There was no reference to a shape, or four colors, or numbers.

"What does it mean?" Dom said.

"I don't know," Jack said. "Form the shape, the heart is there. Do you know how to make a heart with the tangram?"

The befuddled look on his face was enough of an answer for Clara.

Dom said, "No, but I'll research it when I get home."

"Great," Jack continued. He looked tired. "Clara, do you have time to read through more of the documents?"

"Sure," Clara said.

"Okay, you hang on to the thumb drives. Keep them safe."

"We should go," said Clara. "That loco Thor might drive up anytime and find us." Hearing no argument, she stowed the laptop and thumb drives. She would find out what she could and give the information to Renn. She would show them that TacoCat was useful—and trustworthy.

Dom wiped the excess powdered sugar from his mouth and took a deep swig of water. "Wow, what's this?" he asked, holding the bottle up to inspect it.

Renn looked ready to burst.

Jack laughed, "Dude, that's like twenty-proof jalapeno juice."

Dom raised his eyebrows and appeared to consider the beverage. He took another drink of the tainted water. "Not bad. Pretty good."

Chapter 29

Clara shooed her youngest sibling from her room and shut the door. Her family was such a contrast between loving and infuriating, endearing and annoying. But it was the only family she had. She flopped onto her queen bed and took a deep breath. Outside her room was noise and chaos, inside, her only sanctuary. And she was exhausted after the events of the weekend. It had been a very exciting Saturday, and today had been Mass, chores, dance class, more criticism from her mother: a normal Sunday.

Her leg had cramped a little at practice, probably from running at the zoo. Clara pulled out one of the white dresser drawers and used its curved top edge as a makeshift ballet barre. She thought about the email Renn had sent her, or rather, had sent TacoCat. It summarized the new information that Clara, in fact, already knew. First, they knew Sam's real first name—Sameer. Second, they suspected that Thor worked for Silver Labs. And Sameer had some kind of connection with Jason Silver. One thing she knew for sure; TacoCat should not know what Thor looked like. She'd have to be careful how she handled that.

She switched legs and leaned into the stretch until it hurt, focusing her attention on the pink and lavender patterns in the quilted comforter on her bed. This was getting complicated. If she wasn't careful, she'd slip up and say something to the others that would give her away. Even as she thought it, another part of her brain proposed a different thought. Why couldn't she just tell them? It wasn't like she was doing anything wrong. She was helping.

Clara shoved the thought down and grabbed the laptop from beside her bed. Propping herself up against frilly pillows and stuffed animals, she fired it up and tried some simple searches. It was no use; she got way too many hits with just the name Sameer. She brought up a simple Python script she had written with the Beautiful Soup library. Clara turned it loose on the Silver Labs website, but it turned up nothing.

What else did they know? Something nagged at her, something she was forgetting. She picked up the closest teddy bear and interrogated it. "What am I forgetting? Qué?"

When it didn't respond, she tossed it back on the bed and turned her attention away from the Sameer problem to Thor. She didn't know how she would even proceed without a picture had she not seen him herself. So she browsed the Silver Labs website for photos and searched her scraped data for employee profiles.

Ten minutes later, she huffed in frustration at her failure. Her patience fraying, she slammed her laptop shut and threw herself back into a prone position with arms splayed wide. Clara Flores, TacoCat, hacker extraordinaire. If she ever revealed her identity to her new friends, they would laugh her out of the school. She needed to shoot some stuff.

She took up position her desk and donned her gaming headset, logged in to see who was online. Aha, her acquaintance who had gotten Owen's information was on. They had not yet played their matches together. This was an excellent time to take out her frustration on some hapless noobs. Clara pinged him and he scurried off to gather the rest of his team. Soon they queued for a new match and she felt like a racehorse, restless and skittish in the starting gate.

Clara ran through her mindful moment and opened her eyes. It was like flipping a switch; it put her in a different world. And then the game really did drop her into a new world. She was in an abandoned, shelled-out building. She planted a beacon at the best rendezvous for her team and began making her way to it. Someone from the other team had roamed out ahead, hoping to catch them emerging from their starting points. She took him out with a head shot.

She stood waiting at one end of a long bridge for the others to arrive. Based on her starting location, at least two of them should be there by now. The avatar of her acquaintance hopped over the husk of a burned-out car and waved at her. Together they defended the bridge against three opponents. The rest of her team must have been lost or re-spawning.

Five matches later, their team traded digital high fives, singing the praises of their new teammate. They had lost the first match but won the next four after Clara had figured out how to take up the slack. It had almost been too easy, but it was exactly what she had needed to let off some steam.

She went into private chat and typed, "Hey, how did you get that information I asked for?"

"The license number? Oh, easy. I work for the DMV out here in the driver's license office."

"Where you at?"

"Coeur d'Alene. You?"

"Idaho? I'm in the Midwest. Isn't that, like, invasion of

214

privacy or something?"

"Nah. Well, I mean, yes, but you'd be surprised how loose people are with information like that. Plus, it's so boring. Gotta have a little fun, right?"

"Right, I guess. Say, what would you do if you only had a picture but no other information?"

"You could do a reverse image search on the off chance it will turn up pics from social media—long shot. We don't have any facial recognition software. That's like NSA stuff, I don't know. They're recording this chat right now. They have *everything*. Trust me, I work for the government, lol."

"Okay, thanks again."

"Hey, I'm Pete. What's your name?"

Clara pondered this simple question for a long moment. Finally, she typed, "I'm very grateful. Thanks for the games, Pete, gotta run."

She yawned, stretched, and looked at the time. It was getting late. Still, Pete had given her an idea. She didn't have any scripts to crawl social media feeds, another brilliant idea she would have to look into.

It was unlikely that Jason Silver would be on Facebook; who used that anymore? What did professionals use? Twitter, perhaps. What was that other site... LinkedIn? Clara shut down the game and created a LinkedIn account, tried searching for Jason Silver. There were a lot of them, but it wasn't hard to land on the right one. Jackpot. It gave his complete employment history, education history, skills. It didn't list any of his LinkedIn friends, though. She couldn't trace his network.

She looked through his professional history. He'd been CEO of Silver Labs for a decade. Before that he was in some other company, and before that he attended Stanford. It showed a college logo, an 'S' with a Christmas tree sticking up through it. Green on a maroon background.

She clicked on his company name, Silver Labs. Several other employees were on the network, too. She saw Lewis Edmunds and Julia Bouchard. She didn't see Owen, or Thor, or Sameer. Still, there was something... she returned to Jason's profile.

It hit her in the face like a head shot. Jason Silver attended Stanford University. When they had met Sam, or Sameer, he had been wearing a maroon sweatshirt with a logo. A simple Google search, 'Sameer Jason Silver Stanford', turned up a few hits. There was a news story from around twelve years ago.

"Jason Silver and Sameer Bakshi, students at Stanford University, partnered to form a new company based on a rec-ommendation engine they created together. Recommendation software, like Amazon uses to make personalized product recommendations..."

The article had a picture of the two of them, and Clara once again looked into the face of their blackmailer. "I've got you now."

Chapter 30

Dom waved goodbye to Jack and Noah before turning into study hall. He offered an additional wave and soft hello to a couple of Math Club people and found his usual desk near the back of the room. He felt confident for a change, and why not? He was the kind of guy who shared a laugh with popular football players. He had friends.

Mr. Baumgarten sat at his desk grading papers. Students trickled in as the bell rang. Strange, the environment hadn't changed, only his perception had. Mama always said his altitude would only be as high as his attitude.

Dom cracked open his backpack and pulled out his childhood tangram. Without the printed GPS coordinates, he couldn't solve the puzzle, but he might be able to figure out the right shape. Most of the lines in the last riddle didn't seem to involve the tangram at all. It didn't even say anything about observing the four-color theorem. He would try to obey it anyway, just in case. The key line was obviously, "Form the shape, the heart is there." He shifted pieces around and racked his brain for memories of a heart-shaped solution.

Motion near the front of the room drew his gaze, and he was immediately sorry for looking. Bernie's friend, Ryan, sauntered in and lazily scanned the room. He caught Dom's eye with a wink and crossed the room to an empty desk. Dom returned his attention to the puzzle and tried to focus. It didn't take long to sink into his usual zone of concentration, a cocoon of isolation from the distractions of the world. His fingers moved pieces around the desk surface even as his mind raced ahead to scout out new possibilities.

But as success eluded him, Dom daydreamed. His mind drifted back to the last incident with Bernie and Ryan in the hallway. They had set him up to be tackled like a sack of potatoes and he had collapsed like one, too. He replayed the incident over and over in his mind, like a broken record. But each time he varied the events to produce different endings. One time he sidestepped and tripped Bernie as he lunged for his tackle, sending him sprawling on the floor instead of Dom. The next time, he didn't even wait for Bernie to finish counting. He rushed him, knocked him on his butt, and ran for freedom. The next, he took evasive action the moment they tried to remove his backpack, using their momentum against them and putting them into painful joint locks, both kneeling on the hallway floor begging to be released. The next time he faked left and went right as Bernie came in for the tackle, breezing right by him, ran a few steps and turned to receive the imaginary pass that Ryan was now releasing. Dom caught the ghost ball and spiked it. All three of them laughed and high-fived each other. Dom shook his head. God, the things his brain came up with.

"Hey, buddy."

Dom jerked back to reality with a start, accidentally knocking a piece of his tangram to the floor. He had not noticed Ryan walking down the row towards him. He glanced up to Mr. Baumgarten, but the teacher's head was bent over the papers he was grading.

"It's okay. I asked him if I could come back and ask you a math homework question."

"But... we're not in the same math period."

Ryan stood on the right side of Dom's desk, the side that the desk wrapped around his torso until it attached to the chair. He kneeled by the desk and Dom noted that he was out of sight of the teacher. Ryan picked up the fallen puzzle piece with his left hand but didn't even spare a glance at it. His right hand he rested on Dom's right leg near the knee.

"Don't worry 'bout it. I didn't have a math question, anyway. I just wanted to see how you're doing. You been okay, buddy?"

Dom swallowed, his mouth suddenly dry. What was Ryan up to? He sounded like he was being nice. Why was his hand on Dom's leg?

"I, uh, okay, I guess."

"Good, that's great. I'd think so, you being in with the cool kids now. You know Jack's taking real good care of you. He's a good guy that Jack. I bet you and I could be friends, too. Would you like that?" Ryan's right hand gave Dom's leg a light squeeze. "Hey, whatcha working on here?" He held up the piece he was holding and looked at both sides.

Dom was still wondering how to answer the unexpected question the quick change in topic took him by surprise. "Um, it's a puzzle. It's called a tangram."

Ryan looked at the pieces on the desk, with real or feigned interest, Dom couldn't tell. His right hand never budged from Dom's leg. He was awash in emotions and didn't understand what Ryan was trying to do. He shifted in his seat as if that would remove Ryan's hand. Dom was embarrassed but didn't know why. He was afraid of other people around them noticing his predicament, worried about what they might think. Ryan looked as if he had not a care in the world.

"Wow, looks good, buddy. I mean, I was doing five hundred–piece puzzles when I was nine, but whatever. Hey, who're you going to take to Homecoming?"

The question almost didn't register with Dom. He was focused on the fact that Ryan still had a tangram piece in one hand and another on his leg, making any thoughts of extracting himself from the situation remote. He looked plaintively up at Mr. Baumgarten's desk, but the teacher had his head down, his red pen flying. Dom's attention jumped back to Ryan as if he dropped out of warp drive into the middle of a raging battle.

"You should ask her out. She wants you to."

"Who? What?"

"Sharonda. I heard her talking about you, dude. She's hot for you."

Sharonda Jones. Cheerleader. Beautiful. Smooth, dark skin. Dom thought she had dated half the football team. She wasn't in any of Dom's classes. Sharonda Jones was out of his league. Nevertheless, Dom allowed himself to consider for the briefest of moments the idea. Now he felt doubly uncomfortable that Ryan had taken up residence in his personal space and made Dom think about a girl in *that* way.

"I could put in a good word for you, buddy. Let her know you're interested. Dude, guaranteed base run. You ever been to first base with a girl?"

Dom's face flushed with humiliation. He realized that was Ryan's purpose here, to make him uncomfortable. Ryan wanted Dom to know that he could manipulate his emotions, jerk his chain. A flash of anger added to the cocktail of other emotions. He ran through various ways he could fight Ryan, attack him fast and hard, but rejected them all. He was no match for Ryan in a fight, and he didn't want to get into trouble. But maybe he could make him regret this encounter. Regret it and remember it. Dom's attention focused on his leg, almost numb, where Ryan's hand rested. There were a mere two or three inches from his hand to the underside of the desktop. He wondered how much pain he would inflict if he slammed his knee, bearing Ryan's hand, up against it. If he were lucky, there might even be a screw sticking out in just the right place.

"Can I have my tangram piece back please?"

"This piece? Can't finish the puzzle without it? What picture does it make, anyway?" Ryan leaned in and added, "Is it dirty?"

If he were going to do it, make Ryan pay, he'd have to do it now. He'd sacrifice his puzzle piece if he had to, he could get another. He tensed up, but realized that he was telegraphing his intention. May as well have been using a bullhorn. He tried to relax his legs, his arms. He took a breath and focused on jerking his leg with no warning. Only he couldn't. He was frozen in place. The thought of it differed from the action. He wasn't sure what was holding him back. The fear of retribution? He tried to summon the essence of the lion. He, Dominic Marshall, didn't have to put up with this indignity. Dom tensed up, mentally reprimanded himself again.

Ryan removed his hand from Dom's leg and stood up. He looked at the puzzle some more, but could not hide his boredom. He tossed the piece into Dom's lap and looked down his nose. "Well, you run along home, buddy. One day you'll work your way up to big boy puzzles." Ryan turned and walked back to his desk.

Dom watched him retreat, at once relieved and disappointed he had missed his chance. He saw Ryan take his seat, lean over, and share a laugh with his friend, followed by a glance in Dom's direction by them both. Dom sunk down, trying to become invisible. He had failed again, and Ryan had humiliated him. Dom realized, for the hundredth time, that he couldn't stop Bernie and Ryan with violence. He didn't have it in him.

He was no lion.

Dom laid his forearms across the desk and dropped his head onto them. His face was shielded, hiding his watery eyes. No longer anywhere near the "zone", he let his mind drift, searching for some peace. The scenario replayed itself again and again, but the ending was always the same. He couldn't even visualize a successful outcome. Ryan's taunts ricocheted around his brain like bullets. But eventually, they were whittled down to a bare, essential pattern.

Run along home. First base. Second base. Third base. Home base.

Dom's eyes popped open as the bell rang. The rest of the pieces clattered to the floor, and he scrambled to collect them. He had to find the others; he had to tell them he solved the puzzle.

Chapter 31

Jack sat at the lunch table, staring at a multi-colored shape carefully laid out in front of him. Renn and Clara stared, too, Clara tilting her head this way and that to get different perspectives. He wanted to give Dom the benefit of the doubt, but when the math-wiz had stumbled into lunch mumbling about a home or something, Jack wasn't so sure but had watched with interest as Dom assembled a shape that kind of looked like a house.

The truth was, Jack had been losing confidence in their chances of navigating out of their predicament. Even though they had escaped from Thor, he and Renn had been picked up almost immediately by Sameer. Out of the frying pan and into the fire, as the saying went. He was always the one to keep morale high, fire up the team. Now he was losing his spark.

"It looks like a train," said Clara between bites of mashed potatoes.

"I think you're looking at it sideways," said Renn. "Right?" she added, checking with Dom.

"It's a house," Dom nodded. "More to the point, it's a home."

"Oh, that's a chimney. I get it," said Clara.

Jack gulped some chocolate milk and gestured towards Dom

with the carton. "You said this was the solution to the puzzle. I still don't get it."

"The clue isn't what's in the puzzle, it's what's missing from it," Dom said, pointing to the house-shaped tangram.

Jack was still confused. What he remembered of the puzzle had nothing to do with a house. He guessed that was the point Dom was making, but how? He leaned forward and rested his elbows on the table. "Okay. Explain it to us."

Dom swallowed a tater tot and wiped his mouth and hands with a flimsy napkin. He launched into his explanation with a level of excitement Jack had not yet seen from the shy introvert.

"The word 'home' is missing from the riddle, but the question is why that is the missing word, instead of, say, 'tomato' or 'geometry'." He pulled out a sheet of paper.

Jack could see the lines of the riddle, with editorial markups.

"I'm confident, but I want you to see it. Take a look at this." Dom turned the paper so they could read it. "The first line says 'Congratulations, you got this far' There's nothing there. The second line is 'Score a point and run to (home) base.'"

Dom had added the word 'home' in red pen before the word 'base.' Jack had to admit it made sense, but one instance does not make a convincing argument.

"The next line says, 'Form the shape, the heart is there.' Where's the heart?" Dom asked, looking around the table with a sly smile. "Home is where the heart is."

Clara clapped her hands, and Renn nodded. Jack wanted to hear more.

"It continues 'Down the (home) stretch to end the chase. Now to unlock the final clue,' and finally, 'Get out (home) free and win the race.' What do you think?"

"That's neat, Dom," said Clara, causing him to grin. "I think you solved it."

"What about the four-color theorem?" Jack asked. "It didn't mention it."

"The riddle doesn't mention it. But there's usually some uncertainty in assembling the tangram, so I assumed it as a requirement."

It was worth checking out. Jack pulled the Ziploc baggie with his 3D printed tangram and dumped the pieces onto the lunchroom table. He and Dom quickly duplicated the shape and made it obey the four-color theorem. Then they flipped the tangram upside down. Jack's stomach jumped, just like it did before every game. He was getting excited despite his sour mood.

Dom fiddled with the orientation of one piece, and it was clear when they had a new number sentence lined up. Jack squinted at it, leaning in to get a closer look.

Renn said, "Uh, those aren't GPS coordinates, guys."

Disappointment and frustration welled up in Jack. This thing was designed for the best and brightest engineers and scientists. How were he and his friends supposed to solve it?

"What does it say?" Clara asked.

Dom read the line out loud. "151 3951# *99."

"Smart," Jack said. "They changed things up."

Renn gave him the side-eye, then changed the topic. "I have some news from TacoCat."

Thank God for the TacoCat. "What is it?"

"Sameer's last name is Bakshi. He and Jason Silver were big buds at Stanford. They started a company together."

"Silver Labs?" asked Jack.

"No, it was called... what was it called?" she muttered. Renn tapped her tray absentmindedly with her fork.

Clara fidgeted beside her.

"Oh right, it was called 'Likely.' They made this software that would learn what you liked and make recommendations for buying stuff. Anyway, they apparently had a falling out and Sameer bought Jason out of the company. That's when Jason started Silver Labs."

"So, they're not friends anymore?" Dom asked.

Renn finished her last bite of food and arranged her trash in one corner of the tray. "It's kind of hard to tell. They've been seen together at charity events, so it seems like they still talk. They're both super rich, so it's not like one should be jealous of the other."

"Did TacoCat find out anything about Thor?" said Jack.

Renn shook her head. "I'm afraid not. We didn't have any identifying information to go on, so it was a long shot. He suggested we try staking out Silver Labs."

"That would confirm his employment, but it wouldn't tell us much about who he is or how he's involved," said Jack.

Clara jumped in. "No, but we could follow him home. And if we got inside Silver Labs again, we could find a phone list or a big board with everyone's picture."

"I don't remember seeing anything like that on the tour," said Renn.

Jack listened as Clara pushed her point. She was forceful and insistent whereas Jack felt defeated and discouraged. It seemed like Clara was getting revved up. This girl was up for a good fight. Fine, if the others hadn't given up yet, neither would he.

"If we could just get in there," Clara continued, "I know I... I know we could nail him." She glanced around the table, then

226

suddenly added, "I'll take your trays up for you."

Dom thanked her as she carried four trays, loaded with plates and trash, up to the kitchen window.

Jack took a picture of the tangram and changed the subject again. A memory had surfaced, and his excitement was building. "I remember where I've heard one fifty-one before." He disassembled the puzzle and put pieces back into its Ziploc baggie. "The room number of the giant 3D printing lab was one fifty-one. Remember, they called it Lab 151?"

"Huh, I guess so," said Renn.

Jack continued, "Rennie, you told me once about indoor geocaches. You wouldn't be able to use GPS coordinates to find it though, right?"

"That's right," said Renn. "You'd have to give some other way to find it, like a room number, a mail box..." She drifted off into silence.

"So you think there's a room number in there?" asked Dom.

"I think," Jack said, wagging a finger at them, "it's referring specifically to Lab 151 in Silver Labs. Remember who this game is for."

"Silver Labs employees," said Renn.

Dom sat ramrod straight and shouted, "Home base!"

"Exactly," Jack said. "We're going back to Silver Labs."

"You might be right, Jack," said Renn. "But that only explains the first number, not the other two."

When Clara returned from her errand, they were all quietly contemplating the answer revealed by the tangram. There was a new mystery to be solved, and Jack was getting revved up.

Chapter 32

The bright yellow line of buses snaked around the perimeter of the parking lot. Renn zipped her vest up to her chin and resolved to dig out her winter coat when she got home. Her Kaplan's study guide lay open on her lap as she sat on the front steps. A trickle of students passed by. The flow wouldn't pick up until the final bell rang in a few minutes.

She tried to focus on the trigonometry problems arrayed before her. The exam was this Saturday. True, she had another year to take it again, but this would tell her what she needed to work on next semester and over the summer. If she didn't hit her target score, she'd have to double down on her efforts.

Someone dropped their backpack a step higher and sat down beside her. Clara nodded, blew into her hands, and rubbed them together. Renn reviewed her quadrants for positive trig values: all, sin, tan, cos, all, sin, tan, cos. Clara leaned in close enough to see what Renn was reading.

"Ay, Math. I hate math," she said.

Renn closed the book but let it rest on her lap. Her productivity was plummeting anyway. "It's not my favorite, either. We're not getting away from it anytime soon though."

Clara shrugged. She turned and looked like she was about to say something, but paused. Finally, she broke the awkward silence. "Why do you push yourself so hard?"

Renn pressed her lips together and looked off into the distance. Her loose hair fluttered around her head from the north wind. When she answered, she turned her head over and down to look at the shorter girl. "I want to be a surgeon. I'm not sure what specialty, yet. But to get there I need to get into a top medical school. To do that, I want the best pre-med program I can get into. I'll have to kill it on the MCAT."

"But why?" Clara asked again. "I mean, what drives you?"

Ah, thought Renn, *so we're peeling the onion.* She turned the question around. "Why are you so invested in this little group? You went out of your way to get in and stay in. How come?"

Clara dropped her eyes, shrugged again. She faced forward and appeared to study the line of buses.

Jack and Dom ran down the steps and blocked their view. "Wassup?" said Jack, his usual enthusiasm restored.

"'Sup, boys," Renn said.

"I call this meeting of the Black Hawk Pirates to order," said Jack.

"We are not the Black Hawk Pirates," Renn growled.

Jack leaned sideways towards Dom, lifted his hand to bracket the side of his mouth, and said in an exaggerated whisper, "I told you they wouldn't like that name."

Dom shrugged.

Renn raised her voice to take control. "We need to decide when we're going to Silver Labs. Then we'll figure out the how." Remembering the heavy book sitting in her lap, she added, "And it can't be Saturday."

Jack folded his arms. "Well, it can't be Friday. I've got to be there for the game."

"I'm pretty open," said Dom.

"What about Sunday?" said Renn.

"I can't get away from my family until the afternoon," said Clara.

"Me either," added Dom.

"Oh, wait," Clara said. "I've also got dance rehearsal in the afternoon. Sorry."

"It's okay," Jack said. "It'll be getting dark soon after than. Maybe we can find a time after school this week? Wednesday?"

Dom squirmed and looked like he wanted to hide under a rock. "That's church family night. My mom would kill me if I skipped it."

"I've got soccer practice on Thursday," said Renn.

"Math Club," Dom said miserably.

"We need some time to figure out the other numbers any-way," Jack said. "I don't see how we can go before the weekend."

The walls closed in on Renn. They had to finish this by the end of the weekend, or the clock that Sameer had started would run out. She pulled out her school planner and flipped through her week. "Dom, what time does Math Club get out? Can we go after you finish that, and I finish my fund-raising meeting?"

Clara opened her phone and studied her calendar app. "It's getting kind of late, isn't it? What if we ditch Friday afternoon and go before the game?"

Renn consulted her planner page for Friday. "Okay, let's see. Nope, I've got a test in sixth period."

"Oh, come on!" Jack said in an exasperated tone. "I guess I could give Coach some lame excuse. He might kick me off the team, though."

Renn bit back a retort about him quitting football all on his own. That wasn't fair. He'd been hurt, and yet he sacrificed himself for them at the zoo. All she'd done was try to keep her normal life on track. Maybe it wouldn't hurt for her to sacrifice a little, too.

"No." Renn's voice was soft but cut off the conversation like a knife.

The others turned to pay attention.

"No." she said again. She was gripping the study guide with both hands. Her knuckles were white. "We'll do it on Saturday. I don't need to take the ACT this time around."

Jack gave her a look, and she knew that he, of all people, appreciated how difficult this was. She nodded to him.

"It's okay, really. It's just a delay."

Clara looked at the three of them. "All right. That's settled. Now we need a plan."

Dom looked at the buses, now more than half full. "I need to catch the bus. See you tomorrow?"

"I'm catching a ride with a friend," said Clara. "See you later."

Renn watched the two retreat down the steps.

"We are going to figure this out," said Jack when they were alone. He took Clara's spot on the step beside her.

"We have too many questions, Jack, and not enough answers."

"Yeah. But we still have time."

Renn stowed her planner and study guide in her backpack and zipped it up. "I've been thinking about that."

The line of buses started moving, peeling off one by one.

"I believe I know how to get some answers."

"TacoCat?" Jack said.

"Not this time. He's helped a lot, but I'm thinking of a more direct source."

"More direct," Jack echoed. "You're gonna have to speak plainly. I'm only a football player you know."

She smiled at his self-deprecation. "I don't want you to worry."

"Don't do anything stupid," he said. "At least not without me."

"No. I'll be perfectly safe. It's just that the one person who might be able to help us now is Owen Sutherland."

Jack let out an explosive breath. But then he leaned in, gave her a side hug, and said, "Fine. You want me to come along for moral support?"

She did want moral support, almost as much as she wanted to hide under her covers for a solid week. "No, it's okay. I've already looked into it and I can't go without adult supervision. I've asked Ranger Scott to take me. Promise me you won't say anything to my mom? I don't want her to worry."

Jack made the motion of zipping his lip and throwing away the key, causing her to laugh. "My lips are sealed, but I want to hear all about it."

"Deal."

Chapter 33

Renn sat in a wooden chair on linoleum flooring that looked like it went back to the fifties. Every adjustment of posture caused squeaks to echo through the sterile waiting area. In front of her hung portraits of the governor, lieutenant governor, mayor, and warden. She sat uncomfortably with her hands pressed hard against the tops of her legs.

"You sure you're up for this?"

"Have you ever visited anyone in jail, Ranger?"

"Well, I can't say as I ever have." Ranger Scott bowed his head to remove his hat, revealing thinned gray hair that Renn remembered as blond. When he raised it again, he met her gaze. "But I'd imagine he's pretty much like you or me, made some bad choices is all. There but for the grace of the Almighty..."

"Yeah, let's hope you're right."

"Scott Victor and Adrienne Chao."

Renn stood and turned to see a heavyset female guard in the doorway. She looked bored, annoyed, and ready to tase someone at the drop of a pin. Renn determined to stay on her good side.

"Yes, ma'am."

"Follow me."

She led them down a hallway to a security door. Next to the

door was a desk with a guard. Arrayed in front of him were various monitors showing locations within the jail. Renn saw inmates sitting, walking, and lying on their beds. The station guard took out two plastic bins, removed their lids, and placed them on a narrow counter between them.

Their chaperone said, "Remove all jewelry, chains, electronics, wallets, and watches, and place your personal effects in these bins."

Renn hesitated, raised her hand, and asked, "Ma'am, does that include makeup?"

The large woman glared down at her in a way that said, *really*? She drew in a deliberate breath and began her recitation again. "Remove all jewelry, chains..."

Renn feared her ire was ramping up, so she quickly emptied her pockets into the bin. "Okay, I'm all ready."

The hulk of a woman, whose name tag read "Daisy," reached into Renn's bin, slowly pulled out a package of Kleenex, and held it out between two sausage fingers.

Renn took it back and muttered, "Thank you."

After they passed inspection, the station guard pressed a button, and the security door buzzed open. Daisy yanked open the door and let them through. Renn expected they would see chain link fencing or barred cells, but instead they were in another white hallway with occasional doors to the left and right. At the second right, Daisy opened the door and showed them into a room with a large, long table. She instructed them to sit on one side of the table and wait.

In the few minutes they sat waiting, Renn felt the walls closing in. This would be a horrible place to be. In the distance they heard a security door buzz and slam shut. Five deep breaths later, the door to the room opened and a new guard entered with Owen trailing him. The guard led Owen to the other side of the table and, after Owen sat, locked his handcuffs to some unseen hook below the table.

This new guy spared them a smile. "All you folks have to do when you're done is say so and I'll be back to let you out. You need anything?"

They shook their heads and Ranger Scott said, "No, thank you."

The guard shut the door, and they were alone with Owen.

Ranger Scott began the conversation. "Thank you for meeting us, Owen. We appreciate your time."

At this, Owen scowled and leaned back in his chair. "Oh, I got plenty of time, don't I? No trouble at all, Ranger. Nice to see you again."

Renn, who had kept her head down, so she didn't have to look at Owen, glanced at the ranger in puzzlement.

He explained, "I'm on retainer at Silver Labs as a wildlife consultant. I go over there now and then to meet with their groundskeeper."

Renn nodded and fixed her gaze on the table between her and the man she put in here. She didn't know what to say, but a small soft voice escaped her lips anyway, "I'm sorry you got arrested. I never meant—"

"Never meant to go snooping around my house? Never meant to call the cops on me? Spare me the excuses."

There was a moment of awkward silence during which Owen looked everywhere but at them. He sat up in his chair and his handcuffs rattled. "Listen, why don't you just tell me why you're here."

Renn forced herself to lift her head and look the prisoner in his eyes. He was staring at her, his face now an impenetrable mask. She cleared her throat and spoke again. "I know you have no reason to help me, Mr. Sutherland, but we need it, my friends and I. We've gotten dragged into this mess with geocaches and company secrets, and we're in over our heads. I was hoping you would help explain some things?"

When Renn mentioned the geocaches, Owen's expression became more curious, but he didn't take the bait. "Maybe you've forgotten why I'm in here. I took a bald eagle, and the authorities determined that I should stand trial for a federal crime. That's it."

"Well, didn't you?" Her anger at Stella's abduction boiled up in a flash. "You took Stella. What in the world did you mean to do with her?"

Owen's voice raised in response. "I wasn't going to hurt that bird. I was just holding on to her for a bit. For her safety."

Ranger Scott practically fell out of his chair when he heard that. "Bucky's balls! What do you mean for her safety?"

Owen withdrew a little and calmed himself with some effort. "I would never have hurt Stella. I love animals. Did you know they took Rosco..." his voice choked. "They took Rosco to the shelter 'cause I don't have anybody who would take him in."

Owen's obvious love for his dog softened Renn's attitude towards him. "Then why?" she tried again.

"I don't have to explain anything to you two," Owen practically shouted. As if of two minds on the subject, he added in a quieter tone, "Please, believe that I was protecting that bird from an even worse fate."

As passionate as she was about all things Stella, Renn felt it was leading into a dead end. She tried to steer back to the main topic. "Listen, you work at Silver Labs, right?"

Owen answered simply, "Yes."

"Well, somehow this all has to do with Silver Labs. We've been threatened and chased. Now we have to get these caches for this guy or he's going to ruin us!"

After a moment of chewing on his thoughts, Owen said, "Little lady, you're either a lot smarter or a lot dumber than you look. You've got no idea of what you're into, though."

"Exactly!" agreed Renn. "If you know anything about this, could you find it in your heart to help us out a little? I could, I don't know, maybe there's some way I could help you out in return."

"And how do you propose to do that?"

"I can tell you love your dog. I could take care of him for a while until you're out or find him a good home."

A flash of some expression, perhaps hope, flickered across Owen's face before disappearing behind the mask. "You'd do that?"

"Sure. I love animals too. I bet he and Bear would get along great." Owen looked concerned, and Renn added, "Bear is my Newfie."

"Oh, I had one of those once. Great breed."

Ranger Scott leaned in and tapped his watch. Renn remembered that they were on the clock and there was a time limit on this visit. Fifteen minutes and no longer.

"So, will you help us?

Owen bit his lip, obviously tempted. "Listen, I can't just spill the beans. But if you tell me what you know, I might be able to tell you if you're in the ballpark."

Renn glanced over at Ranger Scott, who shrugged.

"Okay." And she launched into the story of Jack and her finding the first cache and solving its puzzle, leading to the next, and the next. She told of Sam, or Sameer, confronting

237

them at the Village Inn and demanding that they bring him all the caches. She told the story of Wappoke Zoo and being chased by a very large, very blond man. At this, Owen hissed out a breath and muttered something. "What?" asked Renn.

"What?" said Owen.

"You said something, a name, I think. Eric?"

"So, what? You said he chased you around the zoo."

"Yes, but we didn't know his name. Does he work at Silver Labs, too?"

Owen must be kicking himself for letting out that bit of information, but he was true to his word and nodded yes to her question.

"You worked in the security office. Does Eric also work in security?"

Another yes.

"And Sameer, does he work for Silver Labs, too?"

No.

Renn's mind was racing now, trying to decide what to ask and in what order. She took a slow breath and tried to calm down. "How high does this thing go? All the way to Jason Silver?"

Owen snorted. "I can't tell you that! You have no idea of what's at stake here. And maybe I don't know.

Renn thought furiously and tried to piece things together. "When you were arrested, that messed up somebody's plans. Or maybe it was when we found the cache. I don't know. Is that why Sameer approached us?"

Owen nodded and said, "Now you're getting it."

"The second cache was very close to the Raptor Center. Is that why you were there?"

A pause, and a slight nod yes.

"Was Eric your partner?" A piece clicked in Renn's mind, and she experienced a visceral and emotional reaction. Her eyes watered and her hands flew to cover her mouth. She looked at both of them but she could not speak. Three breaths later she said, "Oh, my God." She stared at Owen and continued, "You weren't there alone that day. You were with Eric."

Owen shrank even further into himself before the words came in a bare whisper. "We were supposed to be in and out, no one the wiser. Ranger was there, and we were waiting for him to get out of sight. Then, that infernal bird starts chirping at us. She must have thought we had food or something."

She may have imagined it, but he seemed relieved that someone else finally knew his secret.

"You were protecting Stella from Eric. For some reason you had to take her, or Eric would have done something worse."

Owen shifted in his seat and glanced back and forth between them. This time he whispered his answer. "Yes."

Renn's perspective shifted in that instant, and she was suddenly more concerned with the future than with the past. They only had a couple more minutes with Owen. "Listen, we're stuck on the last puzzle. We know we have to get into Silver Labs. We think to Lab 151. Then there are two more numbers that we don't understand."

"You kids are very bright to have gotten this far. Listen, I'm not certain the last cache is important. That is, I'm not sure if you'll find any, ah, extra goodies in there. But if there is, it would be in the lab's lock box. That's what the second number is for. It wouldn't be sitting out in the open."

"And the third?"

"You won't need the third, but maybe you'll figure it out."

"Let's see, how do we..."

The door opened and the friendly guard came back into the room and said, "Time's up folks, please step this way."

Before Renn could spit out another question, Owen shouted to her, "Don't forget Rosco! He's allergic to peanut butter, he'll puke it all over. But he loves liver. Don't forget!"

The guard ushered them out into the hallway and closed the door behind them. They were escorted through the security door where they collected their personal effects. They signed out on the log and Daisy showed them back to the lobby. There was nothing left to do but hike out to the Ranger's pickup truck.

After they had stepped out into the bright daylight, Renn turned and hugged Ranger Scott around his chest. He patted her head with one hand and said, "Well, that was quite a story, little wren."

Renn smiled at the special nickname that only a few people in the world had called her. One was her dad and one was Ranger Scott. She stood up and wiped tears from her cheeks. "I didn't think I'd ever see him as anything but a lowlife, but I actually feel sorry for him."

"Me too, darlin', me too."

The sun and breeze hit her and she thought about Owen locked up. She thought about Sameer and his threats. She thought about her friends and the puzzle that was leading them around like they were on a leash. And now it was leading them right into Silver Labs, the one place she wanted nothing to do with.

"Ranger Scott?"

"Yes, ma'am?"

"You mentioned you did some work for Silver Labs. Have you ever considered taking on some interns?"

Chapter 34

Jack parked the Green Machine in a visitor's spot at Silver Labs and the four stepped out into the cold, crisp autumn air. They stood between his car and Ranger Scott's ancient F150, two spots away. The ranger strode around the back of his truck. He was in full uniform.

Ranger Scott tipped his hat to them and addressed Renn, "Adrienne, I've been thinking about this here matter and have developed a bad feeling about it. You all have been put into some dicey situations, and you've been very brave. But if you go in there and get this cache, you're stealing just as much as the people you're mixed up with. Why do their dirty work for them?"

Jack had thought about this; he imagined they all had. He and Renn had talked about it. She appeared ready for the argument.

"I know, and I'm sorry to involve you in it. We don't want to steal anything, and we have no intention of turning the caches over to Sameer. But the fact is that we don't know who we can and can't trust in there." She pointed to Silver Labs.

Jack picked up the thread. "We could call the police, but their first call would be to Silver Labs' security. That used to be Owen, and now it's Eric. Sameer seems to know almost everything we're up to, so we have to go through with this."

Clara said, "But at the meet, we're going to turn it around, set up a trap for Sameer." Her eyes gleamed. "We're going to have a reporter there and livestream the whole thing."

"To avoid embarrassment, Silver Labs will be forced to go with our story," said Dom. He looked at Jack and added, "Uh, what's our story again?"

Jack clapped him on the shoulder. "That we were helping them the whole time to expose an embezzling operation."

Renn pulled out her Ziploc bag and opened it for Clara, who dropped in the thumb drives she'd been carrying. "In fact, I think it would be better if you held onto these for today." She offered the bag to Ranger Scott, who received it with a solemn nod.

"Just one more to add to the collection," said Clara.

Ranger Scott put the bag into the glove compartment of his truck. He stepped back, shut the truck door, and gave all of them a long sober look. "Well, we'd best be about it then."

They filed into the lobby, which reminded Jack of the tour. How far they'd come since then, and they'd done it together.

A perky young receptionist greeted them from behind a long counter. "Welcome to Silver Labs!"

Ranger Scott stepped forward, explained his business, and introduced his four "interns."

She pulled out a contractor badge for the ranger and four visitor badges for them.

"Are there many folks around today?" asked the ranger.

"At this place? Always," said the receptionist. She lowered her voice to a whisper and said, "These people are workaholics, if you know what I mean."

The two shared a laugh at this. The receptionist said, "I'll let Mr. Morris know you're here."

They waited for about two minutes until Clara whispered something to Ranger Scott, who sauntered up to the reception desk again.

"I'm so sorry. A couple of us need to use the restroom. If you'd be able to buzz us in, that's right where we'll be when Wilbur comes up."

"Oh, I'm sure that'd be okay." She reached for something, and a buzzing came from the door that led inside. Ranger Scott opened it and thanked her again. The five of them slipped into Silver Labs.

The bathroom was just around the first corner, and they huddled at its entrance. The hallway continued a short way before opening up into a large area of cubicles with walled offices and conference rooms behind large windows. Beyond this area, they remembered that one of the doors on the right side was for Lab 151.

"Okay, we've all been here. We can do this," said Jack.

Ranger Scott said, "You all hide in the bathroom until Mr. Morris comes. Chances are he won't even know it's more than me unless the receptionist mentions it."

"And if she does, I'll come out and we'll convince him it's just the two of us," Renn added.

Ranger Scott said, "Good luck, kids. All y'all got moxy, I'll give you that."

Jack watched the girls disappear into their bathroom. He and Dom did the same into the men's room.

They waited.

Jack washed his hands and ran his wet hands through his blond hair, shook them and wiped them on his jeans. *Well, this is getting real*, he thought. He looked over at Dom who had been pacing the bathroom for five minutes, his lips moving as he muttered to himself. For the thousandth time, Jack considered the wisdom of bringing him into this affair. He had come a long way already, though, and Jack was proud of him.

"Hey, Dom, how you doing?"

"I'm okay, a little nervous."

"What's our probability of success?"

"Am I a robot or something?"

Jack laughed. "No, no. I think of you more like *A Beautiful Mind*."

Dom stopped pacing. "*A Beautiful Mind*. Yeah, John Nash was cool. Except you know what the difference is?"

"What?"

"Nash only imagined people were out to get him. There really is someone out to get us. At least two."

Jack had to give him that one. He closed the space between them and faced his friend. "Listen, Dom. Sameer is just another bully, right? He's going to get his due."

"Great, just what I need. Another bully. But our biggest concern right now is Eric, isn't it?"

Another point for Dom. Not only was there a very good chance that Eric was in the building, he might be sitting in front of a row of monitors looking at camera feeds. He might have already seen them for all they knew. They might have to get out of Silver Labs fast. "When we get to the lab, let's scout out the camera situation so we can stay out of its view as much as possible."

"Or we could use lemon juice."

Jack looked over at Dom and tried to figure out if he was joking or serious. "What?"

"There was a man who tried robbing a bank and got caught. He asked the police how they identified him and they said the security camera. He insisted that wasn't possible because he had the 'juice.' Turns out, he heard somewhere that if you rub lemon juice on your face, cameras can't see you."

"Ha, that's hilarious. Criminals are so stupid."

Dom's voice was soft and frightened. "Jack?"

"Yeah?"

"Are we criminals?"

Oh boy, talk about splitting hairs. "No, Dom. We're not criminals. I promise."

The ranger's voice came from the hallway, talking to someone else. A knocking sound reached them and Jack made out that he was calling for someone. He was asking after Renn.

"I don't think this is good," said Dom.

The voices receded after a minute, and they stayed put just in case, counting the seconds. There came a light rapping at their door. Jack looked at Dom and his worried expression mirrored Jack's own. He cracked open the bathroom door. Clara stood alone in the hallway. Jack exhaled and motioned for Dom to follow as he swung open the door and stepped out to join Clara.

"What happened?" asked Jack.

"The dude who met the ranger knew there was supposed to be more than one person and asked where the others were."

"Great. Well, we expected that might happen. So, Renn had to go with them." Jack laid it out as a cold, hard fact. "Five minutes in and we're down a person. We still doing this?"

Clara and Dom nodded, and Jack tried to offer a reassuring look. The stakes kept growing in this strange game they found themselves playing. Jack walked to the open cubicle area and surveyed it. He didn't see anyone. The cubicles were the kind with tall walls. If someone was standing up and tall enough, you'd be able to see the top of their head, but only from far enough away. He turned towards the others, shrugged, and beckoned with his arm.

Together they walked through the area towards the next section of hallway. At the corner on the right was a conference room with large glass windows, the widest section facing them as they approached. Three people in their twenties sat around the table working on their laptops. Whether they even noticed the three teens, Jack couldn't say. He kept his face forward and his stride purposeful. Ten seconds later the right side of the hallway became a large, long window and after the window, next to the long room's door, was mounted a placard that simply read "151."

Jack looked up and down the hallway. All clear. He opened the door, let Dom and Clara in, and slipped in behind them. They had made it to Lab 151.

Chapter 35

Jack's heart jumped up to his throat and thumped a few extra beats. He stared into a white half-dome security camera mounted on the ceiling in front of them. It was impossible to tell if the camera inside pointed at them or if someone was monitoring its feed. He pushed Dom and Clara forward until they stood beneath the dome. He didn't think it could tilt to look straight down. Maybe they were in a blind spot.

They were at one end of the long room, near the far wall. Looking down the length of the room, Jack saw the four large 3D printers standing away from the walls. Each one must have been four by six feet, and at least eight feet tall. The walls, metal on the bottom, became clear Plexiglas around the top half. The large printing mechanisms were visible through the transparent sides. At the far end of the room, on their side, another half-dome surveyed the room with its lidless eye.

Jack stifled a curse and guided them in between the middle two printers, where they ducked low. This appeared to be a blind spot for both cameras. If there was a third camera, he didn't know what they would do. Dom shook Jack's arm and pointed to the wide front of the room and up. Jack mentally kicked himself. Most of the front wall consisted of window. They had looked in here from the outside not two minutes ago.

"Aren't there any blind spots in here?" he whispered.

Clara got on her hands and knees and crawled around the front side of a printer, keeping it between her and the cameras. By hugging the front wall, a passerby would have to look straight down, and still might not see them. Jack tagged Dom and motioned for them to follow Clara's lead.

Clara kept crawling until she was able to peek around the corner of the last printer. She turned and waved. Jack joined her and she whispered, "I think I see the lockbox. It looks a little like a mini-fridge in the far corner."

Jack leaned out to look. Sure enough, there it sat. He could tell it wasn't a refrigerator because of the keypad on its front, and the turning handle. "Okay, I'll go open it."

Clara nodded and switched from her crawl to sit against the wall.

Jack checked the numbers on his phone and wondered what would happen if he got the code wrong. He pictured lights flashing red and a wailing siren. He shook off the thought and scurried over to the lockbox where he was most likely in view of a security camera again.

"Here goes nothing," he muttered, punching in the numbers and the hash symbol. A soft, satisfying click came from the door and a green light came on. Jack turned the handle and tugged. The door swung open. If only Renn were here to see this.

The lockbox had two shelves, giving it three levels of storage. It looked to be about two feet deep. Stacked on each level were papers, blueprints, and folders. Jack didn't bother looking through any of these. Renn had told them what Owen had said. If there was any stolen data in here, it wouldn't be in plain sight. This made sense. Lots of people used this safe, and someone would notice papers that didn't belong. He bent over to look deep into the unit, stuck his hands in and reached around. Jack lifted the stacks and looked under them. He assumed they were looking for another thumb drive, but it might be in some other form.

Jack crawled back to where Clara and Dom hid.

"There's nothing there," Jack said, resting his head against the beige metal surface of the printer. "There's nothing there."

"Let me look," said Clara, even as she scooted towards the lockbox.

Jack thought about stopping her, but waved her on. "Be my guest."

While Clara searched, Jack turned his attention back to the nearest printer. From his kneel, his head was level with the machine's control panel. To the left of the panel was a slot that contained a book. He slipped it out and inspected the thick user's manual. He sat back beside Dom and started skimming the pages.

This was all so crazy. He would have loved to come back and look around Silver Labs some more, but not this way. And they were a person down already. He hated that Renn couldn't be here with them. They needed her, but she was outside walking around the grounds with Ranger Scott and the groundskeeper.

Jack flipped the page, saw something interesting. A list of function codes for the printer ran down the page. Different codes did different things, like run a self-maintenance function, or a diagnostic, or print a test model. They were all three-digit numbers preceded by an asterisk. And that made him think of the puzzle's last number, *99. He scanned furiously but could not find any numbers below 100.

"Are these the bio-printers?" asked Clara.

Jack looked up to find that Dom and Clara had switched, and she now sat beside him.

"No." He pointed to some spools of material with colors ranging from silver to gold. "I think these printers all use metal. They probably make parts for some of their products."

"Maybe they make other printers," said Dom, his arm disappeared in the recesses of the lockbox. "Like machines making machines, reproducing."

"Dom, this may be the only time I tell you you've been watching too many movies," Jack said.

"Hey, I found it!" Dom said. He withdrew his arm and held out a small object. He crawled back, and they all tried to get out of view of the security camera.

"Where?" Jack said.

Dom showed them the small case he'd retrieved. "This is magnetic. It was stuck to the underside of the bottom shelf, about halfway back." He slid the cover off to reveal a thumb drive with a Sliver Labs logo on it.

"How did we miss that?" Clara wondered out loud.

"I used spatial reasoning," said Dom matter-of-factly.

Jack chuckled at this. "Dude, I have good spatial reasoning."

Dom shrugged his shoulders.

"I have spatial reasoning, too!" insisted Clara.

"Yeah, but men have more of it than women do," teased Jack.

Clara elbowed him in the ribs. "You can take your spatial reasoning and..."

Jack coughed and held up his hands. "Okay, okay. I give up."

"We don't have a way to see what's on here, do we?" asked Dom.

Clara pulled out her phone and a little adapter cable and said, "Here, let me have it."

Dom handed her the thumb drive, and she plugged it into the wide end of the adapter. The narrow end she plugged into the charging port on her phone. She messed with her screen a bit and smiled.

"Here's a list of files. I don't have the right apps to open most of them." She whistled. "Wow, they're working on flying cars!"

"No way," whispered Jack. "Don't show me, I don't even want to know anymore." He turned his attention back to the printer and started fiddling with the control panel.

"Uh, are you sure you want to do that?" asked Dom.

"Well, it's part of the puzzle. I figure that last number is a special function code that makes it print something."

The control panel was different, and more complicated, than the one at school. But it was similar enough for Jack to feel familiar with its operation. He flipped a rocker switch that made the machine come to life, thankfully without much sound. It looked like he just needed to go into settings and poke around for... aha. He punched in the function code 99, but nothing happened and the number remained on the screen.

"I think it expects to get three digits," said Clara, who had been looking over his shoulder. "Try *099."

Jack smirked, but he tried her suggestion. The printer whirred into life. The print head danced around behind the Plexiglas and lay down a silvery material.

"We should get out of here, guys." Dom craned his neck to see through the window behind them.

Jack understood how Dom felt. He was nervous and a little scared, just like before a big game. Every atom in his body vibrated a little faster. If you didn't understand how to harness that energy it would eat you up alive. But the way Jack saw it, if the cameras had seen them, they'd have already been caught. They should be okay for a few minutes longer.

He turned his attention to Clara, who still scrolled through cache files on her phone. How did that even work? "How do you know so much about this stuff, Clara? You figured out the printer code. You've got a dope laptop and know how to use it."

Clara shrugged and avoided eye contact.

Pieces clicked into place, like the tangram, and he blurted, "Wait, I've got it!"

Clara looked like a caged bird. Her eyes darted every direction, as if looking for escape routes.

Jack continued, "You took Mr. Ahring's computer class, didn't you? My friend Noah took it last semester and learned a lot."

Clara let out an explosive breath and said, "Yup, you got me. I'm actually interested in computers."

"Do you game? I'm guessing you do or you wouldn't need the Alienware."

Clara shrugged again. "A little."

Jack's perception of this girl was changing moment by moment. "I'm sorry, Clara, I judged you by your cover when we met. I was wrong."

Clara's face flushed, and she made brief eye contact with him. She mumbled, "Thanks."

"Can we *please* go?" said Dom.

He was right. Every minute they stayed was a risk they didn't need to take. Jack perched on his knees to look through the Plexiglas window. It was so much faster than the one at school.

It might only take ten minutes. The piece was already an inch high. Jack couldn't yet make out what it was.

The door to Lab 151 sprung open with a loud bang and Thor strode into the room. Not Thor, Jack reminded himself. The name was Eric. He wore a security guard uniform. It didn't look like he carried a gun. Two other guards followed him into the room and waited for instructions. Eric reached across his body to a walkie-talkie clipped to his shoulder. He turned his chin towards it without ever taking his eyes off the three intruders. "We've got them."

Jack tensed up like a steel spring. He was smaller and weaker than Eric, but he was also responsible for Dom and Clara, and he intended to protect them.

"Hi, kids!" Eric said cheerfully. His smile looked painted on and didn't come close to reaching his eyes. "Let's go. Don't make a scene."

Dom looked resigned to his fate, and Clara was nowhere to be seen. There was no hiding in here. What was she doing?

Eric motioned one of the guards to the far side of the room to look for her, but she stepped out from behind the printer. She had a wild look in her eyes, like she was ready for a fight. Jack knew then, if he tried to fight his way out, Clara would be right there with him. He didn't want to risk her or Dom getting hurt.

Jack stood and raised his hands above his head. "Okay, okay."

The three of them shuffled out of Lab 151 under the watchful eye of Eric and the two guards.

They'd been caught a few minutes from freedom.

Chapter 36

Renn followed Ranger Scott and Mr. Morris down the hallway. She was disappointed she didn't get to stay with her friends to investigate the final cache. This was the first indoor geocache she'd ever hunted. Renn felt ready to be done with her hobby. Look what it had gotten them into. Plus, she had found all the caches in Black Hawk Bend, legitimate and illegitimate, so there was that.

"Scott, I was thinking we could talk in my office today. We've already walked the property together."

Renn looked up to see Mr. Morris talking to Ranger Scott. He was tan, even this far into the year, but also overweight and out of shape.

"Why, that'd be just fine, Wilbur. They've given you an office finally, have they?"

"It's not the Ritz, but it does the job."

They passed Lab 151 and Renn looked in wistfully at the empty room. But they kept following the hallway to its end. Mr. Morris opened the door on the left and led them into a stairwell. Renn followed the two men down a level where the stairs ended. Great, the basement. They would put the groundskeeper in the basement where nothing important ever happened.

The basement of Silver Labs wasn't anything like the basement of the hospital. Instead of concrete walls and exposed lighting fixtures, this was a finished hallway that looked the same as the one above. The ceiling seemed lower and created a slightly claustrophobic feel.

They walked a ways and Renn heard the ding of an elevator. She didn't remember seeing an elevator on the first floor. It must have been off the main path. Instinctively, Renn positioned herself on the far side of Ranger Scott, using him as a screen. She wasn't sure why; in her role with the ranger, her presence here was completely legitimate.

They arrived at a room, or suite of rooms, with long windows to the hallway on this level, kind of similar to Lab 151, at least from the outside. Renn looked in and saw some monitors, similar to the hospital. They passed the main door to the suite. The glass was stenciled with the word "Security." The hair on the back of her neck stood up, and she hugged even closer to the ranger's side. She caught a glimpse of two men emerge from a side hallway on their left. The three of them did not stop, but Mr. Morris said, "Eric. Got any money on the game?"

The voice that replied belonged to Thor and chilled her blood. "You know it, Wilbur. It's going to be a great weekend."

"Good luck."

Renn shivered and felt goosebumps on her arms. She heard Eric and the other man enter the security office and breathed a sigh of relief. She wondered if he had seen her; chose to believe that since she had not seen him, it worked the other way, too. It was the only thing keeping her from having a cardiac event.

She almost ran into Mr. Morris, who had stopped short two doors down from Security. He unlocked the door and showed them inside. His office was tiny and had no windows. Adding to the claustrophobic effect, his desk was overflowing with topographical maps and surveys. Other than his chair behind the desk, there was only one other chair in the office, which Ranger Scott offered to Renn. She was still contemplating the fact that Eric was only a couple of rooms away when she heard her name.

"Huh?"

"I said, what are you doing for your internship with Ranger Scott?" Mr. Morris said.

"Oh, I, um, I'm interested in learning about conservation. And sustainability."

The ranger described conservation efforts at the park that Renn had never heard of, watersheds and prairie grass. She tried to pay attention in case she was quizzed about them but couldn't stop thinking about Eric. Of course, they knew there was a chance he'd be working, and there was no way they could avoid all the security cameras all the time. They had hoped to minimize their time in the building and their chances of being seen. With any luck, the other three were already on their way back out.

The bigger question in Renn's mind was who at Silver Labs could they trust? She didn't believe for a minute that Eric was the mastermind behind the embezzlement plot. He was the hired muscle. He and Owen had complete access around the building in which put them in a perfect position to smuggle secrets out of the lab. Chances were, any random employee she talked to would be on the up and up. However, they would run it up the chain of command and it might run right into the ringleader. It was an impossible situation.

"I'm also interested in other things Silver Labs does. I've been writing a paper on how 3D printing can be used to lay down organic tissue."

Mr. Morris' eyes glazed over at the shift to tech. "Does anyone here do that, Adrienne?" he asked.

"Well, they have lots of 3D printers, but I don't know what kinds of materials they use. I wanted to ask someone about it. Do you think I could do that today? I mean, after this meeting?"

Mr. Morris gave Ranger Scott a look, amusement or consternation? "We can check who all is still in the building then. Even though it's the weekend, the hardcore folks might be about."

Renn conjured her best charming high school girl persona and clapped her hands in joy. "Oh, thank you, Mr. Morris."

The two men resumed their conversation. Mr. Morris pulled a map from the stack on his desk and gestured to a marked location. Renn leaned forward and feigned interest, but she strained to hear anything outside the room. Sweetly, she said, "Mr. Morris, I'm so sorry, is it getting hot in here? Do you mind if I prop the door open a little?"

"Oh, of course. Sorry, it does get stuffy in here. There's a doorstop on the floor."

She used the doorstop to prop the door open about three inches and walked back to the desk. Now she could listen for activity from the hallway. She wanted nothing more than to text Jack to see how they were doing, but she knew it would be rude to user phone at the moment.

She thought about Stella and wondered how the sweet girl fared back in her safe cage at the Raptor Center. Another revelation struck her about two of her favorite places in Black Hawk Bend. The Raptor Center and Wappoke Zoo involved animals in cages. She didn't quite know what to make of that, except that she could relate with them at the moment. It wasn't a good feeling.

Soft voices leaked into the room from the hallway, and Renn strained to discern the words. Something, something about—Jack!

"They showed up on camera in Lab 151 about ten minutes ago. We think there are four youths involved."

Eric's voice sounded authoritative, controlled. She heard none of the rage they had experienced at the zoo. Well, they had given him some trouble that day.

"Vasquez, you check the logs in the lobby and find out names and how they got in. I'll take Finn and Smitty to the lab and retrieve the kids."

Renn pulled out her phone and sent a quick message of warning to Jack, prayed that he would get it. What should she do? In a minute they could be in custody and Eric would know where to look for her and Ranger Scott. She could use Mr. Morris' help, but didn't think he'd want to stick his neck out for them.

"I'm so sorry, is there a restroom nearby?" It worked once, maybe it would work again.

Mr. Morris barely looked up from the map he and Ranger Scott were pointing at. "Sure, just down the hallway on your left, not the way we came from."

"Oh, thank you, Mr. Morris. I'll be right back, Scott." She laid her hand on the Ranger's arm as she spoke, hoping he would take the unusual familiarity as a sign that all was not well. Then she stepped out into the empty hallway and jogged back towards the stairwell they had descended earlier.

Renn sprinted up the stairs back to the main level and pulled open the door to the long hallway. All seemed quiet. What did that mean? She poked her head out of the stairwell and looked down its length. She saw the door to Lab 151, but there was no activity. Where was Eric? She stood frozen, racked with indecision. If she entered the hallway, she would be very exposed.

Capturing her courage in a deep gulp of air, Renn stepped out into the hallway. Jack and the others depended on her warning them about Eric. She took one step, heard the ding of the arriving elevator, and dashed back to the protection of the stairwell. She cracked the door to peek out. Her chest tightened and she clamped a hand over her mouth. Three security guards marched into Lab 151. Precious seconds ticked by. Renn could hear talking. Then Jack, Dom, and Clara emerged from the room, escorted by the guards. They headed to the elevator, probably back down to Security.

Renn slid down against the cement wall into a sit with her knees drawn up to her chin. Watery pools threatened to spill onto her cheeks. What had gone wrong? She'd tried to warn Jack. She should have stayed with them, or they should have canceled and tried again later. Everything was going wrong.

Renn sniffed and wiped her eyes. This wasn't the time to lose it. She knew as well as anyone that it had to be today. This couldn't be how their story ended, it just couldn't. Renn had to find a way to take back control of the situation. But who could she trust?

She only knew a single employee of Silver Labs who hadn't tried to capture her or who she hadn't put in jail. Now, please let him be "hardcore" enough to be here on a Saturday.

Stepping out into the empty hallway, Renn took a few tentative steps, broke into a jog, and then a run, until she reached the staff cubicles. Where was it? Right turn, halfway down, cut across the cubicles. She kept her head up, tried not to care about the few people who stared at her from their walled-in workstations.

Where was his office?

She stood in front of the glass window of an office, but it was empty and she did not recognize the name next to the door. Renn leaned her forehead against the glass and ran through the maze of cubicles in her head. A tap on her shoulder startled her, causing her to jerk around, eyes wide.

A young woman offered a friendly smile. "Can I help you? Are you lost? This place can be kind of like a maze." She glanced at Renn's visitor badge. "Who are you supposed to be with?"

"Oh, thank you." Renn tried to sound lost, and it wasn't much of a stretch. "I went to the restroom and got all turned around in here. I was looking for Dr. Edmunds' office. I thought it was right here."

The young woman offered an understanding smile. "Ah, that explains it. You're just off by a mirror image. I guess you zigged when you should have zagged. Come on, I'll walk you over."

Renn followed the woman towards and across the main hallway. Halfway through this section she turned, knocked on a door, and opened it.

"Lew, I found a lost puppy. I guess she's one of yours."

Renn looked in through the office window and saw Lewis Edmunds hunched in front of his three-screen computer setup. Strewn around his desk and shelves, pictures and little figures, some still in boxes, marked this as the office of a true geek. The man had quite a pop vinyl collection. He glanced towards the door, then at Renn, bemused. Renn nodded her head and mouthed the word "please" through the glass. After an agonizing few seconds, he waved them into his office.

"Thanks, Shelly. I just got distracted here, I guess."

Renn hurried in and said, "So sorry, Dr. Edmunds. I got lost after going to the bathroom."

Shelly waved bye to them both and closed the door behind her. Lewis studied her, trying to place her. "You look familiar. Star Wars or Star Trek?"

"Um, neither?"

"Nonsense. Mythic hero's journey or technological humanist allegory?"

"I guess the first one."

"Great. Star Wars, then. I remember you from the school tour. What brings you back to Silver Labs?"

"Dr. Edmunds," Renn began.

"Call me Lewis."

"Uh, Lewis, are you loyal? To Silver Labs, I mean?"

"Of course, I've worked here my entire career."

Renn glanced out the office window behind her to make sure they were alone. "My friends and I discovered that someone has been sneaking intellectual property out on thumb drives. Two of the security guards are involved and Sameer Bakshi is blackmailing us to collect the information for him. We're trying to stop it, but we don't know who to trust. My friends just got captured by one of the security guards and I don't know what's going to happen to them."

The words rushed out of her as if from a burst dam. There was no use trying to filter them, and she didn't dare breathe until they were all out.

Lewis leaned back into his chair, causing it to roll back across his working space. "Sameer Bakshi!" He spat the name as if it were a curse. He rolled back up to his desk, pulled a notepad and pen from the drawer and leaned in towards Renn. "Okay. Slow down and start again from the beginning."

Chapter 37

Jack tried the door one more time, putting all his weight into the effort. In frustration, he slammed his body against it.

"Is that making you feel better?" asked Clara.

"Yes. Yes, it is." The frustration and helplessness had been building up inside him ever since Eric had found them in Lab 151. They were so close. How much earlier could they have left if Jack hadn't messed with the printer? Probably only half a minute, but it could have been enough. They might have gotten out of the building. He wondered for the hundredth time how Renn was holding up. She must be bored out of her skin walking the grounds with the ranger and groundskeeper. He had hoped he might send her a message, but Eric had taken their phones before sticking them in this room.

Clara looked annoyed. Dom looked scared.

Jack felt guilty and responsible. "You guys see anything we can use in here?"

Dom picked up the receiver of an office phone. "The phone is dead."

Clara, who had opened every desk drawer and cabinet door, said, "No, there's nothing here, unless you can use a stapler or a marker?"

Jack forced a degree of lightness he did not feel. "Who

knows? We beat Eric with a little jalapeno juice last time. Maybe we could staple them all to the wall."

This room was part of the security suite. It opened into the main security office that looked out into the basement hallway. There was a window and they could open the shades and look out into the main office, for all the good that would do them. For now, Jack was content that they couldn't see outside and Eric couldn't see in.

How could this be any worse? "Hey, Clara, did they take the thumb drive off you?"

At this Clara smiled and shook her head from side to side. "Nope. I had time to hide it."

That must be what she was doing out of sight. "Was anyone able to close the lockbox? Did we leave it open?"

"I think it's closed," said Dom. "I swung it shut. I'm not sure it locked, though."

"Well, that's something, at least. I guess now we have to sneak back into Lab 151."

"After escaping from this place," Clara reminded him.

Jack stretched out in his chair and set his feet up on the desk. "There's nothing to do at the moment. Try to relax and not go crazy. Renn and Ranger Scott will be here to bail us out soon." He closed his eyes and focused on his breath. A headache was forming, and he still needed to be on his game.

A pounding on the door interrupted his meditation. Cracking one eye, he saw Clara standing at the door with raised fist.

"I want my phone call!" she shouted.

Jack heard the lock turn and sat up in his chair. The door opened and one of the security guards, not Eric, stepped halfway into the room.

"What's the commotion in here? I thought we told you to

keep it down."

"Sorry," Jack said. "How long are you going to keep us in here?"

"Not much longer," said the guard. "Just chill. I don't want to hear any more out of you."

"Or what?" said Clara defiantly. "And when do I get my phone call? I have rights!"

The guard laughed and shut the door, leaving them once again alone.

Dom leaned forward on the desk, resting his head on his arms. From his hidden face, Jack heard his voice and caught a note of despondence. "We're never getting out of here."

Jack wasn't too worried. Renn and the ranger might not even know they'd been caught. Once they did, it wouldn't be long. They would make up some story about kids exploring and it would be okay. Everything would be okay. But Clara and Dom seemed to be suffering from the stress. He needed to keep them occupied on something else.

"So, Dom. You ever wonder how GPS works?"

Dom lifted his head from his arms and looked thoughtful. He recited everything he knew about GPS satellites and how they made geocaching possible.

Jack tried to listen as his thoughts swirled around, touching on Renn, Sameer, Lab 151 and the printer, football, caches. His head ached dully, but it was better than the zoo.

Chapter 38

Renn had to break into a jog to keep up with Lewis. Boy, that man could walk fast when he wanted to. They covered the distance to Lab 151 in silence, but as he opened the door and invited Renn to enter the lab he said, "This will not stand. That snake Bakshi isn't going to get away with it again. No way."

He went to a back corner of the room and tried the door of a cabinet. It turned out to be the lockbox. He punched in the code and it buzzed open. He spent half a minute rooting around through it before sitting up on his knees. "Do you know if they found the cache?"

"Sorry, I don't."

He extended his hand, and Renn helped him up to his feet. Lewis noticed the printer buzzing around behind its Plexiglas case. Renn looked at the piece and thought it looked like a small trophy, about four or five inches tall. It appeared to be almost complete.

Lewis put his fingers on the Plexiglas window and watched the printer head do its mesmerizing dance for a few seconds. He turned and gave Renn a smile. "I designed this piece, you know."

"You did?" Renn replied. "What is it?"

"We needed a reward for our game, so I designed this little

trophy in about twenty minutes. I wrote one of the poems, too."

Renn distinctly remembered mocking each of those poems, maybe more than was warranted, but they were pretty dumb. "Really? Which one?"

"It was something about thirteen types of complexity, I can't remember. Did you like it?"

A memory came flooding back of beat-boxing as Jack read it aloud. But it was sort of catchy. "You wrote that? It was pretty good, but I'm no judge of poetry."

Lewis chuckled. "Somehow I don't think I have your honest opinion. Anyway, I had recently seen Hamilton and I remember channeling it, like it was inspired or something."

He seemed to be caught up in a reverie of the time when Silver Labs first opened this campus and they put together the team-building game. Renn felt funny about interrupting, but something had been nagging her.

"What do you mean 'again'?"

"Hmm," Lewis murmured.

"You said Sameer wouldn't get away with it again. Has he done this before?"

Lewis grunted and said, "He's tried. Jason and Sameer hate each other, ever since their falling out."

"When Jason left their company," Renn interjected.

"Right. Now they try to poach talent from each other as much as they can. It's almost like a competition. I've been recruited by Sameer's people more times than I can count now. But Sameer is dirty about it. I mean, he just doesn't have any limits. He'll lie, cheat, and steal if it gives him an edge over Jason. No, this scheme doesn't surprise me one bit."

Lewis spun around and kicked the lockbox door closed. He

swept past Renn towards the door and waved her to follow. "Come on. Let's get some more help." He led them up a flight of stairs, taking two at a time. They entered the large common area with its comfy couches, egg chairs, and ping pong tables. Two people reclined on couches with open laptops.

Renn caught up with Lewis. "Do we need to tell anyone else? The more people who know..."

Lewis held up a hand. "We're going straight to the director of operations. She's Jason's right-hand person here. She's been on a fast track ever since she graduated MIT at the top of her class. She loves this place as much as any of us and would never let anything happen to it."

As on the first floor, offices and conference rooms lined the perimeter of the space. Lewis led them to a large office with a panoramic view of the woods outside. He knocked and waited for a faint "come in" before opening the door.

"Julia, Sameer is up to his old tricks again." Lewis began explaining even as they entered the office, and Renn saw that Julia Bouchard sat across a large metallic desk from them. Her workstation stood behind her, facing the woods, and it was elevated so she'd have to stand to get any work done. The atmosphere seemed very austere and sterile to Renn. She didn't see any family photos or personal knickknacks like Lewis had in his office.

Julia beckoned them in and stepped to the interior windows, where she closed blinds to obscure their view of the common space. The three of them started talking in hushed tones. Julia encouraged Renn to share the whole story. How had Sameer contacted them? What exactly was he asking them to do? At moments during the story, Renn thought she caught real emotion flash across the woman's face, but very quickly, a mask of perfect control covered it up.

When Renn finished, Julia reoriented to face Lewis and said, "You did the right thing in bringing her to me, Lewis. This needs to be handled delicately, and I know just what to do." She reached out and set her hand on his shoulder. "How long have you worked this week? You look tired."

"Oh, just my normal schedule."

"You should go home and get some rest. You work too much anyway. I'll take care of this. Listen, before you go though, I need you to do something for me."

"Sure, what?"

"I won't have time to drop these reports off in Jason's office. Could you do it for me? He's going to be in on Monday morning." She gave Lewis a sugary sweet smile, and he grinned and nodded in return. Renn rolled her eyes at how easily Julia manipulated him. Then she remembered how she had played the same game with Mr. Morris and the nachos vendor.

Julia handed a folder to Lewis and opened the door for Renn to exit the office. Renn turned back and said, "Thank you for helping me. And believing me." Then they were walking across the open area away from Lewis, towards the elevator.

Julia's hand rested on Renn's shoulder, firm and strong. Her voice was gentle, maybe even compassionate. She spoke in soothing tones as they walked. "We're going to go find your friends, okay? Everything is going to be all right."

In the elevator, Julia punched the button for the basement and bent at the waist, bringing her face closer to Renn's. She flashed a reassuring smile and said, "Listen, Adrienne, I'm going to make sure that Sameer doesn't hurt you or your friends, but we're going to need all the evidence you've collected so far. Do you have the drives with you?"

Something about the question made Renn uncomfortable. It reminded her that she, and her friends, had been sneaking around, collecting secret, stolen data from Silver Labs, apparently for Jason Silver's main competition.

"We don't have it with us. It's safe though, and we were never going to give it to him, I promise."

"I know, dear. You're not in any trouble." Julia patted Renn's shoulder in the stiff manner of someone who has never actually had to comfort a child.

The elevator doors opened, and they walked towards the security office. Renn's discomfort only grew. How would Eric react when she strolled in with Julia? About the only thing that reassured her at this point was that Ranger Scott was here, too. He was her lifeline. On impulse she said, "Just a minute, I need to check something." She broke Julia's grip and darted to Mr. Morris' office.

Julia shimmied after Renn as quickly as her heels would allow. "Adrienne, wait! What are you doing?"

Renn tried his door, but it was locked. She knocked and called his name, but there was no answer. Then Julia was there, her hand on Renn's shoulder again. "Whose office is this?" she demanded.

"Mr. Morris, the groundskeeper. I... I met him once. Never mind." Renn turned and walked the two doors down to the security office with Julia at her side. At least she would see her friends and they'd be able to get out of here.

Julia opened the door and let Renn enter before her. Two guards sat at a table drinking coffee, and Renn recognized one of them as Eric. Another guard sat at a counter scanning a row of monitors.

Eric looked up, and seeing Renn and Julia, leaned back in his chair and raised one eyebrow in question. "Good day, Ms. Bouchard. What can we do for you?"

"We've come to reunite Adrienne with her friends. Are they here?"

"Yes, ma'am. We caught them up in Lab 151 messing around."

"Have you contacted the parents or authorities yet?"

"Not yet, ma'am. We were looking for this one still." Eric nodded towards Renn.

"Well, she's found us. Can we *conference*?"

Renn picked up an odd vibe from Julia's choice of words and the strained tone of her voice.

Eric nodded and stood. He walked over to the counter and picked up a clipboard, studied it. He said, "Smitty, why don't you do your rounds now. Take Vasquez with you." The guard sitting at the counter returned a terse verbal assent, and then the two guards left the room.

When it was just the three of them, Julia released Renn's shoulder and started pacing. "You idiot! How could you let this happen?"

Eric's smile, his general sense of amusement, did not change, and perhaps increased. "I don't remember letting them into the building and giving them free range of the place."

"You're security!" Julia shouted it, but regained control after a brief glance towards Renn. "You were supposed to put an end to this before it got this far."

Eric's smile dimmed, and he shot a predatory glare in Renn's direction. "Well, we've got them now."

"Yes, but not the drives."

The realization had already come over Renn, like a dark

shadow blocking the sun, that she should not be here, but it was too late. She inched back towards the door while they talked, froze when Eric glared at her. Renn decided she had one chance to make a break for it, so she did. She turned and lunged for the door. It opened a crack before Julia was there, slamming it shut again.

"Whatever are you doing, Adrienne? I told you you'd see your friends again, and you will." Julia nodded towards Eric and said, "Put her with the others."

"You, you, how could you?" Renn sputtered, caught halfway between anger and panic, between attacking Julia and hyper-ventilating. Julia's dark laughter rang in her head. Then Eric's meaty hand was on her back while his other unlocked a door to a side room, opening the door, pushing her inside, shutting it behind her.

How could she have been so fooled? Her worst fear had come true. She had trusted the wrong person. She focused on slowing her breathing, and gradually, her heart rate slowed as well. The sound of pounding blood in her ears faded. What just happened? It was all so surreal.

She surveyed the room but didn't comprehend the scene. Jack, Dom, and Clara huddled around an office desk. Dom had a black dry erase marker and was writing something. In fact, the whole desk was covered in black markings, pictures, and equations. Jack was asking Dom questions. So was Clara, only she seemed to have forgotten English because hers came out as a steady rapid stream of Spanish. She didn't think Jack or Dom knew Spanish. Surreal.

Jack turned from the desk and rushed over. "Renn, you're here!"

"What's going on here?" she asked.

Dom replied distantly, "We're trying to figure out how they can use nine satellites to solve for three variables." He added something about too many equations.

Clara waved at Dom's scribbling and said in a pained voice, "Ay!"

Jack gripped Renn's shoulders. "So are you here to get us out? Where's Ranger Scott?"

Renn slumped in Jack's firm grip. "I was, but now I'm in here with you." She broke Jack's grip and made her way to a chair, sagged down into it. "Jack, it was Julia Bouchard. She's the brains behind this whole thing. And she's working with Sameer, and we're all trapped in here."

Chapter 39

Renn leaned against the wall, slumped in a low-backed office chair, lost in her own thoughts. How long had it been, ten minutes? Fifteen? Dom still studied the desk, tapping its surface with the marker. Clara lay on the other desk, set against the wall, her hood pulled up around her head. Jack had his chair tipped back on its hind legs with his feet propped up on the central desk, his head lolling back.

At first they heard shouting from the other side of the door. After several minutes, the noise died down, and then nothing. Despite her worry, fatigue set in and she drifted in and out of consciousness. She half expected that Ranger Scott and Mr. Morris would come through the door any second. They had been only two doors down the hallway a little while ago. She wondered if the ranger had sensed something wrong. She had never called him by his first name in her life.

Renn heard the lock turn in the door. She jumped up, hoping to see the ranger, but it was Julia. She stepped into the office prison and carefully shut the door behind her. Not one hair was out of place, and she wore freshly applied lipstick.

"My man is just outside the door and will deal harshly with you if I don't return safely in five minutes. In case you had any bright ideas."

"Your man, Eric?" Renn hissed.

Julia shot Renn a disapproving look but did not respond. "I've been thinking about what to do with you. You've all caused me a significant amount of trouble, and I'd like nothing more than to dump you in the Mississippi." She ran one hand along her hair, checking for loose strands. "But I'm a reasonable woman. All I want is to get out of this miserable hick town back to some kind of civilization. I have a position waiting for me once we clear this unpleasantness up."

Instinctively, Renn understood what Julia meant. "You want to go work for Sameer. Well, it seems to me that he's been trying to get Silver Lab's secrets without you." Her tone of voice, the look in her eyes, her posture, all held accusations. "Why would you go work for him?"

Julia was unperturbed. "The data he tried to blackmail out of you was—is—going to get me my signing bonus. He thought if he could get it from you directly, he could weasel out of paying it. Just business, you see? If I were in his position, I might try the same tactic."

Jack had sat up and turned his chair to face her when she came in. "You're kidding. All for a signing bonus? That couldn't possibly be worth embezzling or blackmail. What are we talking about here?"

Julia told them the figure and Jack whistled and slumped in his seat. Julia continued, "I don't tell you this to impress you. I only want you all to understand the stakes at play. We will come to an agreement before you leave this room." Her matter-of-fact tone left no doubt about the veracity of her statement.

"So how much is it worth to you?" asked Clara.

"Clara!" Renn's head snapped around to stare at Clara, who

still had her hood up but now sat erect on the edge of the desk.

Julia laughed, a husky, deep-throated sound. "That's more like it! Let's start with Sameer's deal. You will turn over all data you're in possession of. Otherwise, his promises to ruin your young lives will be carried out. On the other hand, if you do deliver the data and promise to forget this ever happened, I'll reward you for your efforts. It has to be something that won't draw attention. How about $10,000 cash for each of you? A little spending money that will keep you in Air Jordans, or whatever it is kids are into these days."

Renn snorted in disgust, and so did Clara. Dom sat silent and slack-jawed at the desk.

Jack said, "Can we have a few minutes to talk it over?"

"Of course," said Julia. "I'll give you fifteen minutes." Then she knocked on the door three times and slipped out when it opened for her.

The moment the door closed, Renn turned on Clara. "How could you roll over for that woman? What's your number, Clara? What's your price?"

"Oh, get off your high horse, Adrienne! For your information, I was just playing along. She has to believe that we're willing to accept her deal, right? What's your plan, to play the martyr? Besides, if I had a price, it'd be a lot higher than that."

Renn couldn't believe how quickly Clara had given in. She heard only betrayal and selfishness in the words. Now her anger burned again as Clara put her on the defensive.

Clara's eyes flared as she muttered, "A lot higher."

Jack stood and stepped between the girls. "Enough, guys, come on. Thirteen minutes to go, what are we going to do?"

Renn sat back down in her chair and turned her head away.

Dom, who had been quiet for a long time, cleared his throat

and asked, "So are we going to take the deal?"

Renn and Clara turned their heads and yelled in unison, "No!"

An uncomfortable silence descended on the room like a cloud. Jack began pacing back and forth. After a minute, he pushed his chair against the center desk and used it to step up and onto its shiny surface. Renn's curiosity overcame her anger, and she tried to figure out what he was up to.

Jack had to stand hunched over to avoid hitting his head. He probed a ceiling panel and pushed it up and to the side, exposing whatever was hidden up there. It looked to Renn like a dark hole.

Renn walked over to the desk and tried to see what Jack saw. "Whatcha thinking, Jack-o?"

Jack lowered himself into a crouch on the desk. "Well, we may be in a security office, but I don't think these rooms are meant to keep anyone in. These ceiling panels are the drop-in kind, which means there's a bunch of empty space up there. I'm trying to see how much space. Anyone have a light?"

No one did, so Jack stood up and stuck his head all the way through the hole in the ceiling. Renn assumed he was giving himself some time for night vision to kick in. After a couple of minutes, he ducked back down and climbed off the desk.

"Listen," he said in a hushed tone. "There's a cable tray that runs into the room from the hallway and then turns into the main security office. It looks like the best option to get out, but it's kind of narrow. I think both the girls could fit, no problem."

Renn shot Clara a glare. She'd rather go alone.

Clara said, "Wait, what will you do?"

"Yes, what will we do?" said Dom.

"Dom and I will barricade the door and buy as much time for you as we can. We'll say we need more time to talk about it."

They pondered in silence for a moment.

"Wait a minute," said Clara again. "What will *we* do?"

Renn groaned. "I can go. I know my way around pretty well, and I know who to contact. Clara can stay here."

Clara crossed her arms and looked ready to put up a fight when Jack jumped in. "Renn, look. You should both go. You'll have twice the chance of success. We only need one of you to get out."

Renn chewed her lip as she considered. "Before I ended up with Julia, I met with Lewis Edmunds and told him our story. I don't believe he's in on it. I think he got duped into turning me over. We could try to find him. Or we could try to find Ranger Scott. I don't know where he'd be now." After more lip chewing she added, "If we can get to a phone or computer, we might be able to contact TacoCat and get some outside help."

Clara grunted, but said nothing.

Renn shot her another glare, but continued, "We have the evidence out in the ranger's truck. Maybe we should just try to get it and call the police. We know everything now, right?"

"But will the evidence be enough to connect her to it?" said Jack. "It's not like it says Julia Bouchard anywhere on it."

Renn nodded, realizing the truth of it. If they were going to get out of this, they had to take down Julia. If they were put into a situation where it was their word against hers, she feared they would lose. He was also right about Clara, as much as she hated to admit it. "Well, if we can't find help inside the building, we'll make for the truck."

Renn looked over to the desk against the wall where Clara still sat. Her face was blank. That girl was such a mystery.

Right now, the only weak part of Jack's plan stared right back at her.

"Actually," Jack cut through the tension. "Could you all help me rearrange some furniture?"

Under his direction, the four of them moved the desk against the door so it ran along the wall and extended towards the hallway wall. They had to lift the desk rather than slide it to be as quiet as possible. They brought the desk that Clara had been lying on and set it against the first desk extending towards the wall opposite the door. After they finished, the room looked something like a Tetris game in progress if viewed from above. There still remained a couple of empty feet between the second desk and the far wall, but Jack said he could fill that space with chairs, making it impossible to open the door.

Renn watched with growing fascination as Jack climbed back onto the repositioned desk and removed a ceiling panel close to the hallway wall, adjacent to the cable tray. Could this crazy escape plan actually work? His head disappeared through the hole for half a minute, then he crouched and waved Renn up.

She took Jack's extended hand and climbed up onto the desk's smooth surface. She stepped under the hole in the ceiling and stood up straight. Her head plunged into darkness and she waited for her eyes to adjust.

Directly in front of her was the tray Jack had described. It was a hanging platform on which cables were routed around the building. Long rods connected the tray to the actual ceiling, still a foot and a half or more above her. The rods were thin, and the tray looked flimsy. It was anyone's guess how much weight it could hold.

She ducked down so she could see Jack again. "Are you sure we're going to get through here?"

"Yes, keep moving. Seven minutes until the deadline." Jack pulled a paper clip he had found while moving the desks out of his pocket and handed it to her. "You might need this. You're going to have to pry up a ceiling panel from above, and there may not be room to get leverage with your fingers."

Renn took the paper clip and tried to muster a confident smile. "Okay, thanks. Well, let's do it." She reached up and felt for handholds as Jack turned around and got on his hands and knees. It took precious minutes for her to figure out how to get into the space. She needed Jack to get on his knees and shove her legs up into the hole. Once in, she started wriggling forward like a worm, and soon she was in almost complete darkness.

She heard Jack's voice from behind her saying, "Spread your weight out," and seriously considered warning him not to make comments about a girl's weight. Instead, she kept wriggling and reached a point she imagined was well into the hallway. She chose a panel and started prying with her paper clip—a brilliant idea, as it turned out.

She sensed the vibrations through the cable tray as Clara climbed into the space. It felt even more claustrophobic than before. She displaced the panel, creating a bright open square into the hallway below her. Renn decided she ought to crawl forward a little more so she could go through the opening legs first.

She was making an incredible ruckus and expected to see Eric and Julia the moment she emerged from her cocoon of cables. Instead, just as she lowered herself through the hole in the ceiling, she heard pounding on the door of the office and Jack's voice as he said, "Yes, who is it?"

Chapter 40

Clara lay in the dark, cramped confines of the cable tray, stuck between the proverbial rock and a hard place. The rock was a pair of grubby sneakers about a foot in front of her, attached to Renn's feet. The hard place was their office prison, about to be breached by Thor and a nasty uptight woman. Not that she was claustrophobic or anything. She didn't mind close spaces, in fact she loved nothing more than to pull up her hood around her face and block out most of the world. It helped her focus.

It also gave her a sense of anonymity that she craved. But she had begun to feel like this was a security blanket she needed to outgrow. It provided some protection but was hardly bullet proof.

After an eternity, Renn looked like she was ready to make her exit, and Clara started inching her way up to join her. Then the pounding started. She heard snippets of the conversation between Jack and that horrible Julia woman. At this point, Clara would rather stomp on her toe and punch her in the mouth than take any amount of money. She hadn't liked her when she was giving them the tour of Silver Labs, and now she knew why. Clara reached behind her head and pulled up her hood, preferring its familiar confines to those of her current surroundings.

A bit of light that leaked in from the holes in front of and behind her and, for the first time, she noticed the cables stretched beneath her. She isolated one with her fingers and lifted it closer. It was round and smooth, and in its shades of gray she thought she picked up a hint of blue. Of course, it was an Ethernet cable. This was how they wired the building for Internet and data. How nice it would be to jump into this little cable and zap out of here.

"Psst!"

Clara raised her head and resumed her ten-foot journey. Renn was no longer in front of her. From behind, she heard pounding and yelling. It was time to get out of here. She scooted forward until she could see down through the hole. Renn stood there, her hands cupped around her mouth. She whispered loudly in an effort, Clara was sure, to give helpful advice.

"Keep going until your waist is past the hole, like I did," said Renn.

A guard might come through the hallway at any moment. And she had a better idea. As she scooted forward, she used her hands to position her torso over the hole. She lowered her face into the light and grinned at Renn. "Put your hands up. That's right, hold your arms up straight and don't bend them."

"What?" Renn hissed. "What are you—?"

Clara lowered her right hand and clasped Renn's left hand. When that was solid, she scooched some more, getting her waist and pelvis out of the cable tray, and lowered her left hand to clasp Renn's right hand. She gave Renn a nod. Then in one fluid motion, she put as much of her own weight as she could onto Renn's arms while straightening her own, like a Cirque du Soleil handstand.

Once she had hefted her lower body free from the tray, she bent her elbows until her head dived behind Renn's. She completed the movement by tucking and rolling and landing on the floor behind Renn, who had wisely released her vice grip. She hadn't quite stuck the landing, but it had been quick and mostly quiet.

"Are you okay? Why are you lying on the floor like that?" Renn whispered.

"I'm fine, thanks," replied Clara as she sprung to her feet and dusted herself off. She pointed to the gaping hole in the ceiling and asked, "Should we close that?"

"No, let's get the heck out of here."

"Finally, we agree on something."

They jogged down the hallway to the stairwell. Next to the door, a placard on the wall suggested the best escape route in the event of a fire. At least they were out of the frying pan. She didn't know yet whether they were heading out of, or into, the fire.

Clara let Renn lead them past Lab 151. At intervals she saw a security camera up in a corner and cringed with the thought that Eric and Julia might be watching every move they made. Whatever they did now, they had to do it fast. She wondered if there were something they could do about the cameras. There couldn't be that many around.

As they headed through a maze of cubicles, Clara wondered how Renn kept her bearings. They arrived at a windowed office. There was a name placard that read "Lewis Edmunds" by the door. The office was empty, but the lights were on. Renn said something under her breath, looked up and down the hallway, and started chewing her lower lip. This was bad. It seemed like Renn's main plan just imploded.

They needed to make a move, something bold. Otherwise they'd never get on top of the situation. But Renn wasn't about to listen to her. Jack had risked a lot to let them get away at the zoo. Renn had sent them on to the gas station while she went back to rescue Jack. Maybe TacoCat had been of some help, but what had Clara Flores done?

Renn still stood in front of Lewis' window, her shoulders slumped. "Right. Let's get out of here and find Ranger Scott. He can call the police."

"Wait. I have an idea. If we take out the security cameras…"

Renn started moving past her, towards the lobby. Clara, not knowing how else to stop her, grabbed one of Renn's hands. She twirled and tried to reclaim it with a jerk.

"Listen. We can still save the boys and get out of here."

"I know you're trying to help, Clara." Renn paused long enough to lecture, "But the only person we can trust in this building is gone. We have to go too."

"You can trust me." It came out as more of a plea than a statement.

"Can I? Really?" Renn tugged her hand from Clara's grasp and started for the main hallway once more.

This was the end. The police would come, and they would be exposed as nothing more than vandals and thieves. Julia would completely control the narrative. Sameer would take away their futures. Unless they could find a way back into the game.

Unless Clara did something right now.

She ran after Renn and pulled her back again. If it weren't for the need for stealth, it would have turned into a brawl; she saw it in the other girl's eyes. She led Renn into the nearest empty cubicle, where they knelt in secret.

"You need to trust me. You need to trust *us*."

Renn furrowed her brow and stared at her in confusion. "What?"

Clara's heartbeat doubled and she thought she was going to hyperventilate. She grabbed Renn's hand and squeezed. Renn looked more concerned than angry. But her eyes still smoldered.

"I have to tell you something and I'm sorry I didn't tell you before. I thought I could keep it secret and it wouldn't matter. I didn't think..."

Renn looked around, then held both Clara's hands in hers. "What in the world are you talking about?"

Clara blurted out a sound that sounded something like, "Imtacocat."

Renn stared at her blankly. "Huh?"

Clara took two deep breaths and tried again. "I. Am. Taco. Cat."

Renn's eyebrows went up and her eyes slowly widened until Clara saw white all around her blue irises. "Shut up. You are not."

In a small, hushed voice, Clara told Renn about the text for help she received, the emails she had sent, the locker she commandeered as a drop site, and its combination. Renn's expression had become stony; she could not read it. Faced with this blank wall, her own emotions started to swing and gyrate uncontrollably. As she spilled out her truth, she felt by turns liberated, embarrassed, clever, and stupid. Heat radiated in waves off her skin. Renn's stare bored into her like a laser. If it went on like this, she would go supernova.

Clara ran out of words. She wasn't built in the image of your typical hacker, gamer, computer geek. Maybe she'd blown

Renn's mind. Clara couldn't sit like this anymore, exposed in front of Renn. She pulled back, tried to retreat to anywhere but here. "Forget about it. Let's just go."

Renn stopped her. Her hands, which had tried to pull away a minute ago, now clamped down solidly on Clara's, keeping her in place. The stony expression softened.

"I get it, Clara." The other girl was serene now, her voice calm and soft. "We all have secrets. Hidden places that are too raw, too wounded to show to people." Renn's mouth opened and closed twice until she found words to continue. "My dad was an immigrant. He came from China with his family when he was twelve. They worked hard doing the kind of work you'd expect in restaurants and dry cleaners. He put himself through college, the first of his family to make it. That's where he met my mom. They settled here when he got his job teaching physics at the community college."

Clara studied Renn, wondering where this was going. None of this had been in Renn's school file.

"He used to call me his little wren, like the bird, you know?" Clara nodded.

"He made me feel safe, always. Anyway, he got sick about five years ago. Cancer. He got treatments here and up at Mayo Clinic. He fought it for a couple of years, we all did as a family." She wiped a tear out of her eye. "But it got him in the end."

Clara whispered, "I'm sorry."

Renn leaned in and pulled Clara's hands closer. "He did everything right, Clara. Everything he was supposed to do to succeed. And he was a success. He lived the American dream until the point he got sick. Then he was just... gone. That's when my plans switched from veterinarian school to medical school."

Her grip on Clara loosened. Renn pulled out a sleeve and wiped her eyes with it. "It's probably also why I'm such a control freak. I refuse to let things just happen to me."

"I get that," said Clara.

"But this whole situation..." Renn waved her arm around, "is totally out of my control."

The moment lingered, and Clara wondered if they had resolved anything about their current situation. A switch appeared to flip in the other girl and her normal, driven attitude returned. "TacoCat said he, I mean *she*, had our back. Is that true?"

Clara nodded vigorously.

"All right. What's the plan?"

Chapter 41

Renn braced against the wall and struggled to keep her balance. Clara sat on her shoulders. The weight of her kept shifting around while she did God-knew-what. "Would you be still up there?"

"This is not easy. I'm trying."

Renn heard the rip of plundered duct tape separating from the roll. For a blessed couple of minutes, Clara stopped shifting around. Then she cursed in Spanish. A sticky wad of duct tape fell in front of Renn. Another sound of tape ripping from the roll.

Renn tried to do the math in her head. It would take them forever to find and cover all the cameras in this place.

"What's going on?"

Renn froze and Clara's legs stiffened around her neck. The voice had come from behind her. Slowly, she spun in place to face it. There was a twenty-something Indian guy standing between cubicles, holding a mug of steaming liquid.

"Ah, I'm. Um," said Clara.

Renn interrupted in a low, conspiratorial voice. "We're helping Lewis punk one of his guys. I don't even know who. But it's going to be epic. Right, partner?"

Clara echoed, "Yeah, partner. Epic."

"Cool. Can I help?"

This response Renn did not expect, but she rolled with it. "Um, sure. Got a roll of tape?"

"I can get one. How many do we have to do?"

"All the cameras out in the open on this floor and the second floor. All except one."

The man didn't even blink. "That's seven minus one, so six cameras. Easy. But it will take forever this way. We should pre-make the covers and lift them into place with a broom handle. We can do it in ten minutes." He lifted his mug to his lips and sipped. "I'm Gopal."

Renn did a mental double-take. That would totally make this work. She had to admit, Silver Labs hired the smartest geeks around. "Wow, thanks. I'm Adrienne, and this is Clara. Do you know where we can get a big piece of poster board and a marker?"

Less than ten minutes later, they finished up a conference room on the second floor. Gopal had left them to return to his work. Renn laid a large piece of poster paper on the table. In marker, they had written a message for Julia and Eric. "We have all the caches. We're taking them to the police in 15 minutes unless our friends are set free."

Everything was in place.

"That was amazing!" Clara half spoke, half giggled.

"I know. Can you believe Gopal helped us out like that?"

"Do you think it will work?"

"I don't think they'll just let the guys go," said Renn. "And that means they'll try to find us."

"And they'll need as many people as possible to look since they don't have their precious cameras," Clara added.

"Yeah, it should work. Where do you think we should hide?"

"Let's try to find a janitor's closet, a bathroom, or something."

They walked through the large common area with the ping pong table and couches, looking for any place to hide, finding nothing. The executive offices were all enclosed with glass, as was the conference room they had just vacated. They stood in the middle of the large area, looking for a closet, when they heard the ding of the elevator.

Clara tugged at Renn's arm and pointed. Renn nodded, and they sprinted for the only hiding place they could think of. They spun the two egg chairs to face away from the open space. Clara climbed in one while Renn took the other. She was cocooned in a shroud of darkness; she would have felt safe if not for the fact that anyone walking in front of the chairs would see them.

The area had been empty a moment ago, but now Renn heard voices from behind. "Let's spread out and look for them." Eric's deep voice buzzed with static through the guards' walkie-talkies. "When you're done on two, we'll sweep the first level together."

"We'll be there in a minute."

Renn heard the faint sounds of movement as the guards opened doors and checked rooms. She held her breath as one guard came into partial view. He peered into Julia's office through the glass wall. Then he disappeared again.

The elevator dinged and Renn heard its door slide open and shut. The voices were gone, and her breath escaped in a relieved sigh. She had to stifle a shriek when Clara ran into her field of view, grinning.

"You almost gave me a heart attack."

"Come on, let's go," said Clara. "We have to get back down

to the basement before they're done searching."

The guards seemed to prefer the elevators, so Renn figured they ought to use the stairwell. They raced to its entrance, but Renn stopped short and broke out in a cold sweat of panic. Did the stairwells have security cameras? She racked her brain but could not remember.

"Cameras?" she asked Clara, pointing to stairwell door.

"I don't think so, but what choice do we have?"

When she put it like that, it made Renn feel better. There was no best choice to be made. They had to do this, and fast. Renn opened the door and they listened for sounds from below. Hearing nothing, they raced to the basement and found the hallway empty.

Luck was with them so far.

The hole in the ceiling was still there, but someone had leaned the ceiling panel against one wall.

Clara would have a big role to play in the next part, riskier and scarier. Renn studied her, gauging whether she was up to the task. To be honest, Renn wasn't yet over the shock of finding out that the petite dancer standing beside her was the very same hacker, TacoCat. It would sink in later. Clara was a girl of hidden depths, more capable than Renn had given her credit for. She could do this.

"Ready?"

Clara nodded, bent at the waist, and touched her toes. Her knees did not bend at all. "Remember to wait for the signal."

Renn kneeled and let Clara climb onto her back for the second time today. They were bonding out of necessity. She stood under the hole and Clara pulled herself up into the ceiling. Before wriggling out of sight, Clara flashed her a grin and a thumbs-up sign.

Renn leaned back against the wall that separated her from Jack and Dom. She slid into a sit and waited.

* * *

Renn heard, or rather felt, two light taps against the other side of the wall. It was the signal. She pushed herself up and brushed her long black hair out of her face, fixed it into a ponytail. She straightened her shirt, brushed off her pants, and gave herself one last affirming self-talk. This was her role, and she could do it.

She started by peeking through the window of the security office. As they had hoped, Julia was alone. Holding her chin a little higher, Renn marched over to the door and tried to enter the office.

It was locked.

This was not a huge surprise, but it would have made things easier had she been able to walk in. Julia glanced up, and Renn relished the look of surprise that registered on her face. The woman masked her emotion and put on a sly smile. She rose elegantly from her seat and cocked her head as she regarded Renn.

Renn shook the door handle and pointed at it. Who knows, maybe she would be cocky enough to let her in. Julia approached but made no move to open the door. She crossed one arm across her stomach to cup the elbow of the other, the fingers of which drummed against her cheek. She did not move to open the door.

"I'm giving you one last chance. Are you going to let my friends go?" Renn wasn't sure how loudly she had to speak to be heard through the glass. Julia seemed to understand her, as a look of amusement crossed her statuesque features. "Clara's outside right now with the police. She'll lead them to the caches in less than ten minutes."

Julia dropped the hand from her face to cross her arms. "She'd be committing professional suicide then—and dooming you and the others to a life of pumping gas at Casey's. If you don't go to prison, that is."

"Good. We can have cells next to each other. You can show me how to do up my hair."

"Oh, Adrienne, nothing on those caches can be tied back to me. I'm afraid I'm going to have to call your bluff."

Renn rattled the door, causing Julia to take a step back. The woman cast a quick glance over at the counter with the monitors. Renn followed her gaze. A walkie-talkie stood on its corner. She could call for Eric and the other guards anytime. Renn had to be smarter.

"Listen, I just want this to be over. Isn't that what you want, too? I want my friends and I released, and you want the caches. Can't we work something out?"

"That's what I was trying to do before you and your little friend decided to go gallivanting around my building." She took a step closer to Renn and her voice hardened. "This is my facility. You are trespassing and trying to steal my property."

"That's your story, but we both know you're trying to steal from yourself. Why would you do that?"

Julia's laugh was husky and wry. "You wouldn't understand. You still think you have this unlimited future. You haven't hit your head against a glass ceiling, yet. You haven't been banished to the middle of nowhere by the one man who you..." she trailed off and swallowed her thought, like a poison pill.

Renn tried very hard not to let her gaze shift to the hole in

293

the ceiling over the conference table that was slowly getting wider.

"My advice," Julia addressed Renn once more, "is don't go into tech."

Renn had to keep her attention front and center for a couple more minutes. "You hypocrite," she said, louder than necessary.

Julia's eyes snapped onto hers, and the woman couldn't hide the fury building behind them.

"What makes you think it will be any different with Sameer? You're just jumping from one guy to another. You're not changing anything. You could go start your own company or something. Control your own future."

"Oh my dear, you are so naive. It's almost cute. There's always someone who controls your future. If it's not the CEO, it's the venture capitalists, and the board, and the press. You have no idea what it means to set goals for yourself, and control for every possibility, only to have some random twist of fate screw it all up."

Renn staggered, stunned by the woman's words that hit too close to home. She slapped her hands against the glass and braced herself, trying desperately to stand strong. Her mouth opened and closed, like a fish out of water, but no words came.

In the moment of silence that followed, Julia turned around, reacting to some sound. Clara's upside-down head poked through a hole in the ceiling. Julia scrambled for the walkie-talkie while Clara dropped onto the table, wielding the stapler from the office prison.

Julia squeezed the button and yelled, "Eric, get back here now!"

Clara leapt off the table and swung the stapler like a club

at Julia's head. During the back swing, the stapler unfolded, doubling its length and making it a slightly more effective weapon.

Julia shrieked in pain from the blow, and Clara took advantage by grabbing on to the woman's hair and kicking at her knees from behind. Julia crumpled onto the thin office carpet. Clara pushed her aside and rushed to the door, unlocking it for Renn.

Renn had recovered enough to gather her wits. She slipped into the office and locked the door behind her. At least it would slow Eric down a little. Renn tried the office door where the boys were, but the knob had a keyhole and no apparent way to unlock it.

She ran back to Clara, who was trying to wrestle the walkie from Julia's grasp. Renn grabbed hold of it and helped to yank it out of the woman's grasp. "Key," Renn hissed at her. "Where's the key?"

Julia answered with an insult that made Renn's ears turn red. Feeling the back of her head, she added, "You stapled me."

Clara ran back to the conference table and grabbed a small ring of keys off it, held it up for Renn to see. "Got it," she said.

As Clara tried the keys in the locked door, Julia struggled for the exit. Renn was younger and more athletic, but Julia was desperate, trapped, and had nothing to lose. Renn soon had to throw up her arms to block repeated wild blows.

Suddenly the blows stopped, and she heard Jack's reassuring voice. "It's okay, Renn, we've got you."

Renn lowered her arms. Dom and Clara dragged Julia, who had given up all airs of resistance, over to a chair. Jack found their phones and distributed them.

When Clara got hers, she tapped and swiped its screen until

a recording started. It was Eric's voice, then Julia's. Julia groaned when she heard it. "Got you," Clara said brightly.

Clara must have had her phone recording the entire time it was in the office. Clever girl.

No sooner had they gotten Julia under control than a group of people appeared outside the security office. Ranger Scott was there, and so was Lewis. The sheriff and a deputy accompanied them. The sheriff escorted Eric, whose hands were behind his back. Even Mr. Morris was there, looking very out of sorts.

Chapter 42

Jason Silver's secretary reminded Jack of his grandmother. She seemed to be the right age and had a similar immaculate gray hairdo. A chain ran from one earpiece of her thick-rimmed eyeglasses to the other so she could remove them and let them dangle like a necklace. Mrs. Fields had greeted them warmly and offered each of them a soda while they waited. Jack half expected her to have a plate of cookies on her desk, but no such luck. Also different from his grandma, Mrs. Fields' desk was not decorated with doilies and Hummel figurines. Instead, it was empty except for two framed photos facing away from him.

Jack sipped his soda and looked over at Renn. She sat beside him on the hard couch. They were next door to Julia's office. The glass office wall gave them an expansive view of the casual working area on the second floor. Monday morning traffic was picking up and several people worked on laptops and chatted over coffee. Jack offered Renn a reassuring smile, which she returned.

Dom and Clara sat in chairs against the adjacent glass wall. They looked very small in the spacious outer office. Dom bounced his knee while he studied his can of soda. His navy blue suit hung on him like a football jersey without any pads.

Clara looked relaxed. Well, why not? She had saved their bacon with her camera ruse, and then by crawling through the cable tray and dropping into the security office with only a stapler. She was freaking TacoCat. He and Renn had misjudged her on so many levels.

Mrs. Fields took off her headset with the jutting mic and rose from her rolling chair. "Mr. Silver will see you now. This way, please." She opened the door behind her desk and waited for them to follow. Jack gulped the rest of his soda and resisted the habitual urge to crush the can. The others followed him as he stood and rounded the secretary's desk. They filed into Jason Silver's office, the inner sanctum of Silver Labs.

Glass also dominated the wall opposite them. It was almost all windows, offering a panoramic view of manicured lawn, trees, and flower gardens. The wall to their left was wood-paneled and lined with bookshelves. A break in the shelves revealed another door. There was no desk, even though the office was enormous, the largest Jack had ever seen. A ring of comfy chairs sat near the bookshelves with a small round coffee table in the center. Along the window wall was strewn exercise equipment: free weights, a squat cage with pull-up bar, an exercise bike with a large monitor.

Mr. Silver was nowhere in sight, so Jack proceeded to the ring of chairs and sunk into one. The wall they had entered through had a huge flat screen monitor mounted on it. The Silver Labs logo watched over them from its large screen.

He'd begun scanning the spines of some books when the paneled door opened, and a man stepped out and introduced himself as Jason Silver.

"Hi, guys," he said. His tone was welcoming and his smile sincere. He rounded the circle and leaned against the side of a chair. "Thank you for coming in again so soon after the events of the other day. I hope you've all had a chance to calm yourselves and assimilate your experiences."

To Jack, he looked to be in his mid-thirties. His short black hair was neatly trimmed in a trendy style. He wore black jeans and a black form-fitting V-neck sweater over a white tee. He was, by any standard, good looking and in great shape.

They all mumbled variations of "No problem, sir."

"Good, I'm glad to hear. We've begun an internal investigation into who was involved and how our systems were compromised. So far though, we just know about Julia, Eric, Owen, and the intern."

He pushed off the chair and paced around to stand at its back. Jack got the impression that Mr. Silver didn't ever remain seated for too long.

"Julia has been with me for ten years. She was part of my inner circle. I put her in charge of bringing this facility online and she did a great job. Very disappointing."

Jack did not doubt it, but Jason's overall look remained relaxed and confident, and only a hint of tension was visible in the crow's feet around his eyes. They sat, not moving or speaking, as Jason paced behind his chair and contemplated Julia's betrayal. Then he noticed them again, rounded the chair, and resumed his perch on its edge.

"So, tell me, who found the original cache?"

Renn raised her hand as if she were in class. "I did, sir. It was still in the database and so it came up on my app. It was the last one for me to find in Black Hawk Bend."

"Ah, yes. I had instructed my assistant to decommission the cache site after we built the building here. I never followed up, so that's on me. Still, wasn't the big, tall fence with the

'No Trespassing' sign a clue? Didn't you know that it's against the geocachers' code to break the law or trespass while cache hunting?"

Renn wilted at the accusation. "I'm sorry, I guess I was just being stubborn. I'm... really sorry."

Jason rose again and walked over to the bookshelves, where he retrieved a box and brought it back to his seat. Jack recognized it as the tin container from the first cache. He retrieved the log book and flipped it open to the last entry. "So you're Wren. Nice to meet you. I'm Unicorn."

Renn's eyes widened in understanding. "Nice to meet you too."

"I started geocaching during my Stanford days. It took us all around the Valley. We all wanted to strike it rich; start that one-in-a-million company with a billion-dollar valuation. It was heady times."

Jack found his voice enough to ask, "You and Sameer?"

Jason did not hesitate or look at all uncomfortable at the association with the man who had tried to steal his secrets and recruit away one of his top people.

"Me, Sameer, and a few others. The dot-com bust was still fresh in people's minds, but we thought we could do it better, change the world."

This time Clara spoke up, "Haven't you?"

"Oh, we've made a dent, I'll admit. My priorities have shifted a little. I don't keep score with money anymore. My definition of changing the world has matured. Take this place, for instance. You won't find many other Silicon Valley firms with Midwest offices, but I know there are good people here. It's too bad Julia couldn't see that, too."

Jason held out the tin to Renn. "What did you leave?"

She took it, fished around, and pulled out the tag from her old dog's collar, told Jason about Sparky. He laughed with her before returning the tin to the shelf. He was handsome, charming, and rich, but Jack thought he sensed uncharted depths to the man. They hadn't even scratched the surface of Jason Silver.

"I admire the persistence, imagination, and cleverness you've shown in tracking the caches all the way to the heart of Silver Labs. You know, that team building exercise was put together for our scientists, programmers, engineers, and mathematicians, many of whom hold PhDs. And, I can tell you, they had trouble with some of the puzzles. But of course they had to do the whole thing in a couple of hours."

Jason took a small step away from the bookshelf and folded his arms. "Here's my problem, guys. At any time during this ordeal, you could have come to us and brought us into the loop. Those were my secrets being passed around, after all. Instead, you held on to every thumb drive you found, and told no one. At the end of the day, I only have your word that you weren't planning on handing them over to Sameer or Julia, or selling them to the highest bidder. Why shouldn't I turn you in and have you charged for theft?"

Jason looked at them as calmly as if he were chatting about the weather. Jack felt like he'd been punched in the gut; he could tell with a glance that Renn felt the same way. They'd turned in all the drives, including the one Clara had hidden in Lab 151. Did Jason think they'd made copies or given the data to anyone else? Didn't he understand what a precarious ledge they'd been walking along?

None of that mattered. Jack had to think of something to say now to convince him they were on his side. If they thought

Julia or Sameer could ruin their lives, Jason could do at least as bad, and probably worse. He lined up his best arguments and drew a deep breath.

"Mr. Silver, my friends and I risked everything to do the right thing."

Jack blinked and sank against the cushion of his deep chair. The voice had not come from him. He looked over at the source. Dom had risen from the edge of his chair to stand, ramrod straight, in his droopy suit. His arms hung stiff at his sides and he looked straight ahead, only occasionally throwing the merest glance towards the billionaire.

"You know we were being blackmailed by your former colleague. We could have turned the data over to him anytime. You also know that we were held captive in this building by Ms. Bouchard and offered a deal. We could have turned over the data to her. Instead, we held out in the hope that we would find somebody that we could trust. With all due respect, we didn't even know whether you could be involved in this somehow. We didn't ask for any of this, Mr. Silver. I'm sorry if that's not good enough for you. I'm sure we'd all like for you to believe us. But either way, I'll be able to go to bed tonight with a clear conscience."

Dom stood rigid for another second, as if trying to think of something else to bolster his argument. Suddenly, he sat back down on the edge of his seat. Jason, arms still folded, regarded him thoughtfully. Jack could see in him the measured evaluation of a coach and felt like they had been given some kind of test.

Jason stepped towards Dom and extended his hand. Dom shook it, still not making full eye contact. "Dominic Marshall," said Jason. "I'm told that you have some aptitude for math, and apparently puzzles." Releasing the handshake, he turned to face all of them once more. "I hope you understand, it's practically impossible to know who your friends and enemies are in business, and in this business, in particular. When billions of dollars are on the line, your closest friend can turn out to be your worst enemy."

Jason walked back to the bookshelf and picked something up from it, a small silver trophy. "Now, who's my 3D printer?"

That was the piece Jack printed in Lab 151. He never got to see how it turned out. He raised his hand. Jason held it out for Jack to take. It was a trophy, gleaming silver, in the shape of a man with his hands on his hips. It was the most beautiful piece he'd ever printed; no seams or sharp edges anywhere to be seen.

"The first team back to the lab after the exercise got to print this trophy as a memento of their victory. So, here you go, Jack."

The puzzle they had stumbled upon hadn't led to buried treasure. In fact, it had gotten them all into a bunch of trouble. Still, getting this small token at the end cemented it for Jack. They had won. "Thank you, Mr. Silver. I'll never forget this."

Jason chuckled and selected another chair to sit in. He leaned forward, resting elbows on knees. "I'm sure you won't. I hope none of you will. In fact, I'd like to offer some additional motivation towards that end."

Jack hefted the little trophy, still admiring it. It had some weight, not like a little plastic thing.

"First, in thanks for saving my property from embezzlement and choosing the honorable path, I'd like to offer each of you a twenty-five-thousand-dollar college scholarship."

Jack dropped the trophy and coughed. He looked around at

the others and saw that Dom's eyes were watery.

"Additionally, to any of you who are interested, I'd like to offer internships here at Silver Labs during your high school and college careers. I'm always on the lookout for talent, and I see promise in each of you."

A chorus of exclamations and thanks gushed from the four friends as the words sunk in. They weren't going to be charged for theft. They were being rewarded! It was an outcome they could hardly have expected and were finding it difficult to absorb.

"Don't thank me too soon, guys. You'll find I have pretty high standards. And there are a couple of stipulations."

"What stipulations?" asked Clara, always the first to chafe and challenge authority.

"First, you and your legal guardians will have to sign non-disclosure agreements that you won't talk about any of the products or plans you saw on those thumb drives."

That wasn't too bad. They all shared looks and agreed.

"What's the second thing?" asked Jack.

"The second thing, Mr. Henderson, is that the trophy you're holding was meant to be printed with brass, not platinum. That's about three thousand dollars of precious metal, and its cost will be deducted from the amount of your scholarship."

Jack pursed his lips in a silent 'O'.

Jason laughed and rose to his feet. He pulled a phone from his back pocket and pressed a button. A few seconds later, the main door opened, and Mrs. Fields walked in.

"It was nice to meet you all. My assistant will show you out."

Jason shook each of their hands, but Jack could tell he was already thinking about whatever meeting or plan was next. Some new million-dollar deal or world-changing invention.

With that, they filed back out of the inner sanctum.

Chapter 43

Renn held on to the slender birch and let it take her weight. Most of its leaves had fallen, creating a colorful mosaic on the trail. She raised her face to the sun and closed her eyes. The crisp November air bit through her vest and sweatshirt and nipped at her skin. The sun warmed her face and filled her with warmth. Somewhere between the two was a comfortable balance.

"Hang on. We'll be right there," Jack's voice called out from behind her.

She hadn't even noticed that they'd fallen behind. Renn looked around to see Jack and Clara marching along the trail, followed by a huffing Dom. "Sorry. I'll slow down. I just got carried away by the woods, you know?"

"No, I really don't," said Clara, who started rubbing her arms after catching up to Renn. "I'd like to be carried out of the woods."

"Very funny. Thanks for joining us today. I know it was a sacrifice."

"At least we're here to keep you out of the sticky burrs," Jack said, causing Clara to wince.

"Tell you what," Renn said, "why don't you two lead for a while. I'll follow with Dom."

"But where are we headed?" asked Jack.

"I don't know," said Renn, "doesn't matter a whole lot. We left Stella about ten minutes ago, so maybe go for another ten?" She thought about the last time they were in these woods and added, "And let's stick to the trail. I don't want to make it too hard for campers."

Jack and Clara set a more leisurely pace, and Renn chose to slow down and hang with Dom. They had eaten lunch together more than half the time since Silver Labs, but she hadn't had a chance to have a heart-to-heart. "Have Bernie and Ryan left you alone?"

Renn's mention of the bullies who had tormented Dom the entire semester didn't visibly phase him. He shrugged and said, "Mostly, I guess. Bernie caught me alone in the hall after Math Club. This was when Jack was gone, playing at state. Ryan was there too. Anyway, he found me at my locker."

"Oh, my gosh. What happened?"

Dom shrugged again. "He pushed me a couple times, tried to provoke me. I think he stopped because I wasn't giving him what he wanted."

"Which was?"

"Fear, I suppose. I reported him the next day and he got detention."

"Good for you, Dom. I think you picked up something from that lion after all."

Dom smiled at the mention of his new spirit animal. "I also thought of a name for Bernie. Whenever he calls me Dominique, like a girl, I call him Bernice."

Renn shrieked with laughter, causing Jack and Clara to pause and stare. "I love it!"

They passed a dead tree that had been split by lightning.

Its top half drooped away from the trail. "Hey, help me out with this." She left the trail and studied some medium-sized branches, about two fingers in width. Finding one she liked, she kicked at it near its connection point to the dry trunk and was rewarded by a satisfying crack. "Okay, help me pull it."

She and Dom yanked and twisted the branch until it separated from the dead tree. She leaned it against the fallen trunk and instructed Dom to kick it again. He did, and it broke cleanly near the other end. Renn picked it up and tested its weight. In response to the questioning look she got from Dom, she handed the walking stick to him. "For you. Comes in very handy on long hikes."

"Wow, thanks," he blustered, studying the long branch. He stabbed it at the ground a couple feet in front of him and pulled himself back onto the main trail. "This is great."

A few minutes later, they caught up to Jack and Clara. The other two were studying a tall, old oak tree. He beckoned to them as they hiked up. "Hey, come look at this."

Renn joined him and saw what he meant. At the base of the ancient tree, there was a recessed nook between two gnarly roots that broke the surface for a few feet before diving underground.

"This is perfect, Jack. Excellent find." Renn shrugged off her backpack and let it drop to the ground. "We're here, guys."

She removed a white plastic container, very similar to the one they had pulled from the creek. Next, she took out a small notebook and pencil. These she handed to Jack. "Everyone sign the log book with your trail name and the date."

Renn went on the geocaching app and started typing entries to register the new cache site. "Okay, last chance, guys. Are you sure you don't want to make this a mystery cache? We could make clues, write a few riddles?"

"No way," said Clara.

"Sure," said Dom.

Jack glared at her with the heat of a thousand suns. "For the hundredth time, no. I never want to see another riddle again."

Renn laughed, having received the response she was going for. "Fine, fine. A plain ole cache it is. And... we... are... done." She put her phone away and took back the log book and pencil from Dom. On the first page, fourth line, she signed her name "Wren" and added the date. Above her name, Dom had signed his name "Dom."

"Very original."

Above Dom's name was the entry "TacoCat."

"Clara, aren't you afraid that people will figure out who TacoCat is, just by association?"

Clara shrugged. "If they do, I can always change it to something else. It's easy to be anonymous on the Internet."

On the first line was the entry "Jack-o."

"Nice, Jack. And do you have some swag for the cache?"

Jack stuffed his hand in his front pocket and came out with a small, bright orange, plastic thing. Renn held out the container and in dropped his football mouth guard.

"Oh, gross. I hope you've washed this," said Renn.

"What does it mean?" said Dom.

Jack tucked his hands in his front pockets and kicked at the root. "It means that I'm retiring from football."

"What?" Renn had been trying to pry this out of Jack ever since the zoo. "When did you decide?"

"After state. It wasn't because we lost. I loved playing again. It's just that I realized how much it could interfere with the rest of my life if I got hurt again. And the rest of my life is a long time."

"I understand." She moved the container in Clara's direction. "Got something?"

Clara pulled a small thumb drive out of her pocket. Renn was about to ask the obvious question when she answered it. "Don't worry, there are no secrets on here. Just a playlist of some of my favorite songs."

"Very nice. Dom?" She held out the container to him. He switched his walking stick to the other hand and pulled a Ziploc baggie out of his coat pocket. In it were several colored plastic pieces. After he dropped it into the container, Renn realized it was his personal tangram puzzle. "Haven't you had this since you were a kid?"

"Yeah. Maybe it's time I give someone else a chance with it."

Renn was satisfied with the way this cache was turning out. Her friends had all made fantastic contributions to get it started. Well, except for Jack-o. She knelt and looked in the various pockets of her backpack for hers. When she found it, she ran the red tassel through her hands a few times and held it against her mouth. It wasn't the same one from Mom's Prius; that one meant too much to her. But maybe this one would bring someone a bit of luck.

On the hike back to the Raptor Center, she and Jack led in contemplative silence. Behind them, she picked up snippets of conversation between Dom and Clara.

"It's a feng shui charm," Dom explained. "It's for good luck. I think she's saying that it's okay to not control everything all the time, and we could all use a little luck."

"Yes, yes, I know that part," said Clara. "Cool," she said, drawing out the word for several seconds. "Just one thing.

What's feng shui?"

Renn smiled to herself and hiked on.

Epilogue

I hope you enjoyed The Cache: A Black Hawk Bend Mystery. If you want to keep up with Renn, Jack, Dom, and Clara, you can download a short epilogue for free. Head over to https://chriswernerschwarz/the-cache-epilogue and sign up for my newsletter. I'll let you know when the next adventure is on its way. I promise not to fill up your inbox with emails, and you can unsubscribe anytime.

Review Request

If you enjoyed my first Black Hawk Bend Mystery, The Cache, please consider adding a review. More and more, reviews are critical for authors like me. They allow new readers to find our books and choose them from a sea of new content. I'd be so grateful if you would hop over to the site where you bought the book and leave a short, honest review. It need only be a line or two and it makes a massive difference.

Best wishes,

Chris

Acknowledgement

There are many clichés about writing a book. Writing a book is a journey, not a destination. Writing a book takes a village. Writing a book is a marathon, not a sprint. These are absolutely true. My book-writing journey has lasted over four-and-a-half years; begun in one decade of life and finished in another. And I could not have gotten to the finish line without the support, encouragement, advice, education, inspiration, and collaboration of many people.

I no longer even remember how I got the germ of an idea that I could, or should, write a novel. I do remember seeking some small validation that I wasn't accepting an impossible mission. I soon ran across two podcasts that would steer the course of my writing journey for years to come. In The Creative Penn, Joanna Penn inspired me with her writing journey and introduced me to the renegade world of independent publishing. Thank you for teaching me to think, "I am creative. I am an author." The book, and then the podcast, The Story Grid, gave me a system that appealed to the engineer in me. It gave me confidence that I could apply my analytical mind to the task of creative writing. Thank you, Shawn and Tim, for pulling back the curtain on the mysterious process of writing and editing a story that works.

So I set out on the journey with a faith that was, if not blind, then extremely myopic. I wrote words, but I didn't think they were good words; okay, I know they weren't. Fortunately for me, I live in Iowa City, home to the famous Iowa Writers' Workshop. There must be some way for me to take advantage of that. What's that? There's an Iowa Summer Writing Festival and it's been going on for 30 years? How did I not know about this? Sign me up! The festival was a wonderful way to meet other writers and receive instruction from true experts. I took two classes from Sands Hall that were so helpful. It was also my first workshop experience; reading my words out loud and listening to others read theirs, receiving and offering critiques. Thank you Sands for filling up my backpack with tools for the writer's journey.

I could not have gotten this far without the encouraging and wise words of those who read the book in its various stages. My wife Jill was my first reader and gave me the encouragement to keep going. Thank you, Anna Dizack, for reading an early draft; I hope I can return the favor for you one day. My beta readers, both young and old, included Julie Myers, Megan Zalzala, Rose Schmitt, Stacie Schwarz, Proshanto Kladopoulos, Penelope Kladopoulos, Bennett Solis, and Jackson Roe. Your feedback had a big impact on the final product. Thanks to Sue Lafond for helping me evaluate cover designs.

A big huge thank you to my editors, Maya Rushing Walker, Michelle Krueger, and Claire Evans. Any remaining inconsistencies, clunkiness, plot holes, typos, and abused ellipses are totally and completely my fault.

This book went out to beta readers near the beginning of the global pandemic in 2020. COVID-19 changed my work life dramatically, but I adjusted and have grown to love working from home. Then George Floyd was killed by police and the race riots began. The conversation about black lives rose to an intensity we have not seen in a generation, one that is necessary and overdue. But to a writer who is trying to represent a diverse cast of main characters (including a shy, sensitive, bright, math wiz who happens to be black), this was an existential crisis. I was blessed with a couple of beta readers who also provided me with invaluable sensitivity feedback. I read How to be an Antiracist by Ibram X. Kendi, and it raised my awareness of the structural racism all around us by a notch or two. I recommend it. But it also forced me to question the very setting of my series.

I didn't get any feedback about a key character that pervades my story, but I knew I could not take for granted my use of Chief Black Hawk. Black Hawk is a fixture in my home area (the Quad Cities, located on the Mississippi), in the same way as he is in the fictional town of Black Hawk Bend. I looked to Re-Collecting Black Hawk by Nicholas A. Brown and Sarah E. Kanouse for some education. Flipping through the images and reading stories about Native Americans in the Midwest opened my eyes to the extent of our cultural appropriation of the great chief's name.

Issues surrounding race aren't going away anytime soon, nor should they be swept under the rug. Unfortunately, they represent a rich vein of conflict that we can mine for story, character, and theme. I only hope I will grow into a writer that people consider worthy of doing the digging. (If you've read this far, go check out the poem Digging by Seamus Heaney. Thank you Sands Hall for your stirring recitation!) And thank you dear reader for stopping by. I wish you well on your journey.

C. W. Schwarz

Iowa City, 2020

About the Author

Chris Schwarz was born in Moline amidst amber waves of grain and green tractors. He grew up reading J.R.R. Tolkien and Robert Heinlein, ultimately becoming an engineer rather than a wizard, but not by choice.

The son of an immigrant, he was the first in his family to attend college. Along the way he picked up a Ph.D. in engineering and learned to Salsa dance. By day he writes about research on advanced vehicles done with a big ole' driving simulator, and by night he writes his own stories.

He is the author of a young adult series featuring four high school friends solving mysteries tinged with science and technology.

Fueled by chai lattes and dark chocolate, Chris lives in Iowa City with his wife, son and dogs, and waits patiently for self-driving cars to figure out snow.

You can connect with me on:

🌐 https://chriswernerschwarz.com

📘 https://www.facebook.com/cwschwarz.author

✒ https://www.instagram.com/cwschwarz.author